THE BALLAD OF THE LITTLE PEOPLE

"Then the dream—they never believed it was true?" Faree asked.

Zoror rubbed two talons across his chin just above his first throat wattle. "Oh, they believed. And for a while they had their eyes and ears open. There have always been stories, many of which match each other. The Little Men—the People of the Hills—"

Faree stiffened.

"You have heard that before, have you?" questioned the Zacathan.

Faree shook his head. "I can't remember. But I have heard that name—surely I have heard it!"

Zoror looked at him kindly. "Faree, I must give you a warning. Very few must have seen you and it is true you can fold these"—he pointed to the wings—"amazingly small. By day however, there would be plenty sharp-eyed enough to note a difference.

"And boy—you are not safe!"

Tor books by Andre Norton

ANDRE NORTON
DARE TO GO A-HUNTING

A TOM DOHERTY ASSOCIATES BOOK
NEW YORK

DARE TO GO A-HUNTING

Copyright © 1990 by Andre Norton

A TOR Book
Published by Tom Doherty Associates, Inc.
49 West 24th Street
New York, N.Y. 10010

Cover art by Victoria Poyser

ISBN: 0-812-54712-8

Library of Congress Catalog Card Number: 89-39877

First edition: January 1990
First mass market edition: September 1990

Printed in the United States of America

0 9 8 7 6 5 4 3 2 1

For Ingrid who wanted a story of the People—

Up the airy mountain,
Down the rushy glen,
We dare not go a-hunting
For fear of little men.

—William Allingham

1.

It was warm, too warm for one of the room's inhabitants. However, it was probably discourteous to remark upon the heat though a round drop of sweat gathered just below one of his slightly slanted eyes to trickle down his cheek. There was a small rustle when he shifted position on the uncushioned stool which supported him an uncomfortable height from a floor of tiles matched in brilliant color to form patterns which he could only glance at or it made his eyes ache. That his host not only accepted all this as natural, but took comfort in it was one of those irritating situations which had filled Farree's life for some time.

He had seen aliens a-plenty during his bad time in that sleazy portside district, the Limits, which formed his earliest memories. However, such strangers in their own homes were something he was now only being introduced to by the full swing of fate's finger crystal.

"Hot" Togger's thought, always pitched so high that his

own sense could hardly understand, came testily. Farree's jerkin heaved and wrinkled as the smux crawled out into the open to gaze up into his face with stalked eyes.

"Soooo—it is hot, little one?" Not a thought this time but words uttered with a hissing intonation. At a goodly distance down the room a third inhabitant arose, the extended talons on his webbed and scaled feet scraping across the stone pattern on the floor. "Courtesy is all very well, my little friends, but allow me also the privilege of displaying it." A yellow scaled arm, banded at both wrist and above the elbow with well-worn cuffs of an iron-hard wood, reached out to the wall and flipped a switch.

There was no sound of any winds, yet there blew across the room now a swift breeze, tepidly warm to be sure, but at least better than the slow baking heat it disturbed. He who had summoned that now came threading a path between small tables and large—all piled with learning tapes and scan plates in boxes. Farree gave a, he hoped, concealed sigh of relief. Those folds draped across his shoulders, extending down his back so that their edges swept the floor, rose in turn. He did not flourish the wings in full display—he needed more room for that—but at least he could give them a stretch.

The tall old alien watched Farree almost eagerly. He had swept a whole cascade of scan plate boxes to the floor and seated himself with a little grunt and some rubbing of one scaled and plated knee.

Then he leaned forward, setting the palms of his hands on both knees. Farree did not know how long Zacanthans continued to inherit this plane of existence (which was how they referred to life and death) but he was sure that Grand Hist-Technneer Zoror was indeed a long-time master of that skill which, as with all his species, centered upon the collection of information about oddities in a well-spread galaxy—especially the history of such new races as were introduced from time to time into the records of exploration. They were indeed long-lived, these lizardlike people, but even the oldest of them often asserted that he was only beginning his labors.

"Soooo—" Once more Zoror made a hissing of the word. "You wish now that this old man of scales would come directly to the point and tell you what you are and from whence you have come." The Zacanthan nodded so that the pleated frill of skin which lay about the back of his head and shoulders unfolded into a fan like some large ornamental collar.

"It is not easy, you know," Zoror continued. "We cannot walk to the records and say 'Tell me who is this winged one? From what earth and people did he spring?' These," he again flung out an arm to gesture at the unwieldy piles of tapes and spools fencing them both in, "these are records of voyages, many, many voyages, also contributed by men who tell strange tales, sometimes merely out of their own imagination, but other times bearing a truth which—if the Ever Mighty is helpful—can be traced about this far!" He held up a hand to display a thumb and forefinger with a space between them maybe as big as one of Togger's second claws.

"There—there was nothing then?" Farree had curbed his patience all morning, ever since all he could remember had been fed into the read-all of the big computer. His scant store of information had been recorded to match mixtures of still dubious details.

"No, I do not say that. There are stories of such as you. Those come from the bards of Loel, the Rememberers of Garth, the Dance-think of Udolf. Stories, mind you, garnered on more than a hundred planets. But—it remains that they are stories without concrete proof. Those who retell them gather details on this world or that. But the strongest of all—those come from Terra—"

"Terra? But that is but a tale, too." Farree did not try to hide his disappointment.

"Not so—" Zoror's neck frill fluttered as he shook his head. "However, there is something common to all the worlds from which the clearest and most detailed of these stories come. Those were the planets first colonized by people from Terra. Yes, most certainly there was a Terra. It bred several races, in all of which there was one abiding gift, that of curiosity. Terrans were not the first explorers of the space dark, yet they spread farther in less time than many of those who came before. And with them they brought, as we all do, tales which were old and yet part of their lives."

Farree's face creased in a frown. Zoror, for all his learning, was apt to tell stories, too. Ordinarily Farree would have listened with interest. However, what he wanted now was truths, even if they afforded only a very thin thread to trace. "These from Terra—they were certainly not like me." He put up a hand to touch the edge of one wing.

"No. They were not Farrees—" Zoror assured him. "Only stories of such they did carry. In their tales—much of this was researched and put together by Zahaj in a mist of years ago—in their tales they spoke of 'Little People', which lived sometimes underground—"

Farree unfolded his wings another fraction. "With these they could not!" he countered.

"True, true. But there were different species or races of them. Some were wingless according to the tales. They all had a strange relationship with the men of Terra. Sometimes they were good friends, again they were blood enemies. It is said that they often stole the children of men and raised them, to renew and enrich their own blood. For they were very old so at times their race dwindled until only a handful of them remained. They were supposed to have great treasures—perhaps even records!" Zoror's voice soared high. "Only there always came a time when the men drove them from their homes—perhaps not wantonly (though there are legends about such deeds as that also) but because they held land men wanted. And all know the stories of the ever-living greed of

Terra which spread like a mist-dark cloud wherever their ships touched, until there came the Great Reckoning.

"Before that these winged and unwinged ones fled along the star roads not knowing where they might land. They found worlds to settle for a space. But always the same such worlds drew the Terrans. They would come so that the Little People must once more take to space. This has happened many times over, judging by legends we have recorded. However, at last there were no more reports of them, only what remained in songs and stories."

"Did they war with the Terrans then?" Farree's mouth was dry. He must have squeezed Togger too hard for the smux twisted about and gave a warning nip to a finger.

"There was a war, yes, though we hear little of that—mainly a ballad over some Terran killed by the evil magic of the Little People. From Udolf, for example, there comes a whole set of dance songs lamenting some leaders who died from weapons known to the Little People alone. They must have practiced also some form of mind control, for they would keep men within their hold for what seemed a day or a year and then let their captives go, for them to discover that they had really been gone from their homes for a matter of years. There is also the Mingra report. Come and see for yourself."

Farree followed the Zacanthan to the larger table where there were even more piles of tapes balanced perilously. Zoror began to clear these away, piling them on the floor. Farree stooped quickly to help him, folding his wings tight again lest he cause some disaster.

"This is old, too, by the reckoning of most." The Hist-Technneer was fussing with a reader, making sure the machine was in proper position.

"Mingra?" That was a word Farree had never heard before.

"The darkened world—the world of the dead-alive—" Zoror was more intent on the disc he was fitting into the reader than he was to any question. "Now this"—he gave the roll a last turn, slipping it into place—"was the Shame of Mingra, the Shame of all who are space travelers—though perhaps it has so faded during the years that it is only alive as a poisonous whisper by now. Watch with care—for into it has gone the hate of one species for another and yet there is nothing to explain—"

His voice died away in a final hiss. Farree obediently looked at the small screen. Togger moved impatiently in his grasp until he placed the smux down carefully on the table before the screen. Togger drew himself into a ball and perhaps went to sleep. For Farree there was no sleep. He had seen plenty, since his arrival at Zoror's home which was also headquarters for a whole quadrant of researchers, of such records. Some had been so wildly fantastic that he had been sure they were indeed travelers' tall tales and not any true garnering of knowledge.

A picture formed on the screen. Farree jerked, half arose from his seat. For there was not only an ominous picture of a sphere, half lit at one edge by a red beam. But in his head—

He could not say it was a song, he could not even distinguish what must be wholly alien words. Yet deep into him had struck the thought-feeling that this held a truth which was evil and powerful. Gripping the edge of the table he made himself sit again but he did not loose his sustaining hold.

"Hurt—dark—hurt—" The smux had unrolled from his sleep ball and crouched before the screen, waving his great claws back and forth as if he were facing some dire danger.

That thread of sound swelled and, as if it called for sight, the red light on the screen blazed higher to display a barren stretch of riven rocks which were eroded, or perhaps storm-clawed, into ridges and plateaus. Shadows still clung to the feet of those outcrops and these dark wisps moved as if thrown by some source other than the rocks against which they sulked.

There was fear—a fear which arose and strengthened—which began to twist within Farree. A pile of reading rolls crashed to the floor as his wings answered to the unconscious stimulus.

With the speed of a laser shot a head flashed into the bloody light. It was the epitome of all evil Farree had ever known. It clashed broken-toothed jaws together, and eyes like pits with a fire deep held stared straight at him.

It knew, it hated, it was coming from him! And it was—

"Boogy—" The hissing of Zoror broke that fearful hold which the screened creature had half woven about Farree—either to draw him into its place or to burst forth from the screen—how could it? This was unlike any reading roll he had seen. From whose mind had this horror been shifted for future study—and where—when—?

"This was a collective nightmare," Zoror said. Farree heard him but more than half of his own attention was still centered on that thing. It had emerged from the shadow now. The mist lay shrunken behind as if its substance had been stolen to give the creeper more reality. Creep the creature did. Stunted limbs supported it—no, not limbs but rather thick tentacles; and Farree believed that he could actually hear the sound of suckers being pulled loose from the rock to be set again as it advanced.

Nightmare? This was more alive than any nightmare. Enough to bring death if it struck through sleep.

"Which it did," the Zacanthan said. "Look to the rocks at the right, my little friend."

Farree felt that if he withdrew his attention from the crawler he would leave an opening for attack, even if this was a read-roll. However, he gave a quick glance in the direction the Zacanthan suggested.

There was no shadow at the foot of this standing stone; rather it was crowned with such. The form was humanoid and—Farree sucked in a breath and swallowed a cry. For it was a winged one standing there, and he knew without being told that this one controlled the creeper, was sending it at some prey, not to slay—at least not at first—but to torment with fear. A winged one. He gave it full attention now. Its flesh, shown in limb and arm and face, was a dirty grey. The eyes, like those of the thing it commanded, were red and burning. About its body was tight clothing, also of a red to match the ever-lightening sky. Those wings which lazily fanned the air were not like Farree's, broad and colored, with one hue melting into another, so that full-spread the pinions were things of soft beauty. No, this leader of merciless shadows had wings which lacked the feathery down which covered Farree's. Instead they were the same foul greyish shade as the skin. Spread out they displayed perilous-appearing hooks at the top.

"Winged—" Farree half whispered. To the fear which still coiled within him was added now true horror. Was this what could claim him as kin—in spite of Zoror's talk about true tales and false? Somehow he knew that this *was* a true tale—

"Only to two." Zoror picked up his thought, and, for the first time since he had discovered his gift because he could communicate with smux, Farree resented that this was so.

"Two," Zoror leaned over and one of his well-smoothed finger claws touched a control which sent the screen dead again. Yet when Farree looked at it, he could still see that abomination winged and aloft on the rock waving forward the horror born of shadows.

"The two," the Zacanthan was proceeding, "being he who dreamed and he, or perhaps it, who sent such a dream! This was taken from the dream sleep of a small child, one of the many who were brought for treatment from Mingra to Yorum well over a hundred planet years ago. Five only of those little ones survived. The rest—nightmares such as you have just seen pursued them, until some died of fear alone and some then retreated so far from the outer world in their terror that none could reach within where they cowered. Thus they became the lost which we could not help."

"But you speak of shame—" countered Farree. He had seen what could be unending fear perhaps, but there was no shame that he could understand. Any child, yes, and fully grown adult, too, would have no shame for such fear.

"There was on Mingra a colony of dream-sleepers and they were learning how to control their dreams," Zoror explained. "When they were called upon to help, when children howled and screamed in their sleep—they fled and refused any aid. Those who dream-sleep hover always on the thin line of what most men call madness. They have been known to strike out in their sleep, even take up weapons in their hands, to the hurt of any who may be with them. Thus they are sent into wilderness until they learn to control their powers. If this dream recording you have seen worked upon you, think what it might have done to one who was drilled to be sensitive to such encounters? It was not only themselves that the dream-sleepers sought to protect. However, men and women who had seen their children rave in their sleep, a sleep from which there seemed to be no waking, no matter how the medical officers of that colony tried to rouse them—such are not always answerable for red terror which they wreak on their own. There was a wild descent upon the colony of the sleepers. They were taken and given to pain of many kinds when they said they could not awaken nor help the children. They died, not quickly or easily. It was a ship of the Patrol on a regular duty that landed on a planet where hands were bloody and more than one mind could no longer bear the burden of remembering what had happened. The children who had survived that long, and that were very few of those, were brought to Yorum and there healers of the mind wrought ceaselessly to banish the boogyman—"

"The boogyman," repeated Farree.

"That is the name they screamed out of their sleep. However, it was a name which was already very old—another bit of Old Terra come to the stars. For the boogyman was an old creation designed to frighten children into good behavior. And we discovered that some tales of such had been told on Mingra where they were deemed harmless and amusing."

"Harmless? Amusing?" Farree sputtered. "But that was a scene of evil! What child could build such a dream? Unless his race was one of swift punishment and violent tempers?"

"Which they were not—until the plague drove them into such action," the Zacanthan replied. "Nor were any of the dream-sleepers so unstable that they played thus with their own gift. As you must have heard, those who dream-sleep are under vows which are set in their very innermost spirits so that their work can draw no ill upon anyone. However, all the children we were able to draw dream pictures from were caught in the same general horror. And you did not see the worst of this, my small friend. There are some dream pictures locked in stasis since only the very steady and exceptionally well stabilized dare look at them. To dream alike is possible—the dream-sleepers have brought that to a high art. Those who are trained almost from birth can serve for communication even between worlds.

"Therefore if the children were all haunted by the same dream then that dream had a pattern. The Patrol, my own staff, others with one power and another, strove to find the source of this common dream but to no avail. What we did discover was that through that section of the galaxy, comprising some five solar systems, there was uneasiness, there had been riots, even small wars fought. Also there was a rumor which will have meaning to you—the enemy sought was a winged race. Yet no man had actually seen any such, though our net of inquiry was far spread and touched some sources which were usually closed to authority—the Thieves' Guild for example.

"But the outbreak on Mingra appeared to be the end. There were no more nightmares, even though volunteers of trained tenth class dreamers offered their services to the search. Then the Patrol and the authorities said that the whole thing was doubtless started by either some mischief (those who said that had to lie away the very evidence before their eyes) or by a tendency to sensitiveness which was awakened by the old tales. It was then that authority set upon the settlers the brand of Shame for the massacre of the dream-sleepers, and all was to be left alone, with no more time or trouble about the outbreak which, after all, was a very small happening compared to the violence which is ever snapping at the heels of sanity in all inhabited worlds."

"Then the dream—they never believed it was true?" Farree asked.

Zoror rubbed two talons across his chin just above his first throat wattle. "Oh, they believed. And for a while they had their eyes and ears wide. Many of these," he gestured again to the read-rolls, "are their reports. That is why we have easy access to the material now and it is not buried in some storehouse. We add a fact or suspicion now and then—always stories, many of which match one another. The Little Men— the People of the Hills—"

Farree stiffened. People—of—of—the Hills!

"You have heard that before, have you?" questioned the Zacanthan.

Farree rubbed his hand across his forehead as if he could pluck out some very deeply buried memory. Back—back— He was in the sleazy, tent-board place curled up on the pile of mouldering reeds which was his only bed. And the man who owned him sat at a flimsy table, a-twirling between his filthy hands a broken-handled mug which still contained a mouthful or two of the ill-smelling drink he had been gulping. Lanti raised his head to look at Farree and there was promise in his scowl which the boy knew well. It would please the hulking outcast in a few breaths of time to summon Farree forward and beat him well; most of that storm of blows would fall on his hunched back. He could remember that right enough—but what lay before that tent-hut and his miserable captivity was gone.

"Yes." Zoror nodded. "Somehow, sometime, you were brain-erased. Yet when I mention one name given to the People in the past, you seem to know—"

Farree shook his head. "I can't remember. But—I have heard that name—surely I have heard it! Only in the Limits where all manner of spacers come and go, one hears scraps of many tales, or boastings of ventures."

"Still"—Zoror looked at him kindly—"that is one of the lesser-known names of these people who, it is true, might never have been. Well, it remains, Farree, that I must give you a warning. Maelen and Krip brought you here at night, traveling by air car. Very few must have seen you and it is true you can fold these"—he pointed to the wings—"amazingly small. At a distance in a subdued light they might be taken for a hunched-up cloak. However, by day there would be plenty sharp-eyed enough to note a difference. And—boy, you are not safe!"

"The Guild?" It was true that he had done enough to break up one plot of those masters of menace. But was he high enough among their lists of enemies to draw their attention? If so—

He frowned. Maelen and Krip Vorlund were his friends. It was by their efforts he had won out of the misery of the Limits. It was with them and working in their service that the wonder had happened to him—his wings had displayed themselves for the first time. If he were so noticeable, then staying with the two who meant so much to him might bring them into danger in turn.

"No." It was plain Zoror had followed his thoughts. Farree had made no attempt to shield them, he was so absorbed in what might be an unhappy discovery. "It is true that the Guild have no reason to cheer any of you." There was a rattle of a chuckle from the throat of the Zacanthan. "Much trouble you caused them, you three, as well as putting them to a form of shame should the story get around. But I believe you are all discreet enough not to talk about what was done. Rather you look forward to what lies next. However, among the many other noisome activities of the Guild is a form of slavery which they indulge in whenever chance offers. They have a list of clients (many of whom could buy this whole planet for their pleasure) who desire to own novelties. You are certainly one such and would bring a very high price on certain pleasure worlds. Then the Guild have their source of information which may not equal ours but is clearer than, say, the information tapes studied by the Patrol. It is quite possible that they have news about the Little People—especially since the Shame of Mingra. One of the often-mentioned tasks of that winged race, according to legend, was the amassing and guarding of treasure. Just suppose the Guild would take it to mind that you were of that mystery race and that you could lead them to a treasure— Ah, I see you understand me. So it is largely for your own sake that I ask you to take precautions against being seen."

Farree's head jerked on his shoulders. He almost stumbled over the stool from which he had just arisen. Zoror's words might be the humming of insects, for Farree's head was now held high, his nostrils were distended to their limit as he drew in a great breath of air. It had smelled musty, of dust and time in this chamber. Now there came another scent in a wave. Just as fear had caught him when he had watched that horror on the read-roll, so now did he welcome this—fragrance. It filled his lungs, sent him stumbling towards the door. All the flowers he had ever known—the spice of bushes—the keeness of water in a dry land. He dodged about a table and his wings raised and opened. Air—he must fly—

2.

The barrier winked out and there stood Maelen and Krip. But where was the other? Not hidden behind the two, for Farree would have still seen the edge or tips of wings. He knew—

Where was she!

"For whom do you search, little brother?" asked Krip. There was a shade of concern in his voice as he studied Farree.

"The one—the gracious one—she who flies in beauty! Where is she, my brother, my sister! Have you hidden her?" He suddenly recalled the warning Zoror had given him only moments earlier. "On the ship? Surely she is not of Gragal! For they have not seen our like before—he"—Farree signaled with a finger—"has told me so."

He wanted to shout—to sing—to fly triumphantly up and up—to meet her above in the clouds where their own road ran. Yet there were no smiles on the faces of his friends. Rather

Maelen's thought reached into him, dampening the excitement that filled him.

"There is no one with us—nor at the ship, little brother. Why do you think—?"

Farree reached her, his hands outstretched, then a chill extinguished all the sudden joy he had known for the first time in his hard and barren life. The scent—no, he could not mistake that! And it came from—

His hand shot out and he grabbed from Maelen's hold something wrapped in a sheet of luxwool such as was used to protect some fragile ware after purchase. The sheet flipped apart, letting him see something which shimmered in a melting burst of color: rose, pearl-white, and the warm grey of first twilight.

Farree continued to stare as the fragrance arose about him in a cloud of scent filling every breath he drew. She—she—

He uttered a harsh cry and dropped upon the nearest pile of dead tapes that wondrous thing—wondrous, yes. But the feel of raw cruelty was a part of it: such torment as to sweep away all he had first felt, giving instead a sense of harsh pain. Then out of that pain grew an anger, fierce, filling him to the point where he threw out an arm and swept to the floor two piles of tapes, his lips drawn back so tightly against his teeth that his face was now that of a snarling animal unable to give vent to anger save through claw and fang. His other hand flew to his belt and freed the short defense knife which was his legacy from their meeting with the Guild. Who could be made to pay for this—this hurt, sorrow—DEATH!

"Where—" The demand came as a slurred snarl. "Where was this?" He dared not touch that thing of many colors again; it racked him now even to look at it.

Maelen moved deliberately, coming up beside him. Farree's whole body quivered as he longed to turn on her, large as she was, to shake from her the knowledge he must have. She picked up the scrap of beauty, shook it out so that he saw, having to watch in spite of his rage and horror, she held a length which might form a scarf. The strip had been cut at an angle which led the colors to play in and out.

"What is this?" Maelen did not try to pierce the turmoil in Farree's mind, rather spoke aloud in a quiet voice such as she would use with her beloved little ones—those beasts, strange or familiar, which shared her life.

"What is it—brother?" she asked for the second time. Farree had given room to too many strong emotions in too short a time. Now he felt dizzy and sick, having to hold onto the edge of the table. Three times he swallowed before he could bring forth a word.

"It is—from a wing!" His own quivered as he answered.

"So!" That was Krip Vorlund who answered. "Perhaps a wing such as yours?" he asked.

Farree turned his head so he did not have to watch that flutter of color which Maelen had taken up again. Memory— did he have any memory of this? He wrestled with his rage and got its explosive force under control. "A wing—maybe like mine." Save that it was far more beautiful in its warm colors than his own shaded green pinions.

"Can you tell us more, little brother?" Maelen, who was the friend of all winged, pawed, other live forms, was watching him very intently.

Farree did not even raise his hand. His mouth twisted and there was a burning in his throat—anger was still there but here now was something else, a sense of loss so great that it bore down on him as had the burden of his wings before time and dire effort had freed them.

"She is dead—" He spoke the words, and in his mind he wept.

"How did death come?" Vorlund's firm voice steadied Farree enough so he could answer.

"I—I don't know. If I try to learn"—he waved his thin fingers inches above the length of the scarf—"I will only feel what she felt, not the way of death, nor where it came for her."

Zoror's neck frill was fully raised. He leaned forward a little as if he could force from the length of wing silk more.

"Smuggled—contraband?" His hiss was nearly lost in the sharpness of his demand. But he did not try to handle the length which continued to flutter even though there were no breezes here to set it in motion.

Vorlund asked the question for them all. "This then is a forbidden import? Why would any one risk exile from space to peddle such a thing? What virtue does it have besides beauty?"

It was true that smuggling was a major crime on all planets, one which brought a full force of all law enforcement officers, on planet or off, to find and punish the miscreants.

"I do not know," the Zacanthan returned. "Because I officially deal in off-world curios, things which might add even a word or two to our records, I have a full membership in the Importers' Guild, not only here but on five other worlds. This is on the forbidden list—"

"And how is it listed?" Maelen laid the strip carefully back on the table.

"As spider silk—a new type—to be reported to the nearest Patrol post at once."

"I do not know this spider silk." Farree looked at nothing but that shimmering mass. "But this cannot be that—"

"No." Krip Vorlund shook his head. "It appears to be far more. Taken from wings—"

At his words Farree shuddered and had again to grab at the table's edge to steady himself. He must wall off that beginning of thought. In the scum of the Limits, where these two had found him, had saved him from rotting with the rest of the drifters bogged there in the mud of evil which the straggling settlement near the landing space really was, he had had the first beginnings of thought to thought—sharing with the smux, also a prisoner. Then these two had come and swept up Togger, and him. He had seen sights a-plenty which were a mingling of fear and horror, but somehow none of those had touched within him as this did—as if it strove to unlock a door which, if he opened it, would sweep him up into another time and place which he must not enter, not yet—

"If it is on the forbidden list," Maelen said, "then its nature and source must be known to someone—it's likely been seen before."

It was Zoror who answered the question. "Wings—brother." He looked now to Farree and there was concern in his eyes, hidden partly by wrinkles of scales. "Could you tell us who or where?"

There was a wave of sickness rising in Farree. "I—"

"No!" Maelen interrupted him. "That is one place he dares not venture—into the past from which this came." She put forth her hand and pushed back a sweat-damp lock of hair from Farree's forehead.

"Where did *you* find this, Daughter of Moon Power," Zoror asked in a formal tone, as if she were to give evidence.

"For open sale at the market. To search bodily, that we can do!" she returned. "There Farree may find a clue that he dares draw into his mind."

"Watch for a spacer, down on his luck, far down," commented Vorlund.

"A spacer who has been to many worlds, perhaps, known and unknown," Zoror added as if he were attacking some problem with the full strength of his own knowledge. "It follows that we must see this spacer again—and perhaps best in his own setting. There may be more—!" He did not touch the scarf which his talons indicated. "But our little brother here—he must have some protection. Let us see—"

"Protection?" Vorlund asked.

"Yes. When we have more time I will explain. But twilight is here and I would say that we had best be about what we would do before the coming of full night."

There was a hooded cloak which Maelen proved adept at

putting about him, fixing the hood above the upper jet of his wing tips, leaving him a seeing space in front. Farree's height now was akin to that of his companions. Before he left Togger leaped from the table where he had been squatting, seeming no more than a fistful of outward pointing scarlet quills, dodged within the eye space they had left Farree and settled down, holding on with all eight of his claws.

As they came out upon the small court where the Zoror's team had their quarters, the Zacanthan spoke into a wrist dial, summoning a scooter. Vorlund shook his head.

"With all respect, High Tech, within that we shall be as bare to sight as a half token on a swept pavement—"

"That is so," Zoror returned as the small flyer set down, waiting orders. "But it will take us to the port entrance. There will be many coming and going—and we shall make us a path through such a gathering to the Faxc entrance—from there it is but a step to the Street of Traders."

Maelen looked at him keenly. "Elder brother, you speak as one who leaves a stricken field and expects the victor on your trail. You say that Farree walks into danger. What pot is boiling here?"

"Of you I could ask the same, little sister," the Zacanthan returned. "But there is a watch which has been placed on this small brother—of that I am sure. Yes, he goes into what may be the very heart of danger. Thus we take what precautions are possible to us."

They climbed into the scooter and Vorlund leaned forward to tap out a destination.

Farree took up more than his share of room because his cloak-covered wings returned to him the hump which had once weighed him down so much. At least they had left that length of wing stuff behind and he was free of the influence which it exerted over him—though he was not free of a nagging ache—the now firm belief that somewhere there had been such trouble as, in spite of all his own sufferings in the

Limit, he had not known. He looked from one to another of his three companions. The Zacanthan by what expression his scaled face could show was the same. Maelen's head was up and there was a spark in her eyes which Farree knew of old, just as he recognized the tightened lips of Vorlund, and the fact that the spacer's hand slipped back and forth along his belt as if he sought the hilt of a long knife or the grip of a stunner, both of which had been lawfully put into a locker by the port officers when they had landed here.

"Where is this trader?" Zoror wanted to know.

"Close to the edge of the stalls," Maelen answered, "near those places which rent at night space to those low in credit." Her hand covered her own wrist dial, which stated what lay behind her in buying credit.

"Then we shall land by the Gate of Unregistered Aliens." Zoror's talons clicked against the scales which guarded his lips "And—"

"We are followed," Vorlund interrupted. "There is a private scooter which flies this line and does not take another course. Merchants have house colors here, do they not, sir?"

Zoror did not turn to look and satisfy himself that the spacer was right, paying Vorlund the compliment of trust.

"They do so, yes."

"Then who among them puts up three red stripes with a sun yellow in the middle?"

Zoror blinked twice. Farree longed to turn and see what Vorlund had reported but was too tightly wrapped in his cloak to try.

"It makes no sense," the Zacanthan said.

"What and why?" the spacer countered.

"You name the colors of a house which trades by sea and would not show such a sign this deep into the continent. The sea-based houses are of a different breed; there are few of them who take to the land for anything but a Call Out from the

Council—and then they do it protestingly. None of them even has a secondary quarter here."

"No!" Maelen's voice was an order; enough to bring all their eyes towards her. There was a grim set to her jaw and on her knees her hands moved in patterns which Farree believed were those of a Moonsinger.

"Do not think," her voice dropped until it was hardly more than a murmur, "there is none who seeks!"

Farree followed the old path of his own. There was a tower, he speedily constructed in his thoughts. One like that on Yiktor where he had come into his proper inheritance and Maelen had discovered the buried history of her own kin, long forgotten. But this tower was not of stone, nor of any of the building materials which he had seen; and it was fast deepening before the eyes of his imagination to a deep rose. Now it lightened slowly from one story to the next, then darkened again into a grey which became the velvety shade of the early night sky—

So intently did he fasten his attention that it was with something of the shock suffered by one who was shaken hurriedly awake from a deep sleep, that he swayed under Maelen's touch.

The scooter had landed. Just behind them was the gate Zoror had mentioned though there was no one passing through now. Before them, not too far away, was the beginning of a sprawling port within a port which was as dirty and unrulable a place as the Limits had been. There were plenty to call it home after a fashion: spacers who had committed such errors as forced them to surrender their active tickets, those who dealt in smuggled wares. Here one doubtless could re-equip oneself with a stunner such as Vorlund and Maelen had surrendered upon landing here.

It seemed to Farree that the very air above the jungle of decaying and half ruined buildings showed against the sky of growing night as might smoke from a noisome fire. He drew the cloak closer about him and touched Togger gently. It might have been that gesture which brought the in and out pattern of the creature's mind to meld with his for a moment or two.

"In—in—!" There was such urgency in that beaming that Farree found himself trotting until Vorlund caught him by the shoulder.

"Not so fast, brother," the spacer said quietly. "They still watch—let them not take such an interest in what we do that might bring them down upon us, if that is what they are prepared to do."

However, Farree's head was up, and the cloak twisted back and forth as he turned from side to side. That scent! Once more he had caught the touch of the same fragrance which had filled Zoror's room. This was far fainter, having to fight against all the stenches of the place. But he could not lose it once he had picked it up.

"Right, brother." That was Vorlund. "Lead us—but with care."

Farree paid little attention to that. He moved to the front of their party, leaving the rest a step or two behind.

"Bad—hurt—bad—" That was Togger again. But Farree did not need the smux's warning. For the scent which was his guide began to change in quality. Fear—yes, certainly fear! Farree paid no attention to his companions as they reached the first stinking pathway which served this new version of the Limit as a street. He gathered up the skirts of his cloak and held them closely about him as he met with two staggering drunks and used all the craft he had learned in the past years to dodge them, though one aimed a blow at where his head might have been had the cloak really covered the tall man he seemed.

There were more and more people on the street. Some slipped quickly and furtively along, taking all advantage they could of every shadow. There were more drunks and some who were heading to become so. The potions and drugs one could get within this maze might be watered down and cut to a lesser strength, but those who must have them headed toward their places of supply.

Two taverns leered crookedly at each other across the filthy street. Farther in there were lights beginning to show and one could hear from there the crash of ear-tormenting music.

"In—" Togger might have shouted, so loud did it seem. Farree put a hand inside of his loose over-tunic to touch the smux's back bristles. He did not need Togger's urging now—the beacon he followed was growing stronger and stronger.

Pain and fear: but now he was almost certain that both those were of the past—that he was not on his way to rescue some captive. However, where fragments of wings were to be found, there also one could certainly learn from whence they had come. Naturally the trader would lie. Farree's pointed teeth showed for an instant as he grinned in promise. However—there were he, and Maelen, and Vorlund, and the Zacanthan, and, of course, Togger. All of them had the reading gift. His own had been honed and polished during the past months when he had traveled with the two spacers—he knew that he was far better now at this ploy than he had ever been.

There was a crowd ahead. Farree halted for a moment and looked to what lay between him and that which he sought. To push into that crowd—it would take only one drunken jostling to have him uncloaked and betrayed to a trader who dealt in wings.

Most of those he surveyed were crowded about a platform set the height of a man's shoulder above the surface of the street. On this a tall and very thin man, who wore such a skin-tight article of clothing that he might be thought to be bones alone, was waving a narrowed hand with six long fingers back and forth. From the tip of each finger spouted a flame. He took up from an upturned box which served as a table a pannikin half full of liquid, turning it as far as he might without spilling its contents so that the crowd, or at least those immediately before his perch, could see that the pannikin did have contents. Having made a portion of his audience believe that, he held the small bowl with a pair of tongs directly above his own flaming fingers, chanting aloud words which apparently none of his listeners could understand. Now he had won their full attention. As they crowded closer Farree was left with a small space to push by. What he sought was very near; the anguish of the message had become stronger and he traced it to a booth right on the other side of the magician. There seemed to be no one in charge there, though a man in a stained and worn spacer's uniform from one of the large company ships stood directly before its entrance, eyes on the magician.

Farree reached the end of the booth, searching with his eyes the wares laid out there. Some of that was trader trash—such as the companies used with natives on planets newly opened, where the inhabitants did not know the true value of off-world things. But this was not what he sought. He felt Togger move and knew that the smux wanted out; but it was better, he counciled with a swift thought, to wait yet a while.

He himself held his hand over the counter, clutching the cloak as tightly around him as possible. Slowly he swung it palm down, fingers straight and together. No, not on the board at all. But close, very close. Farree would have to risk Togger after all. With a quarter of his attention on the back of the man he believed was the trader, Farree dropped the smux on the piles of stuff. Togger could hurry if there was a good reason and he did so now, speeding over the trade goods, though he had to stop once and shake a gaudy necklace of fake Ru crystal off one of his claws. Reaching the other end of that narrow shelf he swung part way out, only two of his hind feet anchoring him to the surface. There was a sudden surge of the fear-torment. Farree braced himself as if he stood in the path of a tempest.

The smux came into view again, dragging a flat package which pushed some of the trade trash before it. Farree was shaking now. The fear-terror was fast changing into anger. He looked down at the stuff but there was no weapon there. No, the unlicensed trader would not want the State Pacifers to find him with such. Instead Farree grabbed up the packet. His trembling had become worse, and his hold had fallen from his cloak so that the garment was ready to slip from him.

Togger sprang, landing on Farree's chest. His claws went out, caught at the cloak and dragged it shut toward him. In Farree's hands the packet shook and nearly fell.

"Hey, you! Trying to get that without a credit, eh? Well, you don't play that game with Ryss Onvet, no, you don't. I can call me a street warden good and clear. We may be trash to your up-nosed crowd from the town but we still got our rights, always being that we ain't on any list."

"But of course that is so," Farree felt the Zacanthan move in on one side of him and Maelen and the spacer on the other. "My friend here wishes to make a purchase. He was waiting to attract your attention. The magician, I must admit, is quite good, very good indeed. Now, if you are willing to conduct business, how much does my friend owe?"

The man had a heavy scar across his forehead which twisted his eyebrows unnaturally, but Farree, in spite of the overwhelming discharge from the package, could sense that the merchant was squinting at them narrowly as if he looked for something or someone who was not there.

He must have made up his mind quickly for he said in a rush of words, in trader tongue for emphasis, that he had no business to do with strangers—

"Do you then," Maelen wanted to know, "deal only with your neighbors here? Certainly that makes your market a very limited one and I should think your sales were few."

"Gentle Fem,"—he got out the polite address as if it strangled him to say it—"I deal with all comers, yet I also take specialty consignments. One of those your friend there has taken up. I can also add theft to my complaint against him since that which he holds is *not* for sale at all."

"No? Look at me, merchant, and at my friend here." She indicated Krip Vorlund with a small gesture. "Did you not sell to us a short time since a curiosity which was indeed better ware than any you show here?"

The man opened his mouth as if to refute her at once and then seemed to look beyond them as if he sought for some help.

"Was this not true?" she pressed.

He coughed and stroked his throat as if he had swallowed something he could neither control internally nor heave out again.

"Yes," his voice was hardly above a mutter.

"Sooooooo," the word was such a hiss from the Zacanthan that, for a moment, Farree could believe that he companioned some great reptile. "What isss sissss sing?"

He reached across to Farree and effortlessly freed the packet from his hand.

"Treasure? Sssso you mussst declare it sssso—" Even as the hiss grew more pronounced the Zacanthan effortlessly put a talon under the top fold of the wrapped package and gave one short pull to display its contents.

Farree already knew what he would see. There were two more lengths of the shining wing stuff. One was a red-brown shading through warm yellows and oranges. And the other—

Green, several shades of green: not the darker shades which made up the glory of his own wings; lighter.

Not green—red! The whole world had turned red about

him. He mouthed a strange cry which he had never voiced before and his hands shot forth—not to seize again upon what the Zacanthan held—but to grasp that throat rising above the grimy collar of the disgraced uniform, to dig into the trader's dirty red flesh and squeeze, squeeze and squeeze!

him and he ... ... at the ... ... We ...
before ... with his ... one ... ...
the ... ...
... ...

3.

Get off—you—!" The trader's hand rose. From somewhere
he had procured a band fitting securely about his knuckles,
the metal plates of it starred with sharp pointed spikes facing
outward. He crouched a little behind the warped board on
which lay his wares, his armored hand moving outward and to
the side.

The red mist which had filled the world for Farree did
not lighten, but of a sudden not only was there the weight of
hands upon his shoulders but in his mind there was a binding
as secure as if he were entangled in a hunter's net. He could
think, could see that which he wanted, but he was being
dragged back by those hands on his shoulders, held helpless
by that swift barrier in his mind—but not so helpless that he
could not catch up the length of green wing.

The grasp which held him then swung him bodily around
and pushed him towards the port end of the crooked street.
Then the hold relaxed enough to let him stumble on as long as

it was forward and not toward the trader's booth. Yet inside
him there was a chaos, first nurtured by anger, and then by
scraps and bits of what were certainly no memories of his!

Heights rising from a green plain into a silver mist: there
was no visible sun and yet there shone a radiance as complete
as the full light of such. What he saw was only snatches, gone
before he could center any in his mind. In his nostrils there
was a medley of scents completely covering the foulness of the
path down which he was being urged.

There was a sudden darkness in this place of green and
silver. No true storm, that much he could guess. If he did
somehow look through another's eyes—memories—then there
had come a swirling of strong evil to tear away all he
witnessed. Nor was he able to see source of the evil. He only
felt—first curiosity, which caught him as surely as if a sharp
blade did cut into his flesh. Fear for himself, yes, but what
was worse, fear for another whom he could not see but who
was as much a part of him as if she were an arm, a heart—

He was gone into that dream place, unaware now if any
walked with him, knowing only that death stalked and he
must stand between prey and hunter.

Then—there was a last thrust of heart pain. He thought
he cried out, while still he sought to face that which had crept
behind him. Only now it was dark, full and complete dark.
When that closed upon him, Farree knew he had been too
weak, too small, too untrained. The blackness was death and
into it she had disappeared. He blinked and there before him
was the Gate of Unregistered Aliens at the port. He looked
behind. Hands were still lying on his shoulders—Maelen. She
was watching him very carefully.

"What chances, small brother?" she asked—and her
voice seemed to come from a vast distance.

"Death—" His answer was hardly above a whisper and he
wiped one hand across his eyes. There were no tears to be so
shaken off, only still the abiding rage. His other hand, the bit

of wing silk about his wrist, strayed to the front of his tunic under the rumpled cloak. Togger! Where was Togger?

Taking advantage of the loosened grip upon him Farree turned so quickly that the robe flew out. Only in a few seconds of time did something which was colder, more exacting than his anger warn him. But he was already several strides away from them all.

"Togger!" he thought, as he might shout aloud for another companion who had only speech in common with him.

"Here—we—" Whatever the smux might have added was gone. All that was left was an emptiness Farree recognized. There were devices known both to the Patrol and to the Thieves' Guild which could clamp down against any thought sending. But in order to use those someone must have suspected Togger—and Farree himself.

He longed to throw aside the muffling cloak, to be in the air and so able to follow his friend, for Togger had been on the thin outside edge of response when he had sent that broken call for aid: for that was what it was.

Farree was no longer aware of their company. The contacts he had made mentally within the past turn of the hour sweep seemed to have in some way severed his close contact with the spacers and the Zacanthan.

Only they had not lost him. He was aware of someone moving up close beside him and swerved, having no desire to be once more bound by superior strength of either mind or body. It was Maelen—but she was making no attempt to lay hands on him again. Nor had he picked up that clear sending which was hers.

"Togger," he thought swiftly, hoping to make good use of his present freedom. "Togger goes with one—"

"They have found your small one?" That was Zoror and the thought came from behind.

"I think not," Farree returned. He was already off the smooth surface of the gate road into the dust which would become the muck of the shunned street. He looked ahead. The trader—the magician—somehow he thought of them both together, as if, like Maelen and Vorlund, they were so closely knit that their thought might blend into a single mind voice.

None of his companions tried to stop him. They might have taken council together and decided that Farree's loss was theirs also.

The ever-present glow-light of the port was behind them, but the road took a crooked turn and the evil-smelling splotch of buildings was closing in behind. There was light of a sort—here and there one of the door lights demanded by law was a small spark. But it was plain that none of these were allowed to emit the full glow of the same lamps which hung in the city beyond the irregular wall cutting the port settlement from the place where law walked and there could be questions asked with impunity.

As he went Farree fought to pick up touch with the smux, but the silence was complete. However, he remained certain that sooner or later he would be steered aright.

Around their party clung that scent which had brought Farree into the maze of stinking lanes. Only now he strove not to heed it, since he wanted a clear mind, with no thrusts of rage, to follow any trail Togger had set.

They were all with him, Maelen, Vorlund, and Zoror, but this time they appeared to be content to surrender the lead to Farree. Here was the magician's shaky platform. Some of the boards of which it had been fashioned now lay on the ground but no one had attempted to clear them away.

Farree wheeled to look at the booth where the trader had spread out his sorry supply of wares. They lay muddled, tossed in small heaps, some of them fallen into the muck of the roadway. He who had displayed them was gone, and strangest of all, as Farree knew with particular vividness from his own life within a port refuse settlement, this seller had left his stock in trade behind. There must have been raids already on the tawdry stuff. Even as Farree came up he saw hands which were more like clawed paws than his own working with lightning speed to sweep off the largest pile; it disappeared on the other side of the improvised table. There was a scurry as something small and dark as a blot of night pressed all together scuttled away.

Farree stretched out his own right hand, passing it slowly back and forth across what was left. There was nothing to answer until he came to the extreme edge behind the table. Then his skin pricked and he spread his fingers wider. Here was a trace of Togger at last. But nothing remained of that length of a second plundered wing.

With infinite care, Farree held his hand above what looked like a broken bone—dull and brown and shaped with a cutting edge into a knife. Yes, Togger! Now he raised the hand and turned around slowly so that the hand swept across and took in both the magician's platform and this deserted booth.

There! Farree's hand steadied, pointing inward toward the deeper reaches of this dangerous district.

"They have not found him." He was convinced of that. Were the smux captive Farree certainly could have read that also. "But he must have gone with the trader."

"To search such a maze and its many lurking places," Zacanthan observed, "may be impossible. Do you receive any more from him?"

"No," Farree returned impatiently, "but— Ah!" He interrupted his own answer, corrected it. "He is there! He does not send except with emotion."

"Yes, that I have, too," Maelen agreed. "Will he leave a trail or guide you—"

"If he can. It is this way!"

"Wait." For the first time Vorlund spoke. "There are baits for traps—if they would take you, little brother, how better could they call you so? It may be that they know Togger is with them, but they will let him do as he wishes and summon you—"

"Well thought," Zoror hissed. "We cannot turn for any help to the guards, for they do not venture here themselves by night, nor even far in by day. If there are deaths here they turn their heads and do not look. As long as these prey upon their own kind, so will they be left alone. It is only the very foolhardy who would venture out of the stew to kill or rob. I do not think that even the Guild have more than a token representative here."

"I go for Togger," Farree answered simply.

"He will not be turned from that!" Maelen said. "But if they lay a trap for one and four arrive—four with somewhat better weapons than expected, may not the plan benefit us?"

Zoror chuckled. "Daughter, that is a thought to lighten the heart. Only I would suggest that we do not go openly, marching like a landing party with a talk flag above us. We do not know what we seek—"

It was Farree's turn to interrupt. "The wings!"

"What do you mean?" Maelen asked.

"The wings—such brought me here. I think there is still a link between those we seek and their plunder—and I wear this!"

"Let us not argue this in the middle of the street," Vorlund warned again. "Slip around to the back of the booth. It is only right to believe that we are under constant monitoring and perhaps have been ever since we left the Place of Long Knowledge. However, what precautions are possible let us follow."

Now Farree heard a small sound from Maelen which might be smothered laughter. "Wise, oh, wise. Just let us hope that we do not tumble into some hole of refuse and smother ourselves with nose lifting stenches."

Farree was around the counter in the booth before she

had finished talking. And he was barely out of the way when the others joined him.

"Now what have you to say about the wings—you are sure these are parts of wings?" Maelen wanted to know.

"I am sure," Farree replied shortly. "And those who once wore them—" He swallowed twice as if he would bite and hold fast the emotion which the thought awoke in him. "Those are dead."

None of them answered that. Perhaps the very tone of his voice made it impossible to quarrel with his statement.

They were behind the booth, going single file down a narrow way between the rear of two lines of booths which backed upon one another. Farree forced from his mind all but the seeking.

At the end of that narrow cut with its soft foul footing rising nearly ankle high he stood for a moment, his head turned a little as if he were listening to something which should be audible to all of them. Then he slipped into the wider alley which ran towards the center of the maze. Not Togger, not yet. But he again caught the faintest trace of the other odor in spite of the stenches about—the scent of the torn wings. Abruptly he turned to Maelen and held out one hand while with the other he drew his concealing cloak even closer about him.

"Give me—yes, give me that other piece! The one you bought before."

She asked no question, but unsealed the long pocket which was part of her suit at the thigh. There came a rustle and then he felt the length of silky stuff she passed to him—felt and *SAW*. For, though here were not even booth lanterns with their dull smoky light—his eyes could detect a faint glow from the stuff he had wound about his wrist. And with both strips so tightly in his hold he felt a drawing again—not from Togger. The green length seemed to wrap of itself about his flesh. There was a bitter chill which crept from it up his arm, down into his fingers. Dead—worn by the dead once—but alive in a way he did not understand—save that he was sure it was acting with him, perhaps for him.

Farree darted across the opening of the wider alley and once more sought a very narrow way. He had to be careful to twist and turn to accommodate his wings. The faint radiance from his wrist band was growing stronger—or was it that he was trusting its guidance the more?

"Here!" He backed a little away and nursed the banded wrist against his body. The shadow against shadow which was Vorlund moved closer.

"There is a door here," the spacer reported. "It is set in as part of a wall—I see no latch or way of opening it."

"Let me, brother." It was Zoror's turn before the wall. Farree caught a glimpse of a larger shadow moving in behind Vorlund. There were always noises in these streets—more so now that night had come and most of the inhabitants who sheltered or swaggered here were rousing for another night's pleasure or darksome business. Yet Farree caught a faint clicking and knew that Zoror must be trying his own way of gaining entrance through the wall door.

"It is ssooo,"—the Zacanthan sank his speech to that hiss which served his species as a whisper. "This is most easy— Thus!"

He was gone and Farree caught only a quick sight by the fading color of the scarf he carried to show that the Zacanthan had gone apparently through the door or wall as if that had been an illusion and not a solid barrier. He himself was quick to follow. There was a narrow hall running before him, but what was most important there was also a flight of narrow and splintery steps to his left. Light came from a globe fastened over their heads wherein luminous insects crawled and spun threads which shone brightly.

The steps were narrow and very steep. Farree wondered if he could take them with the cloak still bundled about him.

He had lowered and folded his wings to the smallest possible size but still they were a bigger obstacle than the case which had once held them and made him a hunchback.

There was a sudden thrust with his head. Togger! Perhaps the smux had been casting out for him all the time but the beamed message had not been able to reach him before.

"Here—bad—bad—" A recognition and a warning. At the same moment Maelen caught at the fold of Farree's cloak and held him back.

"Not yet—" As the Zacanthan had used his voice in whisper so did she use her mind speech in a similarly low key. "There is a cover here!"

Farree stopped. He could beam in on Togger right enough and now he sharpened his contact. The Zacanthan, with the usual silent steps of his kind, was already on the stairs, Vorlund only a little behind. Farree tried a trace of touch. There was nothing—none from his companions and curiously deadened for those beyond. This was not the first time he had faced a mind shield in action, though such would certainly be of great value to any of the dwellers in this filthy tangle of rotting buildings and swampy streets.

Instantly he clamped down on his own thought. Did they have some warning—and he suspected that they might well have—so any who would follow them must be thought proof? Had they picked up the smux's broadcast and were the four of them indeed now entering a trap?

The stairway led the four to an upper hall where there seemed more substantial walls and some pretense of cleanliness. Two doors opened on one side and one on the opposite—all closed. However, the murmur of voices reached them. Zoror noiselessly passed to the farthest room and there stretched out his hand, planting it palm down against the surface, but not before Farree caught a quick glance of what was a small disc. Having pushed that against the door, he reached back his other hand and took firm grasp of Vorlund's;

the spacer in turn caught Maelen's in a similar grip with
Farree ending the chain.

He could hear! By now he should not be surprised by
anything which could happen. Instead he strained hard so as
to not miss a single word uttered within the room.

"It is so." The voice so brought to them lacked any
expression of feeling—it might have been a tape left to run.
"He was in the Painted Street tonight. I tell you, the
information Varis gave was right."

There was still only a murmur from a second voice, a
deep-sounding one which seemed easier to hear yet could not
as well be understood: it uttered words which were disguised
against Zoror's spy disc.

"Three of them with him—"

Murmur.

"A Zacanthan! You would not say go up against that one?
He was carefully watched I tell you—it was the scarf which
brought him—near pushed into an act where we could have
taken him easily. But not with a Zacanthan there. Also those
others—there has been a lot said about them—powers they
have."

Murmur.

"Yes, he seemed to know—there was a killing anger in
him then. They have said these would never go off-world—
well, whoever swore that would take oath to Zambut and then
go and spit in his god's fat face!"

Murmur.

"Certain—yes, I am certain. He might still be shaking the
dust-smoke from the Red Dunes off his shoulders. He wore a
cloak—and underneath were wings! Wings, I tell you! You
heard the report, saw the spin record. He is one of a kind and
he is of his own world—he can play no tricks here. Take him
and you'll find your backwards-running River and Old
Saptal's treasure all laid right to your hand. They all have the
secret—if that is the secret you wish to uncover."

A murmur which interrupted.

"We have tried that before—you have seen the reports. They will die rather than talk—and they will their own minds to crack rather than answer with the truth. Get him and—"

Maelen turned her head a fraction toward the stairs and then she alerted Vorlund with a small pull which he, in turn, passed as a warning on to Zoror. The Zacanthan moved away from the door, but he did not loose his hand tie with Vorlund. He retreated back down the hall and, holding the disc between two fingers, he gave a push to a second door. It swung open upon a small room. Another of the luminous insect globes showed a bed, narrow and stripped of all bedding, a small table and two stools. There was nothing else and the air within seemed stale. Zoror let go Vorlund's hand long enough to shut the door behind them and make a sweeping gesture which took in most of that side of the room. Then he crossed to the wall which separated this chamber from the one which now held the speakers. When Maelen briefly dropped her hand, Farree used the free moment to knot the second wing strip over the first around his wrist.

Their hands linked once more, again they could hear. "Speak it, then! If such action is correct, can you do it?"

Murmur.

"Try then!"

There was the sound of footsteps outside. Someone who had no reason to fear those in the far room had just walked past the hall door towards that same room.

"Gulde here." A third voice. And then it came again, undoubtedly from inside the room itself.

Murmur.

"I have promises, High Ones. Three pieces for covering your capture—"

Once more the murmur interrupted.

"It is not my failure, High One. What I was to do, I did.

That others could not carry through the plan was no fault of mine. You, High One—what is THAT!"

"Bad—bad—" The smux was broadcasting in a calling frenzy which Farree had not heard him use since he had been freed from the cage and the torture of Russtif on that day when a better life had come for both him and Farree.

"Catch it, fool with a head of feathers! Why did you bring that here?" The murmur had become speech, unscrambled by any device.

"I bring it?" That must be the trader. "I never saw it—this rotten wall hive may have many stranger things hiding out. Who can swear the Great Oath that ships landing here do not sometimes carry more than is on their cargo listing? It is nothing but a—a thing. Crush it—"

"It is a key," the growling voice began and then sank once again into the murmur. "The thing thinks." That much arose from out of the low notes.

"High One, it is then a way to spy upon us. Let me crush it—" The magician sounded shaky.

Murmur.

"Bait, High One? But is it possible that this is of *their* company—rather than a creature from a ship?"

Murmur. Then from Togger a mind cry as terrible and hideous as the ones the smux used to make when Russtif used the prod to send it into battle.

Togger! Farree pulled loose from their chain of communication and started for the door. Just as rage had taken him over earlier that day so did it rise again to drive him past all thoughts of safety, leaving only the need to rescue the smux.

There was a second cry from Togger. Vorlund had stepped between Farree and the door. He reached out and caught both of Farree's hands in what could be a merciless grip. There was no chance of evading that. But—Togger!

While Farree struggled fruitlessly against the hold the spacer used, he jerked, his body bending backwards, the cape falling to the floor. His face was a mask of pain.

Through the door, or the walls, or the whole of this warren of a house there sounded a shrill, ear-shattering call. Farree was frozen into the position in which he was held, filled with a torturing pain which spread from his head down the length of his spare body. His wings, now that he could no longer hold command of his body—or his mind—swelled up, to open.

He could hear and he could see, but all else was sealed in some fearsome case even as his wings had been. He rocked on his feet as Vorlund changed grip upon him. Maelen had taken a step toward him, he could see her only from the corner of one eye. The Zacanthan swung closer to the wall. He had broken all contact with the others and stood pressed against the stained surface, only the palm of his hand between his head and the disc. He fanned his other hand—a gesture which could only mean for them to remain in silence where they now were. Farree's panic was drying his mouth and throat. Even if the Zacanthan had not signaled silence he could not have broken through that which encased him now. Vorlund drew him closer, supporting Farree against a fall.

Togger! Though he was cold with fear, with the fear that they might indeed have fallen into a trap, Farree thought first of the smux. He was fearful enough to try mind touch. Instantly there was more movement beside him and Maelen's hands came out to clap upon his head just over his ears.

Now he could not see! Streaks of brilliant light played back and forth before his eyes as did lightning over the heights of Yiktor. She was a wisewoman of her kind and she had knowledge. But to use that against him—No, Togger was his own friend more than any other in this world. For a moment there was fire—fire to cut through the chill of that which imprisoned him. He could see the scarves he had looped around his wrist. Along the edges of the wing-strips there flashed sparks of white, of green—and last of all a sun-brilliant yellow. The force of their coming to life shot through his body.

4.

During all his life Farree had chosen to do the prudent thing and withdraw from danger. The uncasing of his wings but a short span ago had given him self confidence to be sure, but to face up to an enemy infinitely larger and more muscular than himself, an enemy fighting on his home territory who might perhaps call on any manner of forces— Only this time all the common sense had been shaken out of his trapped body. He could summon no strength to lunge against Vorlund, somehow to shoulder the tall, battle-trained spacer out of the way, and win to Togger's aid. He was still dumbly in the toils of that mysterious force which the whistle had laid upon him. Dumbly, then, he allowed himself to be shifted between Vorlund and Maelen till the three of them were again handfast with the listening Zacanthan.

"We are under a silence?" That was the magician who asked. Some sibilance of his trade speech betrayed him.

"Do we look to be brainless muck worms? Yes, we are under silence, only one begins to wonder—"

The murmur broke for a second time and they could catch intelligible speech. "Yes—wonder—there is nothing can come upon us here—or is that also false? What traveller can ever weigh the marvelous strengths and defenses of a new world? Be silent!"

Straightway there came something new to plague Farree. The force which held him was sloughing away as if it were a covering which he could rend from his body. That which had struck him at the whistling broke—was partly gone. On his wrist the yellow light of the scarf bands was shading down the scale of color, green-brown-red, and then a red as true as would come with new shed blood. In his mind there was a queer beat as if some drum or rattle was pounding out a code, while the now scarlet band flickered.

Vorlund shifted his grip again, and still Farree was without the necessary energy to pull free. He saw by the mingled light furnished by the band on his wrist and the single dim lamp a pulsating to match the beats. At first he thought that he was swinging from side to side in the same pattern and then he saw that Maelen, Zoror, and Vorlund himself were all one with him and that pounding. Vorlund's lips moved; he might have been speaking, but the drum beat in Farree's head had deadened his ears to outer sound—only the pattern of the drum remained.

It was the Zacanthan who made the first move. Catching at the purse and sheath at his belt he brought forth not one of the knives forbidden to off-worlders but rather what looked to be a curved and shining talon twice the size of any of those which sprouted from his fingers.

The silver length of it was patterned by bits of blue which sparkled like jewels. Stepping away from the wall Zoror used that talon as if it were indeed knife, slicing it back and forth through the air as he might engage some invisible enemy. The talon weapon began to change color, those bits of blue inlay shading into darker and more violent shades just as the scarves had done. It was difficult for any but his own species to read any expression on the Zacanthan's scaled face; however, one could not mistake his eyes—not dark with anger but bright with interest, as if some new bit of learning had been drawn to his attention and he was about to pluck all or any secrets out of this encounter.

Maelen held her own hands out, palms down, her fingers quirking up one by one until they stretched to their farthest reach in fan shape. She was staring at each finger in turn, as if assuring herself that she still possessed them all.

There was moisture on Farree's wrist. He glanced down. Drops were bubbling out of the double band. He might have just taken it out of a stream or pool. Save what fell was not the clearness of true water, rather it was first a pinkish froth and then took on more substance, becoming the same shade of red as the band now was. Blood! Surely that was blood such as might ooze through the dressing on a wound. It fell, but not to the floor, for it diffused again into small balls of mist before it reached even the level of Farree's knees.

It was as if that moisture filled the air it had disappeared into, for it seemed now as if he could actually taste blood, smell it.

Now the color was draining out of the band. It became wrinkled as ashy spots grew on it. Then both layers of it thinned, flaked away as might ashes from a burning. Only on his flesh there remained a brand, red as a burn. That which had held him prisoner was gone and Farree's medley of thoughts could be sorted out into messages again.

Togger! He quested outward.

"Bad—" He managed to pick up that, but it came very faint and low.

What followed then they all heard clearly, having no need this time for any disc or connected line of search: A cry which was not of the mind but rather had broken from a throat of flesh.

"Ahhhhh!"

Togger! Not that cry from him. Rather another mind send: A sensation of being held tightly, of being flung through the air—

"Fool!" They could hear the snap of that voice without any aid. "Spaquet!" There was a blurred mind image of a pale animal bulk plodding into a thick soup of mud.

"The little one"—Zoror's hiss of whisper came as he moved to restore the silver talon into his belt pouch—"he has struck one—I believe he who was the spider of this net weaving. What weapon has Togger, little brother?"

"Poison—on his foreclaws." There must be more than a lethal dose available now, for Farree had never tried to milk away thin yellow beads of moisture which Russtif had always forced from the claws when he had kept Togger captive.

"Soooo." The Zacanthan crossed the floor with noiseless tread and Vorlund slipped aside to let Zoror reach the outer door. "This one so assaulted will die?" He had put out a hand and drew Farree away from the spacer and closer to him.

The youth was rubbing his hands together, wriggling his shoulders, reversing as best he could the spreading of his wings, back into a burden the cloak would cover once more.

"Will this one die?" repeated the Zacanthan.

Farree shook his head. He felt as tired as if he had marched all day through a Nexus swamp. It took much of the will left in him even to stand and then turn his mind to what might be happening in the other room.

"I do not know," he answered. "There is a poison—but to some life forms it might not be deadly. There is so much difference—" He let that explanation die away while he rubbed his hand across the brand left upon his other wrist. "What may promise death to one kind, may be no more than the bites of a Lugk fly to another. Togger!" He went from words to mind call.

There was an answer, but it was very hazy and he could not understand. At least that meant that the smux was still alive.

"Let him lie," again the voice speaking clearly instead of in a deep rumble. Whatever had cloaked those within these walls must have gone. "He was without a useful thought, a helpful bit of action. Now—get you down to that hole where he burrowed and bring me back—" Not words but rather a series of clicks followed.

"They may be searching, High One." That voice verged on a whine and was certainly from the magician.

"If so it is better that you not be caught, is *that* not the truth? Remember, we have our own methods for resisting capture—the body can fall into the hands of those who would stand against us—but the mind, ah, now, that is a very different thing. You have seen what you have seen of that, is that not so? A certain ship owner from the Circle—"

"High One, no—I will go. But what of that thing which has done this to Gulde? Should we not seek it out and—"

"And die? You seem doubly eager to bring down upon you evils this night, Ioque. Almost one could believe that you yourself had hints of how one might safely use that crawler."

"Not so!"

"You speak that like an Oath of Heart Blood, Ioque. Look out when below where that went out the window if you still tremble with fears. Bring your heel down on its head—"

"But, High One, was it not your saying that this creature might bring to us what we want? Did not the scout swear that the thing belonged to him we have been tracing?"

"At least your memory works, Ioque. But deal with it as you will. We no longer need it."

"How—?"

"With ease." Once more the voice went even higher as if to address a party. "Thus!"

Farree fell to his knees as if his bones had suddenly turned too soft to supply any support. As before he was helpless in the clutch of something invisible which enfolded him both without and within.

It was Maelen who caught and steadied him, once more with her hands on his shoulders. While from the fingers of those hands there poured into him new energy. With a gasp he stiffened and clung in spirit to what she gave him.

There was a new battle in him. He must seek the source of this weakness—if he crawled on his hands and knees to do so—which was a dark urging, and meet it with what remnants of power he still possessed, awakened and armed by Maelen as she fed into his mind belief in his ability.

The room was gone, as if wiped away by a giant hand. He was caught up in a swirl of color, and somehow that in itself made him able to think—or feel—or—what was it—a dream?

There were winged ones in the air. As they dipped and soared or alighted near him he felt a vast peace—or perhaps only the shadow of it—that he was a part of an enduring something which had no failure—which had been, was, and ever would be!

He could not see the faces of those who danced with and on the wind; there seemed ever to be a glittering mist which enshrouded them when he looked too closely. Yet he did not doubt that he was one of them and that this was his own place. He strove to use his own wings, to mount and become a true part of their game, or dance, or the ceremony which he knew was of great meaning and needed only concentration to give up a truth greater than anything he had known before.

How long was he in that place of color, life, and peace? If it were only a moment or two then it possessed a kind of energy which itself vanquished time—the time which ruled the world he knew.

There came a sudden flurry and the winged ones gathered together to face him as if they had but that moment become aware that he was there.

From them came wind-carried bands of color. These swirled around him yet did not touch his body. Instead they wove a pattern as among them spun in turn bits of glitter. This glitter did not float purposelessly but rather came to hang unsupported in the air until he looked upon something which was a distinct pattern and about which there glowed light of another kind, green and white. Each of the bits were stilled in turn and hung quietly before him while he knew, though he did not know why, that this was a thing he must use—

The color, the place, the dancers—gone! What had he seen—with his eyes, or with his mind? He could not have said. But he knew that what he had seen did exist; and there was growing now a new ache within him, an ache like the hunger his body had once known which had come to be a part of him, in the dark days of his previous life.

"Come—" Who said that? One of the winged ones whom he could not see? Or was it an actual voice in his ears? Come—to that place—Yes, with all his heart he would reach for it now.

He was suddenly as aware of a force restraining his body as he had been of the place beyond the darkness. But this was not a holding within him as that other had been, but rather the pressure of hands upon him. He blinked and then blinked again and saw that he was back in the room where Maelen stood behind him, Zoror before, looking down at him with what could only be concern in his large green-gold eyes. The terrible fatigue which had struck Farree was gone. Rather he was filled with an eagerness to be gone—where he was not yet sure, only that he must answer that new hunger which had come.

Without his willing it his right hand twitched. His hand rose and the index finger pointed to the door while the brand the scarf had left on his flesh warmed and there seemed to be even a faint glow from it.

"What—" Vorlund spoke first.

"No!" Zoror shook his head, his neck frill extended to its full extent. "There will be time later for questions and answers. For now we shall find us a way back, one that no eyes shall light upon when we take it. You can go?" He addressed that last to Farree.

Shaking a little the other stirred in Maelen's hold. Her hands moved to help to draw him back to his feet.

He shook his head a fraction and fought for steadiness, for the world about him had a tendency to heave and to flicker. "I can go—but there is Togger."

"Call now," the Zacanthan returned. Farree sent forth that mental signal which had so long made a bridge between his mind and that of the smux. He hardly dared believe that he would be answered. Yet there came to him a clearer signal than any he had used to locate his companion before this evening.

"Out—wait—out. Big one—throw through hole—out—" A longer message than he had ever received and yet one he was certain was true meant, not sent to entice him into the hands of those others.

Vorlund had gone to the door. Now he opened it a crack and stood listening, perhaps for both any sound and with his mind for a hint that they were facing trouble once more. Looking over his shoulder he nodded and slipped quickly into the hall beyond.

There was no one to be heard or sensed. However, Vorlund did not withdraw to the stairs, as Farree saw as they followed the spacer. Rather he slipped along the wall towards the closed door of that other chamber. Maelen reached out and tapped Zoror on the wrist but the Zacanthan was already on his way. As they all wore soft-soled foot coverings and not the heavy metal-soled boots of the space borne, they did not raise a whisper of sound.

Once more Zoror planted his spy disc against the other door and stood statue still, the others as frozen behind him. Then with a quick nod he fingered the door itself and that portal opened, letting them look into a larger room. There was a slit of a window and through that came not only the seething smells of this muck heap, but also the sound of the settlement which was more alive at night than by day.

At first Farree thought the room was empty and he wondered how the inhabitants had gotten past their own hiding place without revealing their passage. Then he came two steps in on Maelen's heels and saw the crumpled body by the far wall. The man's face was swollen and flushed purple on one cheek, his eyes fastened in their direction. Dead eyes! It would seem that Togger's defense against this particular enemy had struck nearly twice as potently as Farree had ever seen it before.

The dead man held no interest for Vorlund. He was across the room in a hurry, edging by the body and coming to the wall against which it huddled. His hands were out and he traced with arm sweeps and the tops of his fingers that barrier itself.

"A hidden door, yes," Zoror nodded. "Though I would say he is long gone."

"Do we go hence also?" Maelen wanted to know. The Zacanthan reached above and beyond Vorlund's shoulder to rasp his talons along that stained and crumbling surface.

"I think not."

"Togger—" Farree had no intention of withdrawal until he was sure of the smux's safety. He certainly could have been flung through that slit of a window but that did not mean that he would otherwise be hidden from harm where he to fall to the way below.

Thought might have been a shout in summons. There

was a hump which appeared at the sill of that window and the smux clambered through, taking off in one of the leaps his kind could make when they were forced to it. He reached Farree and a moment later was clinging to his chest, all but two of the spike-mounted eyes retreating into cover.

Farree was quick to put the smux into a safer perch in an inner pocket of the cape. Only those stalked eyes protruded enough to follow what he did.

They slipped along the outer hall. The light supplied by the bowls pulsated but was strong enough to let them edge safely down the staircase. Again Vorlund took the lead, peering out the door first while holding it partly closed. He beckoned at last to the others, but there was a look of concentration on both his face and that of Maelen, as if they prepared to face a struggle or some wily attack. It was now Zoror who kept a hand on Farree's shoulder under the bunch of the cape, drawing him forward.

They were out again in the muck of the lane and Vorlund had his back against the wall. He had no weapon, but his hands were out in a position Farree had seen before. There were tricks of attack and defense which could be wrought by muscle alone which were as effective as any delivered by steel. Spacers were adept in such as well as in an array of weapons. Those who were prudent never questioned that they could return in full any attack upon them which did not begin with them at once rendered unconscious in some manner.

Just as Farree had been led here earlier by a silent compulsion which no longer existed, so was he now being moved away. He strove to throw off that feeling that he must obey some strange order as delivered by an unknown voice. From that pocket at the level of his chest he felt Togger changing position and there nibbled at his mind a thought which certainly might have been from or relayed by the smux.

"Go—far—"

"We go—at least from here," he returned by mind touch,

setting his own pace to match the Zacanthan's. Maelen was now in the advance of their party and Vorlund was behind. They might have been guards escorting some VIP whose life was under threat.

Farree himself could hardly believe that they were withdrawing without facing an attack, and he was about to question this when the Zacanthan drew him close as Maelen had held him earlier. He saw the lips of the wide mouth shape a word, for they were hurrying past a smoking torch.

"We are followed. Take care."

Farree held out his hand and felt Togger's claws close gently upon his finger not with the poisoned claws but lesser ones. Moving more awkwardly than usual the smux allowed himself to be hoisted out of the pocket and settled on the front of Farree's jerkin. If they were attacked now the smux would have a better chance for defense.

However, the need for that did not come. They were past the trader's wrecked booth. Then the magician's tipsy platform was also behind them. They quickened pace until once more the smooth surface of the port gate was underfoot. Here lights blazed and they must pass in that full glare. If they were still followed their tracker would have no difficulty keeping them in sight.

For the first time Farree dared to try mind seek. Instantly his sending or searching was cut off by the heavy power of the Zacanthan. He did not need any further instructions to keep silence.

They were in the main room of the port now and there were enough travelers, staff, and guards, to form a crowd so that the four from the port slum could weave back and forth among them. Farree knew what they would do. In any place such as this where there were minds in a number—their owners intent on affairs only of consequence to themselves— this should provide shield for their own passage, as long as they could blend their own identities into that of travelers

interested only upon reaching some important destination.
Swiftly he withdrew behind a simulacrum of his own construc-
tive thought, a servant eager to finish a task for a departing
master, then to be on his own for the night. He had not had
much practice in such action but he had been introduced to
part-playing roles by Maelen and knew a little. His companions were adept at this and he was certain that they could draw
about them cloaks of halucination as strong in their way as the
fabric one he clung to. But he longed to turn and look behind,
to test his own power of unmasking any pursuers.

The Guild—of a certainty those they watched for would
be of Guild employment. On Yiktor the game of that mighty
force had been spent by what Maelen and Krip could
summon—with some help from him, and the smux, and the
two other animals who had become Maelen's people in
fur, rejoicing to be numbered so. Only even there the Guild
had had their defense—a man-made thing which could deflect
any mental probe and protect the wearer from such interference.

His memories of that—No! That could provide a counter
to what they needed now. Farree expelled memory. He made
himself once more into the persona which he had seized upon
earlier—a servant, hurrying to deliver a message. Yes, that
was surely who and what he was.

They came down the length of that very long room and
passed through the gate where those only visiting the port
would exit—avoiding the passengers' section. Zoror's talons
on his right hand tapped out a call on the credit dial about his
wrist. A carrier swung out of the line of vehicles moving
slowly towards their take off. Fighting the desire to rush for
the escape that promised, Farree controlled his anxious need
to be away, in order to follow Maelen and the Zacanthan at a
reasonable pace. They had all boarded the craft and Zoror had
tapped out their destination before Krip said:

"Human and yet not—Terran to the eighth degree in body. Something else in mind."

Maelen nodded. "Off-world—and with a different mind pattern from any we have crossed." She looked to the Zacanthan as if she expected he would know the proper answer to the identity of the follower they had detected in their careful search.

"A Plantgon—" Zoror said.

Krip's lips shaped a whistle and Maelen looked as if she would deny Zoror's identification.

"How—"

The Zacanthan shook his head. "His shield is very complete. I might have pried a little and learned more, but then he, too, would be aware that we are not altogether without the same defenses and weapons. Yes, he is one— No, in that I am wrong—*it* is one such as we seldom have here. That it passed the port detectors makes it formidable enough for us. It is plus ten to be able to reach a place where it will have all the defenses known to a great many more races than live or have lived. We may be grateful to some explorer whose wind-blown ashes have fallen into the smallest of tracing and whose race and time can only be guessed at. There is one place where even a Plantgon, and I know all which had been said and guessed about them, cannot pierce with either mind or dream body."

They were winging, at the speed allowed in the fast lanes, straight for the headquarters of the Zacanthan study team. Farree relaxed. He had heard one or two whispers concerning Plantgons but he was not quite sure what they might be. However, if the name meant so much to those about him they truly must be formidable opponents.

5.

"What have we then?" Zoror was settled in an easiseat which accommodated itself to his body. He held in one hand a blackish-skinned fruit into the skin of which had been inserted a tube from which he sucked now and then. His companions of the late adventure were all occupied with restoratives, each matched to taste of the drinker.

Farree rolled his tongue about his own drink tube. The tart liquid was refreshing, seeming to wash out of him some remnants of the ordeal through which he had gone.

"Qun Glude 'p itho." Vorlund looked to the small screen of the reader on the table. "No identification with the Guild. Was second officer on Halfway in last employment—legal one, that is. He disappeared after his flight right was cancelled. That was on Wayland's World near five planet years ago. Activities unknown but was seen in company with Xexepan, commander of a Free Trader under suspicion by the Patrol. Entered into the records because Xexepan has twice been accused of smuggling—mainly in the Wormost slave trade. Apparently"—he raised his eyes from the screen from which he had been reading aloud in trade code the few lines on a val slip—"Xexepan must have been a shrewd voyager. But what was a slaver doing so far into the civilized lanes? He could not have been—"

Maelen leaned a little forward. "There is always kidnapping," she pointed out. "No tie for Xexepan with the Guild?"

Vorlund flicked a switch with his finger and the lines of code flashed on again. "No straight tie, no. Wayland's World?" He looked now to Zoror.

The Zacanthan made reference to his own call screen.

"Fourth quadrant—Ast showing. However, this Xexepan sounds of interest. What was his cover on Wayland?"

"Straight trading. He had some skins, a full cargo of yale sap containers. That was all on the landing permit."

It was Farree who interrupted, for a dark picture had touched him, but not from any screen. "What kind of skins—are they listed?"

They all three glanced at him. In the Zacanthan's eyes there was a sudden gleam.

"Little brother—yes, perhaps you have put thought to something there. Indeed skins may be a key—"

Vorlund turned back to the reader. "No other definition—only skins. We might use a chart, High One," he addressed Zoror.

Zoror swung his seat a little to the right. There was a second screen there, its picture surface now occupied with a viewing of a broken stone slab across which ran a wavy line of nearly time-erased scratches. With a click of a button this was gone. Zoror inserted another plate. This time the screen flared to life with a star map which grew larger and larger, hurtling towards them.

"Wayland—to the left." He prodded a button and one of the dots flared green for a moment.

Farree felt giddy, as if he had been wafted into that screen without any safe anchorage or propulsion. His gaze flickered, almost as if he had been ordered, not to view the planet Zoror had pointed out but to look for another. His wings spread, not from any conscious order of his mind.

"Farree!" Maelen's voice broke the beginning of the spell. "What is it?"

"The chart—there and there!" He had reached the table, edged past Zoror, as his fingers jabbed at the sector far distant from the flashing representative of Wayland to the northeast, nearly at the end of the frame itself where there was only a scattering of stars.

"Why?" Zoror asked. "Wayland is near the rim—there is very little beyond save unexplored worlds, mapped by chart swimmers but with no information taped to draw either First in Scouts or Free Traders, as venturesome as those are."

"No!" Farree pounded impatiently at the table. Togger squeaked and tumbled from his hold on Farree's shirt. He fell on his back and lay for a moment waving his claws, wide spread to show all their vicious promise. One of those scraped along Farree's hand as he raised it to point again at the bright dots on the screen, but luckily did not cut flesh. "There—that is what I saw—the sky dancers! That chart—it was what I saw behind them!"

"Sky dancers?" echoed Maelen. "Little brother, we have not been there."

Farree was impatient now. Within him there was a tug, a need to answer something which was neither words nor mind touch from his companions. "I—when we were there—in the shiptown. I saw—because of this." Now he ran his fingers around that brand the vanished scarves had set upon him. "There were the winged ones—the Mist Dancers—and then before them the lights. I tell you—the lights are those!" Again he pointed to the screen. "They are there!"

Vorlund leaned across to see the chart better.

"You say this Xexepan is a Free Trader—and a slaver?" His tone was cold and his jaw was set. He spoke not to Farree but to the Zacanthan.

"My son, there are rogue traders. And if a Guild man wishes perhaps to find himself a cover—can he not use such a listing?"

"No!" Now it was Vorlund's turn to explode. "We are not dirty handed, no matter what others may say of us. As for this Xexepan—if he wears such a registry mark and is not one of us—then he is an outlaw and no one can stand between him and any trader who calls him to account. We can take his ship, him—" Vorlund drew a deep breath. "There was the affair of the Angol— Surely it is remembered! Those who used her so—they did not space again—unless walking on the emptiness outside an air lock can be considered spacing. The Free Traders take care of their own name—those who would push it into darkness will have every ship against them. I say that your Xexepan was either a liar—or the worst of fools—to name himself so!"

"Well enough," Maelen's calm voice, measured against the heat of Vorlund's, was very cool. "Wayland—let us see now."

It was her turn to survey the chart closer. Zacanthan drew aside for her. "I have been a spacer for a short time but—" Now she tapped the screen with a forefinger. "Look you—a ship riding outward from this"—it was the cluster of stars Farree had indicated—"what is the first planetfall suitable for trade or perhaps for contacting some emissary of the Guild? If one stumbles upon a treasure which is too large for one to handle there are but two solutions—one, to bring forth a part of it and seek a partner, or—to leave it, to be ever more regretted. I do not think that Xexepan is the type to nourish regrets. Therefore with a token cargo he would search for the nearest planet to serve his purpose. It may even be that he was already one of the eyes and hands of the Guild—to search out what will be of meaning to them.

"Somehow I do not think he is a slaver. The Patrol rides the space along the rim. There would be too much risk in slaving. Perhaps he did go to Wayland to hunt what he did not have—a Guild contact."

"He came from there!" Farree held to his own interest. "This Glude"—the name twisted in his mouth—"had—the wings—the parts of them! You say he had skins—what if those 'skins' were wings?"

Vorlund drew a breath which sounded almost like a whistle. But it was Maelen who asked in that calm voice of hers, "What *did* you see, little brother? Tell us."

He frowned, trying to remember every small detail. "There was an open land, very fair—" For a moment he was caught by the memory of that place so totally unlike any world he had seen. "There were mountains—and those who danced upon the air. I could not see their faces in the mist. But they possessed wings"—he put up a hand to touch the outer ribbing of his own—"like mine. They—danced and then came the lights through the mist and those formed that!" Once more he indicated the corner of the chart.

"A far reader." Maelen looked to him. "It could be possible. Try—" She reached out to the top of the table where sat the screen and caught up what must be a lump of earth, or so it looked to Farree. This she pushed at him until, without knowing why, he took it up. Again without the volition of any thought his fingers enclosed it tightly. He looked to Maelen for an explanation.

"What comes to your mind, little brother?" she asked.

Why did she do this when there were other things to be thought of? But under her compelling gaze he looked down at the clod he held. In that part of his mind which could and did speak to Togger and the others something stirred.

He closed his eyes, again not knowing just why.

Before him was darkness, then into that night came—

A creature moved. It was slender of body, and was raised on stiltlike limbs—four of them. Two more jutted out from the body and those gripped a black wand or stick. The slim body was round in comparison to those legs, as was its much smaller head. And it emitted purpose—and that purpose was killing. Behind that no rage nor fear, rather the neutral state of a thing which grew because the instinct of growth lay within it, as might a seed within the earth. It raised its weapon, if weapon that was, to bring it down with what appeared to be the full strength it possessed.

Yet that defense did not save it. Rather it stumbled back as a sharp lance of what might be flame centered on the creature's body. It twisted its limbs as it fell, twitching and kicking. Still Farree knew that it was dead.

He opened his eyes then and looked to Zoror. Choosing words as best he could he was about to speak when the Zacanthan said it for him.

"Death—yes—and a being who knew enough to arm itself and strive for defense." He spoke to Maelen and Vorlund. "You saw—?"

They both nodded. Zoror took the lump from Farree. He tapped it carefully against the table then brought forth that talon instrument which he had used to such good effect in the shiptown. The nearly iron hard covering flaked away, to show a contorted mass of fine yellow bones—hardly larger than a finger.

"This is from my own world," the Zacanthan explained. "Zatan made an expedition when I was but a fingerling. He went into the Canyon of Double Dark and what he found there was this—" Again he slipped a tape holder into the screen rim and the scene vanished to display something else—a bulky cylinder lying on a table, a hand and part of an arm of a Zacanthan resting next to it to show that it was indeed small.

"The remains of a ship," Zoror continued. "Old beyond even our counting, but truly a star ship. The crew must have been both small and limited as to numbers. We sent inner beams to explore and classify. Its like had never been seen before. That"—he indicated the bones still entombed in the stone hard lump—"was found not far from the exit lock. What our little brother here has shown us may be a crew member of that ship. This lump was caught against the ship which our expedition brought back. I have kept it as a reminder that there may be strange things even in one's old world—puzzles which have no solving—as yet. We have talked, Farree and I, about legends and tales, both encased in 'history' as these bones are in this petrified soil, but perhaps still alive in the speech of some races even today. The Terrans have such stories, which they carried with them out among the stars. A winged race, a race which once inhabited the same planet as they sprang from, a race which was feared both for their strange knowledge and its enmity with the dominant species of that home world.

"The legend sprang up again on many worlds as those of Terran descent spread among the stars: Little People sometimes friendly, but mostly to be feared for the powers they possessed, which could not be equalled or understood by those of other blood.

"It is perhaps not mere coincidence that such a story could be known on Wayland. In fact that world was named by a scout who was known to be a collector of legends. He served my people also with what he brought back in strange tales and artifacts. When age caught him he retired to Zorp where he was received with honors and his lectures were deservedly popular. I, myself, attended the one which dealt with 'Wayland,' which world he named after a legendary 'god' or storied hero. There was part of a memory song which he told us then—and it has lingered always in my mind, for to my race it carries a hint of interesting speculation. To his kind it was meant as a warning, to my race a challenge in our quest for knowledge.

"The bit of old lore went like this:

> *"Up the airy mountain,*
> *Down the rushy glen,*
> *We dare not go a-hunting*
> *For fear of little men."*

Vorlund's lips had moved in company with the Zacanthan's as he repeated the rhyme. The Zacanthan nodded.

"So you know this also, far traveler?"

"I heard a part of it once—from a tales teller on Dawn. But it was then part of another story which ended—'because of the grind'—which was a local story monster—one who was an eater of children."

"Little men," repeated Maelen. "And the knowledge of them spread—yet none have been seen?"

Zoror nodded toward Farree. "Perhaps they are seen now. As for gifts which would seem strange and even dangerous to those who did not have them—here is our younger brother able to mind speak, and also to read the past in part." He tapped the broken lump.

Only Farree was thinking of something else. "The wings," his hand went up to touch an edge of one of his own. "The wings—'skins'?"

That rage which had possessed him earlier was returning. Again his hands met before him so he could rub fingers about that brand which had been set on him, as he looked over Zoror's shoulder to the screen where he saw not the miniature space craft still pictured there but rather the star chart. It would seem that the Zacanthan's thought moved with him though Farree was not aware of the invasion of that other mind this time.

"It would seem that there is trouble there."

"The Patrol?" questioned Vorlund.

Slowly the Zacanthan shook his head. "What evidence have we? You have read the data existing on the man with whom we have had contact. Xexepan is under suspicion, but unless more evidence comes to light they would not move. The Guild? One can believe anything of them. What we overheard makes plain that there have been seeing eyes following Farree and doubtless you also. But it is our younger brother here who I think is their main objective. Yet he does not have any knowledge which would benefit them. Thus they want him because he is how he is."

"And who am I?" flared Farree. Sometimes he felt as if he were entangled in words when he wished only the freedom to do—to do what? He could not answer that.

"That is what you have come here to learn," Zoror returned. "A race new to us, save in old legends—"

"A race," Farree repeated, "which was once feared, which has a feud perhaps with the Guild—" His mind sped from what he believed to what might be believed. There were odds and ends which might well be woven to form the truth of that!

"West quadrant." Vorlund might be still staring at the chart but it was plain that his thoughts were speeding elsewhere. "There are journey tapes for Wayland, that must be so. But do those exist which will lift a ship still farther out?"

"Officially?" Zoror picked up his drink again. "That would be only the brief one of the scanner. There may be another—perhaps Xexepan has it."

"A scanner tape," Krip said musingly. "We have operated on such before. It is a chancy way to travel, to be sure. But my people proved that it can be done—over and over again."

"So they have," the Zacanthan agreed.

"You cannot go there." Farree spoke against the surge of

feeling which was filling him. "You have done much for me—" He held out his hands, one toward Maelen and one to the Free Trader. "Twice you have freed me. From the stench that was the Limits, from the hiding place I carried with me." His wings waved as he remembered how he had walked under the burden of his tight-furled pinions, thinking that he was one deformed, a bit of refuse. They had called him, those of the Limits, "Dung," and he had accepted that he was not one who had any future save the days and nights of a scavenger. Not until when venturing with these two into danger had his wings at last broken free, and he had done for his friends what they had done for him—a service beyond their power of body.

They did not look at him. Krip might have been turning over in his mind some problem, viewing it first from one side and then the other, as he often did. Maelen again flexed her fingers—she could have been painting on the air some picture which only she and those of her people might translate.

Zoror leaned back in his chair, putting aside the drained fruit. "Yes." He was not answering Farree but appeared to speak his own thoughts aloud. "There have been expeditions outfitted from just such a thin thread. But two things will be needed—authorization from the Patrol and credits enough to outfit for what may be years of search."

Krip's mouth quirked. "And neither do we have."

Farree stared again at the star pattern. He was without any influence, without any credit save what had been his part of the reward for their smashing of the Guild conspiracy on Yiktor. He wore wings to be sure, but they were not such as would bear him across the star lanes. Yet there was a hunger growing in him, the feeling there would never be any peace for him unless he could find out—

"No, you do not," Zoror conceded. "But—"

Maelen interrupted. "An expedition for the purpose of studying a new race, or ruins remaining: what else do you have but the best reason of all! Your own life has been spent thus, and if you should add something to that great storehouse of knowledge your people maintain—"

There was a throaty chuckle from the Zacanthan. "Sister, you need not tempt me. As all my race would be, I am already won to this quest. You are right, we do not value any reward save that of knowledge gained. We heard those space vermin speak of a treasure. That must be the lever used to move the Guild. However, we can adapt that rumor to our own use. Treasure has many times been found in the remains of a dead and gone race, or even species. Wait—"

He pulled out of the embrace of the easiseat and crossed to a second screen. Before he dropped his hand to the call button there he waved at the others. They caught his unvoiced warning—to scramble out of the range of that screen so that whoever might answer would not learn that Zoror was not alone.

The face which flashed on the screen at Zoror's summoning was that of a Tryistian, her sleek feather crest lying flat, her large eyes half lidded. By the badge on her jacket she was one of the records keepers and also Patrol, but of the Scouts.

Zoror spoke first: "Serve-Wing, is it possible to locate for my seeing the spotter tape covering—?" And he recited a jumble of figures which meant nothing to Farree.

"Your purpose, High One?" she asked.

"Recent information. There may well be a find of note to be made there. Before I make my report I must check this."

"A spotter tape, High One, has little information. However, if anything so reported would be of interest to you, it is freed. Switch to inner files—"

"My thanks-giving, Serve-Wing—" Her picture had already disappeared from the screen. What flashed on in her place was a diagram composed of figures and symbols making no sense to Farree, restraining his growing impatience. However, both Krip and Maelen now went to look over the Zacanthan's shoulder to watch the procession of data.

Impatience continued to eat at Farree, for it seemed that the streams of formulae would never cease. Twice those lines were halted for a moment or two by a sharp motion from Krip. He had taken from an inner pocket a small hand recorder and was holding that up to face the other broadcasting unit, apparently taking notes on some portions which he must believe to be important. Then the date was gone leaving the screen bare except for the flickering light. Zoror typed out an answer which would carry his thanks for the information and list it as Zacanthan research.

"Two solar systems," Krip said. "A sum of twelve planets. I think even Zacanthans might think several times before an expedition was fitted out for such a prolonged hunt."

"Some of those worlds," Maelen pointed out, "are such as would not sustain any life with the same requirements as ours."

Krip nodded but did not answer otherwise. He was busy with his own small record. "There are three Arth-A, six which are borderline, the rest—" He shrugged.

"So you have three now, not twelve," Maelen pointed out.

"Two in one system, one in the other," the Zacanthan agreed. "If you were a far trader—as you once were, brother—to which would you first chart your way?"

"To a doubtful gamble—that one." His finger indicated a choice. "But there was no reading of life on that report. Should it not have checked for that?"

"Some do, some don't," Zoror answered. "The probe making this report was a long way from its home base, or the ship which launched it. Its data banks were nearly full. They are sensitive enough to anticipate a shut down and allow for one as they clear their complete fill up, and it is time for them to return. This was launched on 7546G and it returned on 7869G."

"The time of the Pan-wen War!" Krip cut in.

"Just so. And during that time the Patrol was fully occupied. The report may have just been added to others, lain unnoted for a hundred planet years or more.

"I wonder." He tapped his display of fangs with a talon on a forefinger. "We may not have been the first to be so interested."

"Who could reach that information without authority?" asked Maelen.

Again Zoror gave that throaty chuckle. "A good many, sister. There are many secrets which the Guild hug to themselves. It is said, and with truth, that new weapons and informational devices are often obtained by bribery, murder, thievery. No matter what arms they may run and sell for planet wars, the most effective ones are kept for their own raids and secret attacks. That they have access to sealed information is well understood. So that if they tap into such storehouses of exploration tapes as that we just witnessed they will have their own method of making it profitable. Who knows, they may hold rights auctions to their own newly discovered worlds with outlaws bidding, and a large cut for the Guild at regular intervals. Just as your people, younger brother"—he nodded toward Krip—"buy traders' rights from Survey."

"So," Krip returned, "then we have a secret which may not be one?"

"Our Farree here says so with his very presence," Maelen answered. "How did he come into the Limits? He is mind blocked, and with such an unknown power that even the Ancient Ones of the Thassa could not search far into his memory. Perhaps one of your stolen Guild devices did that. He is here and we—what do we know?"

"Only the bits of legends which are deemed more tale than fact," the Zacanthan said.

"The wings!" Farree burst out. What if the Guild had as

many devices as the stars sprinkled in the night heavens? There were those lengths of beauty which he had held. That dream, or vision, also—the dancers with the wind who were like himself.

"The wings," Zoror repeated. "And a measure of what we overheard this night. So—" His words carried more of a hissing as he spoke faster and with emphasis. "We have a chart, we have the edge of a mystery wherein the Guild may be at odds with all comers. We have a ship." Now he pointed with his taloned forefinger to Krip. "We have a Moonsinger whose talents perhaps even the burrowing, spying Guild do not understand. We have one from an unknown world and his valiant companion." Now he indicated first Farree, and then Togger. "We have an old one who wishes to learn a little for himself and no longer, for a space, pore over the reports of others—" Now the finger pointed to his own chest. "Do we mix the lot of these and what do we do with the sum of it?"

Maelen laughed. "I look to you, High One, and I look to my comrade in adventure, as to our younger brother here. To your questions there is only one answer. Let us go and see!"

6.

Farree hung suspended in the webbing which protected him during take-off and transition into shift. With his wings he could not lie on one of the bunks. As usual he was giddy, with a sickish taste in his mouth, and was for the moment content to remain within the restraints. Around him the walls of the ship vibrated with the force which was its life. It was Krip's ship, Maelen's ship, the one which they had thought to travel the star lanes with those in fur and feathers who would go, to prove to the other worlds they might visit that there was a brotherhood between life forms which must be recognized. They had begun on the world of the Limits with a bartle and Yazz, both of whom had played a part when the Guild threatened them on Yiktor. Nor had those two chosen to remain behind now although Maelen, mind touching, had explained what must be done.

This time, they need not depend upon an unknown pilot, one who might even be a traitor to them as had been so before, for Zoror was himself a pilot and had carefully studied the tape he and Krip had patched together from the data of the searcher. They had lifted off-world recording a goal which was far enough from what they sought that their actual destination might remain their own secret.

Zoror was sure that no spy set by the Guild could penetrate his own library-cum-laboratory. That building was manned largely by robots carefully constructed to obey his voice alone. Though the Zacanthans spoke trade talk, their own language demanded a voice range no other species could project.

However, Maelen had detected a mind search seeking vainly to enter their stronghold several times during the counts of twenty days while they were making their preparations. There had been no difficulty with the authorities. The sector Patrol Commander had stamped his own private seal on their permission papers. A Zancanthan was never questioned when he or she voyaged.

With Zoror's own equipment tuned to a new use, they had inspected—and Farree had been able to join in handling that—every shipment of supplies before it was sealed into the ship. There would be no stowaway surprises to attack them.

Farree himself had lapsed now and then into meditation. To his continued disappointment there were no more visions. He might have been concentrating upon Zoror's own home. On their last night a-planet he at last ventured to speak of this—for if there was no truth in his vision they might even now be acting at a long range motivation induced by the Guild.

He had stood among them, his own wings folded as tightly as possible, and voiced his fears.

Maelen shook her head. "Not so, little brother! Had your vision been a trick its falseness could be speedily read. We who did not see with you might well have seen instead a lashing of the web in which that was bait."

Zoror agreed with her. "There is this too: an object which carries a message may be set to carry such only once. Having made contact with you the charge was exhausted. That one did indeed leave its mark." He gently touched the brand on Farree's wrist. "But only we know of this."

Though he had a great deal of awe and respect for both the Moonsinger and the Zacanthan, and their similar though different ranges of mind send and thought examination, Farree was not convinced. However, he did not mention his fears again. At least on his wrist he did carry proof that there had been power a-plenty in those remnants they had found.

To his shock and disappointment his memory of the dancers and the sky chart did fade even though he strove to hold it in detail. Zoror's story of unknown devices which the Guild could control was part of a private distress. He had been helpless prisoner for a time to one such when they had made their foray into the Field edge town. Could he then have also been marked, even by the scar on his wrist, so that he could prove a guide for others without his knowledge?

They made the change into warp drive easily enough. Farree had to move carefully through the ship, with his wings tight folded, as the passages were narrow, His sleep periods were uncomfortable as he must also accommodate those pinions within another cramped space. Some of the time he spent down on the lower deck with Bojor and Yazz. The huge shaggy bartle that had come from the world of the Limits passed easily into slumber, content to spend most of the voyage in a kind of hibernation. However, Yazz sought mind contact and asked questions Farree could not adequately answer.

Yes, there was a world awaiting them which had open spaces where a fisual could run to her pleasure. Though he himself could not remember too much of the world of his vision, the bright green of the land below the mist clad mountains remained with him. He was sure such a world existed elsewhere—he could only hope that the tape Krip had spliced together would lead them there.

Since the ship was running on a locked voyage tape, with all the alarms for any emergency set, Zoror did not occupy the pilot's seat any longer than it took for him to check at certain intervals that all was well. When hunched back again into the long seat at the end of the bridge, he triggered a small scanner and set a procession of pictures, interspersed with more lines of the intricate script of his own species. Maelen shared his seat and his interest in the records of finds which had been made—Forerunners' long lost works. Rightly she might search such, for the body she now wore was that of a Forerunner—some queen, goddess or ruler of a people totally forgotten until their hiding place of treasure and long sleepers was uncovered in a secret mountain hold where the Guild had come to meddle with that which they might not have been any longer able to command had they gone some steps farther in their investigations.

Dying, Maelen had taken on the body of another long sealed into a chamber to await a waking which had not come in the millenniums between the time when the last barrier had closed and that hour when spoilers had broken through. There she had fought a battle with the remnants of an evil will which still clung to the body, banishing that other after a hard fought engagement. Now she asked Zoror if her present like existed in Zacanthan records, only to be told that she who was gone might have been one of half a hundred races who had sought the stars in years now so far in the past that the numbering of them could not even be tallied.

"It is, you see," Zoror said once when they were all together, Vorlund swung about in the co-pilot's seat to face the other three, "for us a matter of putting together many bits of discoveries, like striving to set in position the shards of a Trysua glass picture which has been broken past redemption. There is perhaps the find of a derelict ship, preserved in space where it has hung past our accounting, or one of the wind-beaten ruins of the Uavan Desert on Tav where one can only guess what the original form once was.

"And there is also the shifting of old tales, of stories told by far travelers. There was that of the Numerod—"

"Captain Famble's find!" Vorlund cut in.

"Just so. Famble might well have been one of my own race, so diligently did he search for that which was only known because of a few sentences gasped by a dying spacer taken from a life boat. The richness of his find on Scar nearly matched that which your own ship discovered on Sehkmet. Only of the people who fashioned those works of art, those things of great beauty, we know nothing more. In none of that treasure was there any hint even of their race or species. They used many motifs of flowers, strange birds—or at least winged creatures—and others which ran six-legged, inlaid with gems to remain for all time. But of the representation of any creature which might be deemed one of the makers—of that we had no hint at all. And Scar, as you know, was a burn-off, half of its surface congealed slag, so imbued with radiation that any close search was impossible, even for one well suited up; while over the rest of the world there was a tangle of vegetation gone totally wild. We have deduced by what we saw and found there that those who had left their belongings in the caverns had done so in haste, yet thought they might come again. However, they did not—"

"There was also," Maelen said, "the skull of Orsuis. Not even your people, High One, had seen such as that before."

"That has proved to be a puzzle which many of us seek to penetrate when we are in youth studies." Zoror nodded. "The skull might be that of a modern spacer of the old Terran breed—but it is wrought from a single lump of Cris-crystal which the experts tell us today cannot be worked by any known method. Yet it exists, and plainly it was in some way a manner of communication. There are many puzzles for the finding here and there."

Farree nodded, rubbing the brand on his wrist. During his time in the Zacanthan's headquarters he had seen many strange things. There were also the legends Zoror had stressed about winged people, the Little Folk who were supposedly known to Terrans, not only on their own world but out among the stars.

Flight time was wearying at best—especially when the ship was on destination tape. However, the Zacanthan used this period to keep their minds alert, holding their interest to more than just winning through to the end of the voyage. During the arbitrarily set ship's hours Farree and the others listened to Zoror's fund of stories of finds and mysterious worlds dead from some war or catastrophe, where ancient weapons yet fought on and anyone trying to land was attacked. Farree paid eager interest at first. The world of his childhood—the malodorous Limits—had had nothing to feed his imagination or instruct his mind—and this was heady stuff.

Only when he was back in his own cabin, Togger occupying the bunk Farree could no longer use because of his wings, he would rub his wrist until the skin was chafed—wishing he had the other silky scraps the booth owner had had, trying, until his very mind seemed to ache, trying to evoke an answer alone, but possessing nothing to read it from.

He shivered now and again when he seemed to be answered by a thrust of pain as sharp and fleeting as if he had faced a laser beam. Each time that occurred he was left sick and hurting.

Farree was squatting on the edge of the bunk, his back to the compartment door, when one such a session had been so sharp and debilitating that he swayed back and forth. Togger gave a claw rattle that made plain he had picked up a strong broadcast of Farree's pain. Nor was he the only one for a voice reached him from the compartment door:

"Farree! That—is death!"

His arms were wrapped over his chest as if he must cling to some part of himself against a fear that was near unbearable. Almost, almost he had been able to pierce that fear, to reach who or what was behind it. His cheeks were wet with drops which gathered on his forehead and ran downward.

Fear—yes, fear, but with it anger— Both emotions seemed to lie as a brand upon his thoughts even as that length around his wrist had put its burden on his flesh.

"Farree." Maelen had moved along the wall until she could look directly into his face. "You must not do this—"

He shook his head. Then he half whispered: "I must know!"

"And what will be good for you to know, younger brother, if it puts its mark so deeply on you that you cannot function? See?" She reached out to draw her fingers down his wet cheek. "You labor and that which you would draw near you is—death. We also have the inner sight, we can follow so far—to go farther means the upsetting of the Scales. Molester gave us the gift of such sight; we are vowed not to use it wrongly."

For the first time he looked at her. "I must know," he repeated; but his voice was dull, that painful awareness gone.

"Perhaps—but not that way—never that way, Farree. None can see beyond when they take the White Path, just as none may return." Again her hand stretched forth as she held it palm down and a little above his wrist. "This—even I can feel what this holds, little brother. That which is implanted with sorrow and death cannot be used lightly. For your own sake do not seek to do that."

There spread into his mind something more than the words she spoke—it was a soothing, gentling feeling, like hands bandaging a gaping wound. Dimly he realized that what Maelen was mind casting was that same assurance that she had many times used with those she called her little ones, whom others might term beasts. Sighing, he nursed his wrist, for, under the soothing thought, he realized that there was truth in what she said. He dare not waste he strength on this search—not when there lay more arduous trails ahead. That there was danger coming he had no doubt.

"Good," she spoke aloud rather than thought. "I promise you, younger brother, that there will be a time for you, and when that comes you shall have a great part in what will follow."

He glanced at her, surprised. There were always hints that those with mind speech could also do more—even as he had proven he might read from touch. Only to foresee was not widely known and all he had ever heard of it was rumors.

"Not foreseeing." She picked that up quickly. "It is rather by reasoning, Farree. This is no easy voyage which we make now. If we raise the planet of your people it is well we be prepared for trouble there—"

He nodded. Yes, it did not take any mind skill beyond thought to understand that. Also she was right, he should not waste what gifts he had trying to compel answers, for that was useless. Any mind skill came and went spasmodically and you could not force it.

So he did not try to summon up again what he had seen so briefly in his one vision. That must have fulfilled its purpose when he had remembered and read the chart which had sent them on this voyage. Instead he set himself to another way of preparing for that which might wait ahead. Not only did he coax more and more reminiscences from Zoror, but he visited Bojor in the cabin which had been specially fashioned to fit the huge furred body of the one-time wild hunter, an animal on its own world so greatly feared that even the stories of its bloody meeting with settlers roused terror.

Farree was learning now from a source which lived and breathed, far from the tapes and scrolls the Zacanthan guarded so dearly. His own short life—or as much of it as he could remember—had been spent in the filthy dregs of the Limits—infinitely worse than even the portside on the planet from which they had risen. He had never seen open country until they had finned down on Yiktor. There events had sped by so fast that he had not had time to think of what they saw but only of what must be done, and as speedily as possible. He had acted mainly from instinct and not from knowledge.

Now he matched thoughts with the bartle and so lived the life of the great furred hunter. He padded down mountain trails, his head up to savor the wind and any message that it brought. Claws were sharpened on a favorite rock which also marked the boundary of Bojor's own hunting ground. And so did he slip from one outcrop of rock to another, eyeing a small herd of grush feeding the shoulder-high grass. Thus he squatted on the banks of the stream, one paw ready to dip in with a gesture seemingly too delicate to be used by a bartle, and bring out a swift-swimming creature which had the sinuous body of a reptile.

It was not a one-way meeting for thought which tied Farree to Bojor during those sessions. For the bartle roused from his hibernation enough to display a curiosity of his own, and demanded that Farree return adventure to balance adventure. The life of the Limits was something which Farree recalled very briefly and from which Bojor turned away in disgust. Those hours he had spent on Yiktor were all he had to offer.

He could still recall the wonder of that time when the hideous hump which had made him a matter of disgust all through his days split and peeled away and his wings were born. The first moments of his beginning flight, when, unsure and clumsy, he had made the attempt to raise himself above the ground, he remembered well—and all the rest of what the wings had brought him—the chance to serve Maelen and her people as no one except he who was so endowed could do.

That memory appeared to interest Bojor above all others.

His own experience with flyers had been only with birds, one species of which had followed him boldly from place to place, feasting on the scraps of any kill. For creatures such as himself and the others aboard this ship (Farree discovered from the first that Bojor looked upon them all as fellow beasts, clearly apart from the hunters who had first entrapped him, even though they had worn the same kind of bodies as his present companions had), flight was very strange indeed. He plied Farree with thought questions as to how one felt speeding above and not across the earth.

There were not only Bojor's memories to be tapped, but also Yazz's. The slender-legged, beautifully coated animal had other information to add to that which Farree was eagerly assimilating. So and so did it feel to come upon a strange track in the muddy bank of a drink-pool. A nose at such times was greater than an eye to tell whether this was an enemy or a stranger who need not be feared.

Farree rubbed his own nose ruefully at that. Though he had been able to trail the wing patches into the ship, he certainly lacked such sensitive and selective nostrils. Thus Yazz added to his store of knowledge about what one might search for in a new territory.

Zoror, Bojor and Yazz all had something to add to his lessoning in preparation for the future. But it was from Maelen, and from Vorlund, that he learned that which would be of most importance if they descended from the stars to discover their chosen world had other menaces—perhaps from those whose interest they had already brushed against.

"They had that wing portion." Vorlund gestured to the mark on Farree's wrist. "It is true that trade after trade may swing from planet to planet, nearly across the space lanes— but those wing portions, while they are rare enough, might have little value in themselves. They might have been brought to back up some story, to entice backing, even as a form of introduction from one Veep to another. Perhaps they thought to use them not only as bait for you—but for all of us, little brother, who must now be well known to the Guild—did we not spoil their game on Yiktor? And they do not easily forget losses and failures. It would not be well for them to either lose or fail without exacting punishment—they have enemies enough who might be so encouraged to fight back. Yes, if this is bait—then we are perhaps heading straight into a trap. So for that we must be prepared."

Thus Vorlund became his instructor in other ways. There was the use of the slender knife which the spacer carried concealed in the top of his space boot. Though their room for practice was greatly curtailed, Farree learned how to throw. In addition he listened as carefully as he did to all his other instructors for useful information which could only come from a Free Trader who had known a number of different worlds. Not the least was Vorlund's collection of Guild information gathered from years of listening in ports and to shipmates.

Farree had thought that life was of little worth in the Limits where not even the peacekeepers walked except in pairs and then with tanglers at alert. However, the more he heard, the more he came to believe that there were dangers he had never dreamed of when he had slunk through the shadows of that pest hole. He had once thought that life in the upper town would be ideal and now he was certain that peril was even more complex and ever-present there also.

Dream— It was one night when he had settled in his cabin hammock that he began to dream.

He was hovering above a rich green spread of vegetation where bright touches of color rose up to the sun as the worlds appeared to spark a star chart. A stream of water bubbled along, so clear that one could well view the stones scattered over its sandy flooring and spy upon the fleeting shapes of water dwellers.

There were taller growing plants along the stream edge and among those fluttered gauzy winged insects, their armored bodies jewel bright. For there was warmth and light—not only from a sun, but also shooting from the mountains which stood high to protect this peaceful cup of valley. Here, too, there was the drifting silvery mist which floated, now and then veiling off one of those heights and then another. Only this time no flyers winged through it—there was only an empty land. Farree was struck of a sudden with a sensation of vast loneliness containing not fear but despair.

He was unaware of his own body—only that he could see—and feel: settling upon him was a need to go elsewhere. There was a flashing of light and he faced an opening of what might be a mountain cave. From the throat of that spiraled the glittering mist.

If this was a natural fault in the rock there had been those eager to re-fashion it, for there were workings to smooth the rock and then overlay it with crystals such as he had never seen. Pure white, like water frozen into clusters, shading downward to the threshold and upward to a squared-off space. Those jutting points near the foot were dusky, yellowish, as if soil had worked into them before they had been frozen into immobility and, far above, the water-clear stones were tinged with a faint shade of violet which deepened into a rich purple.

The doorway drew him and he floated (for he was not aware of flying in this dream) towards the entrance—only to be so sharply and suddenly repelled that he was driven out of dream and sleep in the same instant. He lay, gasping, his heart beating so fast that he felt it must be shaking his whole body. For a space of time which could be measured only by his hurried breaths he adjusted to the fact that he was in the cabin and not before that burnished, gem-studded and open doorway.

Far in his mind something stirred as if a door long and securely locked was shaken. He lay inert and strove to reach that door, only to have a sickening whirling possess him utterly.

While he pressed his hands to his mouth to help control the rising sickness in him, there came a signal from the wall of the cabin. They were coming out of overdrive—if Krip's efforts had been successful, the system they sought lay waiting for them.

Farree moved cautiously, levering himself up in the hammock. The sickness was still with him, but so was that vivid and complete dream—as much of a reality as if he had specifically sought out the crystal door.

7.

There it is!" Krip pushed forward in the co-pilot seat to view what lay on the vision screen.

Green, blue—a round ball rapidly approaching them was before their eyes. For it seemed to Farree that that world was approaching them rather than they were seeking for a landing place on it.

"Ah—" Zoror's hands were busy on the controls. A feeling of tension spread from the Zacanthan to the rest of them. Just as in the dream the crystal door—or something—had warded Farree off—now the feeling arose in him that danger waited—

Zoror's attention was all for the bank of buttons and levers before him, but now he spoke to Vorlund: "Station for entrance—do you use the controls also—" The Zacanthan's shoulders were braced as if he were exerting force against more than buttons.

Vorlund's own hands flew down on the co-pilot's controls and his face drew grim.

Did a flicker on the screen actually waver for a moment? Farree was almost led to believe that it did. In that breath or two out of time it might have been that their ship was warded off, held from entering the inner skies of this unknown world. Then, if there had indeed been a barrier, it was gone. They finned in with the same ease as if the Zacanthan had held the ship in his hand to place it neatly on a solid surface. Vorlund leaned forward to touch the level of the vision screen which would turn slowly to give them a full view of the space where they had landed.

There were wisps of smoke rising which veiled much; the landing rockets must have found something to set alight. Maelen was reading symbols which flashed on a smaller screen near her right hand. Those blazed up in small green flashes, each one of which Farree knew stood to reassure that beings such as themselves dared explore without wearing ponderous equipment meant to battle hostile atmosphere.

The air, the light, all seemed well; there might not be a second warn off. Farree wondered if any but him had felt the first. However, when they prepared to down ramp and go to view this world he saw Vorlund buckling on a stunner belt. Maelen flexed her fingers as if her bare flesh was also a weapon.

That the Zacanthan was also reaching for a stunner was a surprise. So respected were the Zacanthans across the star lanes that even a Guild Veep might consider carefully any idea which included interfering with one. In fact rumor had it that Hist-Techs' continued studies of the past had included experimentation with outré weapons of the Forerunners and that they were better left strictly alone. Farree had his knife in his boottop but he doubted his own efficiency with that in spite of Vorlund's careful schooling.

They came out on the ramp which was slung out over the

strip of burnt vegetation. Maelen paused, fingers lightly clasped and held out as she slowly made a half arc turn, sweeping from one side of the country before them to the other, Vorlund and Zoror pushing back a little to give her full room.

Farree used his mind without any link to an instrument. Of a sudden he took to the air, soaring up above the ship, winging out and away from the circle of destruction its tail flames had caused as it rode those in for their landing.

He headed for a point in the cup of valley in which they had landed—a green-covered hump to the north of the ship. It was the first, he noted, of a series of such which sprouted upward in a straight line. They varied in size, however, some being taller even than Zoror afoot and others so small their presence could be overlooked unless one was searching for any rise in the vegetation.

The careful placement of the hummocks made Farree believe that they were not the work of nature. Burial mounds? Ruins well concealed by years of abandonment? He loosed his mind touch, but there was nothing, not even a fraction of a hint as he earthed on the first one of the line.

This vegetation was thick, curling upward about his feet near to knee height. Hidden by the many three-pointed leaves were small flowers of a dim grey-white, as if the sun, so warm on his wings, never touched them. The weight of his feet loosed scent, sweet-spicy, while from near the patch where he had alighted there burst into the air pellets, some of which struck against him and clung. Those, too, were the grey-white of the flowerets. He pried one loose from his jerkin, finding it sticky, holding now to his fingers. But the moment he took that into his hands he had again a pain-edged flash from that inner part of his mind which had been always sealed until he began this venture. He—he knew this!

Salenge! Ill-bane! It banished ills and made the heart light—only how had he known that? "Salenge," he repeated aloud. His fingers closed of their own accord on the tiny clove he held. It burst under pressure, releasing another scent, sharper, making his nose tingle, the saliva flow in his mouth. Again, without conscious thought, he raised his now juice-coated hand to his mouth and licked the remnants of the burst berry from his flesh. It was cool in his mouth and hot as he swallowed.

Farree flung back his head to look at the sky above the arch of his wings. Salenge—that he knew—and also its use. Only he had never seen this before—or had he? Impatiently he thrust at that barrier in his memory and then swayed at a second bite of pain. No, do not push—Maelen had told him this and she was right. There was nothing but emptiness when he sought. Yet when he let his thoughts settle elsewhere there came hints such as this.

He stooped and shook the plants gently. On his other hand and arm he caught as many of the expelled balls as he could. Then he winged up, to circle the ship in an outward swing, studying the ground below.

They had not landed in what could be thought a valley, rather in an odd formation of ground. It was indeed cup-shaped, a perfectly round stretch which was walled by cliffs and rises, with no sign of any break through which one might depart without a climb. Through the lower of those cliffs were partly masked in curtains of vegetation, as thick-matted as the ground, with many entangled vines, the reaches higher up were of a stone which was of a grey close to silver. Through that ran a pattern of veins of a clear white which in places caught the sun and flashed as if they were embedded with gems.

There were no trees or large shrubs—only the rippling of the salenge which was thickest about that line of undulating mounds, then grew less and less until on the other side of the finned-down ship, beyond the black marks of its landing fires, there was a sprawling of what seemed to be leafless vines across a grey-brown soil, hardly distinguishable from what they rooted upon.

Farree climbed with strong beats of wing until he reached the level of the sparkling stone. The air was clear and the scent of it was the scent of growing things which he gulped, after the recycled atmosphere of the ship, in mouthfuls, fairly drinking it down. The exultation which came with free flight was like a heady draught. Almost he forgot all else when he swung around over that space where the vines made odd ridges, leafless against the ground.

For the first time he centered his attention completely on that. Its contrast to the verdant growth at the other side of the space ship became more and more apparent. He dropped to fly closer. There was something about—

Again a sword of memory cut at him deeply.

Hagger—a hagger run. He could see in his mind a bloated brown body, a thing which ran stomach down on six legs. Yet the shape of its head—! Hagger!

That which controlled his flight did not wait for memory to grow any clearer—it sent him climbing, heading for the gem rocks with wildly beating wings. Then he fought free of that fear, turned back, coming once more to his first perch on the mound. Again around him arose the scent of trampled salenge, soothing—relaxing—

Hagger and salenge—where under the moons of Three did such ever come together? The moons of Three! He dropped his harvest of burst berries and held his head in both hands. Again a memory flash—why did such torture him so?

"Farree!" Maelen's mind call brought him out of that haze of pain. "What is it?"

He did not answer. Instead he took wing, flying back to the ramp outsprung from the ship and there stood before the other three. Plucking a salenge berry from the edge of his sleeve he held it into their full sight.

"This is salenge—what they call also ill-bane for it heals

all ills and wounds if it can be used in time. And"—he gestured to the ship—"behind that are the hunting lines of the hagger. Do not ask me how I know this—I cannot tell." He shook his head slowly. The pain had eased, yet he knew that it was lying just beyond—waiting—

"Where have we landed?" To Farree's surprise Zoror asked him nothing concerning what he did know.

"Thus—" Quickly Farree replied with a picture of the cup in which they had planeted.

It was Vorlund who broke the silence first when he had ended.

"No way out then?"

"Not unless you climb. But I have not had time to search thoroughly."

Maelen let her hands hang free. "No life registers—save our own party."

"Those mounds." The Zacanthan nodded to the humps Farree had first sighted. "Grave barrows, ruins—" He spoke as if to himself. Then he asked Farree the question for which the other had been waiting. "Salenge—hagger—?" Repeating the words he made them an inquiry.

Farree shrugged. "I cannot tell you why," he repeated, "but that much I know."

Vorlund sealed the lock with a word code they all repeated after him and then they moved off, Zoror heading straight for the nearest one of those hillocks. Vorlund stood eyeing the nearest wall, now hidden under that thick coating of vegetation and Maelen held her head up, staring straight northward, as if from a breeze now rising she had gathered a message.

Farree's gaze followed hers. He actually staggered as the strongest hurt from that hiding place of his memory struck home.

"Caer Vul-li-Wan—"

Not part of the barriers which closed them in now,

no—rather a peak upstanding like a narrow tower surmounting a keep. White against the sky which was a rich green-blue— Down its sides he thought he could see flickers of glitter even as far away as it must be—perhaps the same gem light as on the upper reaches of the cliffs about.

Almost as if his small flash of recognition had sent out some unknown message to alert sentries, there was a gathering of haze about that spire, a cover which might have been drawn from clouds too high to be seen, and it was gone from view.

Zoror's thought struck with almost the same force as the memory touch had given Farree. "Caer of the Seven Lords? So—it would appear that we have indeed been caught up by legend, younger brother. But whose legend? Have you come in summons by the 'Little People?'"

Farree paid him no attention; he thought only of the sight of that slim uprise against the sky. No, he had never seen that before— Then where had he gotten that name, and known that it was truly the right one? The haze which hid it now—the Breath of Merl-Math wafted in, to confuse any not of the true blood. But not raised to confuse him.

No, there was other cause to wear the wind veil! Other causes—!

He was airborne once more, hardly aware that he had beat upwards with what was near a leap. It did not matter that the Caer—that which called him—lay elsewhere. Farree wheeled in the air, looking not to the north where the peak was now hidden but to the west. At that moment the ship, those from it, everything which made up the mystery of this new world was wiped away. In him was a compelling call which only he might answer.

Already he had passed above the lip of the cliff which walled in the cup. There was no stretch of green beneath him as he dropped a little lower, skimming across a space filled with many pillars and wedges of rock, where there blazed forth with force enough to make him squint and strive to see only through a narrow slit, flames of light, red, green, blue, yellow, and also rainbows of many colors.

"Farree!"

He blocked that call out of his mind. Beside the compulsion which sent him on it was but a fading whisper. He was needed—he, alone—not those of other blood—those who plundered and took, killed and enslaved—

"I come!" He thought that with all his might, all the power he had learned from Maelen and Zoror. It was as if his own thoughts broke and tore as had that rough skin which had covered his wings, freeing him in another way.

Even as that tatter of some other's wing skin had led him through the crooked lanes of the portside town, so did that appeal, growing ever louder, draw his mind. The stretch of country where the jewel fires blazed fell away. He saw before him now a sloping into another valley but one much wider and more uneven of shapes. There was the glint of water there, and clumps of what might be trees. No bare soil showed the crisscross of hagger ways. Yet there was life here. Across the valley a number of dark animals were apparently grazing the short turf. One flung up its head and pointed that in Farree's direction. On so low a thought band that he almost missed it, he sensed part of what might be a question. He had no desire to linger and answer. The creature reared, flashing forelegs in the air, perhaps in challenge, while those others about it bunched swiftly, before taking off first in a trot and then at a rocking gallop.

Up from the copse of trees not too far from the river whirled a flock of birds taking to wing with the speed of warriors summoned by a chief's horn. They drew near to Farree and he saw that, though they appeared at a distance to resemble birds, this close he could see no feathers. Their brilliantly hued wings were more like his own and their bodies were covered with scales which were as jeweled in this light as the cliff rock he had crossed moments earlier. Their heads were long and narrow, split near the beginning of their sinuous necks with gaping jaws which showed teeth.

He eyed them warily and soared higher. There was a wind now which was chill and had what could be a snow bite to it. Perhaps it had come from the taller mountains to the north. For some reason the bird things did not try to join him. Instead they wheeled as if on some shouted order and headed north, leaving the sky clear.

The sight of this alien life had, in a strange way, dimmed the message which drew him on. Now that was strong again. Suddenly he was looking down at a disturbance of the turf and soil below. There was broken earth, gouges and ruts. Surely those were of such a size as to make certain they were no beast spoor left to be tracked by a hunter. Oddly enough they had sprung from a point in the middle of a bare space of ground as if whatever had left those marks had issued from beneath the surface itself.

Farree flew on. Now he discovered that the call which drew him lay in the same direction as that trail. He winged ahead to where a fringe of small hills were a screen between any ground traveler and the land beyond. But the ruts found a way among these barriers, weaving in and out. Here the valley, which had appeared narrow in the beginning, widened out, though even from the air he could not see what lay far beyond. The same haze which had veiled Caer-Vul-li-Wan cloaked it as fully as if a curtain, hung high in the heavens, lowered folds to hide the earth.

For the first time Farree faltered. That plea which had brought him so far had been cut off—as suddenly as if death itself had been the portion of the one who uttered it. Also there was something about that haze curtain which struck him with a greater chill than even the snow breeze had raised.

He turned track and flew south—only to find there again the curtain in place, while the call was not even a whisper of a whisper. The haze did not hang to the north or across the eastern sky through which he had flown. As he coasted along still a good way from its edge he tried to search with mind call for the cry he must answer, only to shrink backward—for it was as if his own thought, badly distorted, had been thrown back at him. Nor was there anything in his treacherous memory to match this.

To fly above was no answer for, as if it were indeed some weapon aimed at him, the haze spiraled upward also, matching him. From it that deadness reached outward. He was sickened, drained, having all he could do to keep a-wing. The ebbing of energy brought him at last to ground level where, once he felt the firmness of the sod under his feet, he struggled to keep on those feet, unable to do more at first than to gasp for breath.

The haze might have defeated him at this first encounter but that certain stubbornness of spirit which had kept him going as a homeless misshaped creature of the Limits held him now. His wings folded down about his shoulders like a cloak as he crossed to a big rock which showed a deep scoring, as if that thing which had made the road had grated along it. There he sat on the stone, his hands on either side of him, bracing his body as he strove to master the weakness assaulting him in deep waves. His move raised the scent of salenge. There must have been some of the seed globes still clinging to his clothing. He inclined his head to draw that reviving odor into his lungs. A flicker of more recent memory came uneasily— He raised one juice-stained hand to the front of his jerkin. There was no familiar bulge there.

Togger! It was the first time since he had first known the smux that he had actually forgotten him entirely. Now, finding him gone was like losing part of a wing—or a hand. The discovery shattered the spell of compulsion that had kept him seeking westward. He viewed the haze squarely. It appeared to be drifting in his direction. There was a curl of it reaching out to where he perched. Without knowing why he put out his hand and—felt actual pressure against his palm!

Instantly he jerked away. The Wall of the Carrion Wind! There was a faint odor of corruption which flowed from his hand, where it had rested against the unseen, up into him. Farree closed his eyes, and saw darkness shot through with hard brilliant beams of light—light which was as straight as a laser ray. Between those beams there were shadows, some leaping forward as if to drag down a hunted creature for the kill, others falling away because some flash of light touched them and slew. In the midst of the whirl of light and dark someone stood. At first he thought it might be Maelen or even Zoror.

Then he knew that it was neither but one who ruled the Carrion Wind and set it as a barrier against which the living might beat in vain. Only he could not see the one who labored so.

The brand about his wrist awoke to pain, almost as great as that which had first struck him when it had been set upon his body. Farree opened his eyes. He might even have whimpered aloud as the torment grew. He looked down at the hand which he had raised against the force of the haze. There was a blaze of color above the brand mark, hiding that with a brilliance of gem radiance.

He raised his other hand to nurse his hurt, wavering to his feet, feeling as if he burned in a fire from which there was no escape. Farree cried out.

"Utsor vit—S'Lang." His voice seemed to slant outward—almost as if he could see the words take shape and strike at the haze.

There was a curdling of the mist; it might have been stirred by some great ladle. The barrier began to thin before him, first forming a window of sorts through which he might look upon what had been hidden. Then that slit lengthened into an open portal. Farree blinked, shut his eyes. The vision of the darting lights was gone—

Carrion Wind: once more his lips shaped the naming. The stench from the drifting filaments was strong enough to overcome the last trace of the salenge which had revived him.

He did not take to wing again. Instead, with his pinion-cape furled about him, he went forward on foot, picking a way with care because of the deep ruts and holes in the surface of the strange road. The inner call which had summoned him was alive again but very faint and faltering, as if the one who formed it was near to the edge of strength.

Farree stumbled and kept his balance with difficulty. That which tripped him was only half buried in the broken earth. He stooped and dragged it free and stood staring at his find almost stupidly. He knew it—it was out of the past which he well remembered—the hell hole of the Limits. A pulse whip! His finger slid along the indentations in the butt. No weaving of force answered him. Burnt out. Only to find this favorite weapon of slavers here! He made to cast the evil thing from him and then reconsidered. Zoror—the Zacanthan knew such disciplines; it might even be that he could pull out of the torture weapon some idea of who had wielded it last, advance an idea of what enemy they might be about to face.

The haze was near dissipated. Farree had wondered what lay beyond the portal his shouted words had opened. But there was only the churned-up earth, which vanished when it reached a curve of height beyond.

That which had called him faded again and died. He still felt the renewed pain in his wrist but he was no longer imbued with the drive to fly ahead. Instead, with the whip thrust safely in his belt, Farree took wing again, heading back towards the ship.

He half expected to see the haze rise again, to the east, shutting him away from his shipmates. But there was no more clouding of the sky. The sun was farther away—and the chill winds buffeted him. He looked to the north, half expecting to be able to sight the spire of Caer Vu-li-Wan; only it was as if that had been erased from the sky. There were similar heights to be sighted—the one most important was gone.

Farree scowled. Now he could no longer trust his eyes— That calling, was it responsible for this blindness? There were too many questions and no answers he could pick up for himself. What words had he shouted? Now he could not remember. Maelen, Vorlund—to them things like this were known. The Zacanthans closed no doors upon the hope of knowledge, even though it was yet only a hope. What had he? Fragments of a tormenting memory, but so little more.

He shook off his sudden self pity to look around, seeking some landmark. There were the cliff tops ahead, not so alive with flashing colors now that the sun was nearing setting. To him now all looked alike and he had not even the sighting of Caer Vu-li-Wan to set him aright. He was startled by a harsh call—one he heard with his ears and not his mind.

He was not alone in the sky. Above and beyond him a second pair of wings beat, wings as large and wide-spread as his own. But they were not mounted on anything which could in the least be thought his kin.

It was black, that elongated body, which twisted as easily through the air as a snake would cover ground. The head was turned in his direction and he saw a half open mouth, not unlike the ones he had seen on the smaller thing which had flown ahead of him earlier.

It screamed again. Farree needed no other warning, and he flew with all the speed he could summon. That thing also had great clawed feet. Those talons now flexed as if ready to close on prey and as it was fast overtaking him, a third cry sounded almost in his ears.

8.

He was over the cliff top now, streaking at the highest speed he could muster to elude that flying thing. Its body twisted and turned as lithely as that of a snake, matching speed with him, but keeping a little above on a parallel course, while from its open jaws flashed what could have been a tongue of flame. Still, though it hovered above him, giving every indication that if it wished it could attack, it remained two lengths of its own long body behind. Why it hesitated to pull him down was a growing puzzle.

Farree's head jerked up and a lock of his hair flopped across his forehead in answer to what did reach him.

He was meeting a stream of thought which wriggled back and forth as did the body from which it sprung, its message now clear, now snapped just short of fading out with the speed of a breath.

"Darthor, Darthor!" The words burst from him. The stab of memory did not come so sharply this time.

He no longer strove to flee and at the same time somehow keep eye on what had been a menace. Had been—? Of a surety it was so.

"Darthor, varge!" Surging in beat, his own wings carried him higher, brought him around in a glide to face the monster.

The creature cut speed. It veered to the north, though it still kept its large orange eyes fastened upon Farree.

"Darthor, varge!" He shouted as one who has mastered a captive horror from some unknown world and impressed his will upon it.

It squawked, lashing the tail which was a good third of its body length. A shaft of what certainly looked like real fire shot again from between its jaws. It did not spiral away from him, only altered its line of flight so that it flew tandem with him, matching its speed to his.

Farree switched from voice to mind send. "Darthor, servant one, hunting lies not in my shadow." The words came to him in curious formal fashion as he thought them slowly and with the emphasis of one who would be obeyed. A dim picture hung behind that voiceless speech, Darthor a-wing after something which fled in frenzy, while behind him was one who was also winged, who carried a glittering rod in one hand. Himself! No, that could not be— Not him, but one who was his like, before whom Darthor flew as a hunter. Yet Farree's first fear was not quite appeased. He was no master of this creature. Still why did he know it and fear its coming?

For the moment he could do nothing. Darthor was flying in odd spurts even as a land-running thing might give sudden leaps, and always it kept its eyes on Farree. There was a sly sullenness in that gaze, as if the hold he had on it, keeping it from the leap which would tear him from the sky, was only tenuous, that at one moment or the next he might lose that unsteady control.

They were in sight of the edge of the cup valley now. Shadows had crept from the heights to reach out toward the ship. Farree headed toward that mound where he had first trod the earth of this world.

An air-splitting shriek which seemed able to rend the rocks themselves startled him. Even as his feet met the mound he looked up. That creature who had accompanied him was lashing its tail, its whole slender body, back and forth through the air. It would attempt to fly in Farree's wake only to be hurled, actually hurled, back in the air, wings beating fenziedly, other shrieks following the first.

There was rage in every assault it made from the edge of the cliff top. Its clawed forefeet reached out as if to tear the air itself into shreds. Farree was aware of movement beside him. Vorlund came to a stop, his stunner unleashed and ready for firing.

"No!" Farree cried out, striking at the other's stiffened arm as he took aim.

"Darthor—guard—" He fitted together the small scraps of knowledge which he had. "It fears—you!"

Saying that he knew he spoke the truth. The air creature was centering that yellow-eyed stare on Vorlund while lashes of the seeming flame burst from between its jaws. There was rage in it which was as strong a weapon as the one the spacer now held.

"It cannot come here." That also was true Farree knew. There was no billowing haze to present a wall and yet there existed a barrier, unseen, unfelt by Farree in his flight—only set against other things. At that moment there was released from the squirming, flapping thing another kind of attack.

Vorlund cried out. Though the stunner wavered in his hold, he did not drop it even as he fell to his knees. Farree had been on the edge of that blow delivered mind to mind. But not from Darthor—that creature had only released what was being fed to it.

"Fragon, Shadow commander, I name names." The pain in Farree's locked mind nearly sent him sprawling beside Vorlund. "Name names," he thought again. There was a mad whirl of color in his head, but he still held to what was blanking out, or attempting to black out his mind, as a blindfold might have cut off his sight.

"Fragon, Fragon—" He chanted that sing-song aloud as well as holding firmly to what he directed toward the flyer.

"Fragon," he repeated. Then he was chanting: "By the sky hold, by the throne, by the green, and by silver worn, I do call the name—thy name!"

The thing on the cliff top writhed, spinning as if some great fingers had closed upon it to wring it like a rag. It was screaming again. But pain had arisen to blot out what it had been transmitting. Vorlund was shaking, his face strained unnaturally, but he was rising, though the stunner now lay in the thick green growth about their feet.

A new power possessed Farree. He felt a surge of such strength as he had never known. His wings spread wide and he held clenched fists above his head.

"Take your Shadow one, Fragon!" His thought had somehow grown louder, more demanding also. "Take the Darthor, Fragon. There is no meat for its rending here!"

Abruptly the fading turmoil the creature broadcast ceased. It still hung aloft there, its head lower than its coils of body. Farree knew, even without being able to see at this distance, that it was closely observing them, still a tool for another, but one who was wary, angered, yet not ready as yet to take the lead into battle. Then the creature whirled in the air and the steady beat of its wings carried it northward where a thickening haze cloaked height after height, hiding well what might await them there.

Farree caught at Vorlund's shoulder, steadied the taller spacer who leaned forward to catch up the stunner, only to slap it deep into its holster. Then he looked straight at Farree.

"What was it? It would have killed—"

Farree shook his head slowly, rubbing one hand across his forehead where the cessation of that confrontation had ended for him in a dull headache and a mistiness of thought.

He knew—knew what and why? He was unable to sort it out now. There had been contact and now there was emptiness, total withdrawal.

"I—don't know—" he quavered. Within both his mind and his body there was a sickening churning. Pain, which might have been there during the attack but which he had not noticed there, bit deep.

"You named it," Vorlund countered. "There was a second name also—Fragon—"

Farree shivered and then heard another voice, speaking, not intruding into the place of growing torment in his mind.

"A mighty mental power is this Fragon." Zoror came up behind them. Now he looked directly at Farree. "So, little brother, your mind barrier still holds?" He reached out one hand and gently pulled Farree's fingers away from his pain-wrinkled forehead, pressing his own to Farree's head in their place.

It was like a draught of water to soothe a dry mouth and throat: from that lightest of touches spread a cooling.

"I have never been here before," Farree answered in words, "yet I know!"

He felt Vorlund stir beside him, but it was Zoror who spoke: "Know what, little brother?"

"This country—or part of it!" Farree swung out his arms to indicate not only the valley but what lay beyond. Then he looked around to see Zoror still studying him. It was difficult to read expression on that scaled face so different from a humanoid's, but he thought that the Zacanthan's usual one of wide interest was now narrowed into a beam like the Darthor's fiery tongue, reaching out to him with the same force that flying creatures had used.

He closed his own eyes momentarily, in a hope to shut doors against the other's unspoken probe. Farree could not rid himself of the feeling that Zoror was willing an answer out of him.

"Where did you go, brother?" He had been too closely

observant of the Zacanthan to note that Maelen was now also here. Her fingers pointed to Farree himself.

"Up," he answered dully, gesturing towards the gem-banded cliffs. Too much had happened to him. He wanted a time of quiet, or the ability to shut out the lingering tumult in his mind. "There is a large, very large valley over there." Now he gestured westward. "Animals—I think they are animals. Something like a road worn by heavy wagons—then"—he lifted both hands in a hopeless gesture—"there was the fog—the wall—"

He strove to make plain the nature of that barrier but he had hardly finished when it was Zoror's time to question.

"Why did you so leave us, little brother?"

Farree answered with the truth. "There was a—call. I had to answer."

"And—" prompted Zoror.

"With the wall it was ended—that call."

"Ended so that this Darthor might take its place? Perhaps," suggested Vorlund, "you did not answer quick enough. The impulse to incite you was not strong—"

"No!" Farree interrupted sharply. He moved a little so he was facing to the north, to that sky finger of a peak now completely hidden. "They are not the same!"

"What are *they*?" Maelen's voice was soft and low, and she did not strive to touch mind to mind. For that Farree was deeply thankful.

"There is—" He looked down at his hands and then was aware of a sharp tug at his boot. The ill-bane grew in a thick mat but it was trampled here and Togger was easily seen. He stooped and caught up the smux, holding him tightly. In all this maze of wounded memories Togger remained real, alive, and an anchor Farree could cling to.

He cradled the smux, taking pleasure in feeling the creature's body pressed close to his own. "It comes only in bits. It hurts to think," he said slowly. "But I believe that there are two forces here which do not work together.

Fragon—and do not ask me to tell who or what that name is given to—controls the haze—and has spies along the land. The Darthor projects visions of what happens on the ground by cruising along the haze. I think"—he was frowning and the smux wriggled a little as if he were now grasped too tightly for even his tough skin to take—"I think that there is something beyond the haze—that which or who summoned me. And that other is in great peril and needful of aid."

"Which this Fragon would not allow to be given?" Vorlund wanted to know.

Farree nodded. "Only I could not go through the haze—it was a wall. And perhaps another exists here—for the Darthor could not come to us. Two—two forces—" His voice trailed away.

Farree recognized the listening look Maelen wore. This was the Lady as she appeared when in contact with one of the animals or birds which were her lifelong other-being.

Zoror and Vorlund were quiet now, also watching the Moonsinger. Shadows were swinging closer as the sun descended, reaching easily the cliffs they could not climb. Her hands showed the beginning of a flush. Farree guessed that she was taxing to the utmost one of the few defenses her people had kept when they had destroyed a dangerous and contorted past to become wanderers on the earth of the planet they once had ruled.

She began to hum, and that faint sound throbbed also in him as her flush traveled over her skin and grew deeper.

Maelen opened her eyes. "There *is* something there. It does not yield to any search my people know. But it is aware—of us. It—" She did not complete what she would have said then but her hands no longer held straight. Rather they tilted towards the mound on which they stood.

Farree caught his breath even as he heard a whisper of hiss from Zoror. Then from beneath them as they stood—! It was as if something climbed with ponderous movement up towards them, its passage setting the earth to rock with warning.

Farree's hand swept out, knocked up Maelen's fingers. He knew that what might now be awake and stirring was no friend to such as disturbed its slumber.

He dared to shake Maelen hard, as if he could force her to throw off bonds of a compulsion. Then she spoke directly to Farree.

"What comes to my call?"

A source outside his consciousness supplied an answer and as he gave it, he was also entirely convinced of its truth.

"The Sixth Champion of Har-le-don. He who shall rise in the last days of the Far hosting, no longer oath bound to any lord, but shadowed by the binding—" He cried out then, and threw back his head to look up into the evening sky. There was no flutter of wings there, no heart-rousing song of battle to face.

"Come not the dark for our day is not yet dawning!" He knew the meaning of the words he cried aloud, but he did not speak in the common language of the trader tongue.

It was Zoror who moved first. A scaled arm wrapped about Maelen's shoulder and she was swept from the mound top while Vorlund leaped outward, putting a side distance between him and the hillock.

"Farree!" His voice and Zoror's rang together. However, it seemed to the one they had left behind that the herb growing so profusely there entangled his feet and would not free him. Still he sensed what stirred beneath the ground. With that came something else, a thrust—though weak—into his mind. Not painful this time, rather cold, diffused. What or who might have aimed that might be only a little aroused—not yet returned to—

Using all his strength Farree repelled, defended. His wings opened to bear him aloft, but not toward the ship where he had thought to go: rather as if he had received an order he could not disobey. Farree landed on the next of the mounds, then after only a breath or two of resting, he was aloft again. Once more gripped by compulsion he crossed the open space, flying from one mound to the next, some large and some small, until he came to the northern cliff wall. The hold on him was broken there. He turned and flew back to the ramp of the ship. When he touched down there he felt free, as he had not been since they had made landing. What had forced him to make that flight he could not have told. He clamped his wings down into folds and walked, for the first time suspicious of the pinions he wore, back into the ship, trailing after those who had already gone in that direction.

Nor did he wish to look over his shoulder, to see if the Great Mound showed any of the disturbance which was troubling it from below.

He found the others in the pilot's cabin, Zoror holding a reader, his large eyes fastened upon a screen smaller than the palm of his narrow hand.

"'People of the Hills.'" His voice was half hiss as it was always when he was excited. "That is the ancient name— People of the Hills. And their kingdoms, their places of refuge, were often said to lie under mounds!"

"That was glamorie."

The three of them raised their heads to stare at Farree. Maelen and Vorlund wore expressions of no comprehension but Zoror's eyes glowed.

"Ah, glamorie," he repeated.

"Do not ask me questions!" Farree threw at him. His hands again bracketed his aching head. "I do not know where I find these words, or why—"

"It is no question," Zoror continued. "Rather this is a part of the old legend of the 'Little Men.' In many tales and fragments of tales, which have been gathered from the planets where the old Terran breed settled, there are such small scraps to be harvested. One of the stories which is told over and over again consists of two main elements. First, that the People of the Hills (and you were very right, younger brother, in giving them that name) had a different reckoning of time. To be in their presence for perhaps a night took a mortal man or woman away for a year from the life they knew, to stay under the hills for a year meant several centuries passing for the captive or guest from the outer world.

"The other strange gift they had was that of glamorie, of allowing those of the upper and outer world to be deceived easily, thinking they saw something very different from what was real. One of the People might pay for service in coins of gold, the one paid only to discover in his pocket not long after dried leaves or a twist of grass. The People could produce a great dwelling worthy of a high noble and he who feasted there with them would wake in the morning to find himself in a ruined and deserted pen for the safe keeping of animals. Also it is said that if a human was by some chance able to see through these webs they spread he or she might be blasted sightless when this knowledge was betrayed."

"Then they were always avowed enemies of other races?" Vorlund wanted to know.

Zoror's horny fingers rasped along his lower jaw. He shifted his stand a little so he was facing directly north.

"They were, according to the old tales, ever changeable. Some that were not of their race they would aid freely, making common cause with them against danger. Others were for their sport and suffered from their careless cruelty—"

"In other words," Vorlund said as the Zacanthan's voice trailed away, "they were much like us after all—save they perhaps used weapons which we could not wield."

"True," admitted Zoror. "What they would do with us now—for that we must wait and see."

"See!" Maelen was not repeating Zoror's word, but rather summoning their attention.

It was well into early evening. The sun had been cut off so that only the fading of a deeply rose-blue swath across the sky marked it. However, there was other light in the cup valley. Points of glimmer touched the top of each of the mounds as a flame might spring from a candle. They differed in shade or color from one another—here there was a rose shading nearly into crimson, there was one which flared first blue and then green; beyond was yellow, scarlet, even a deep rich purple. Only that largest mound was different yet.

There the blossoming light was not a candle flame; rather it flowered into a circle, from the rim of which shot spears of gemlike brilliance. In color it was different also, being a frosty silver such as might appear on a winter snow bank when a full moon stretched across ice crystals. The points of each of those spears flashed also blue and green.

"A crown," Maelen said softly.

Farree bit hard upon his lower lip and fought for control. Just as that summons had taken him into the air and out over the unknown land, so now was another compulsion gathering within him. Without knowing what he did his hand stretched out—although the mound was far away from him in reach—his fingers crooked as if setting grip upon the crown. Then he shook his head as one who strove to drive away some inner fog, and his hand folded into a fist.

"Staver's Bane—" His voice was hardly above a whisper. "Take up that and the world is one's for the having!" Then he raised his voice in a shout which carried out over that display of jeweled flame. "I do not trouble you, Old One! I want no power from you! Sleep again, Havermut—your time has not come!" He was shivering, one hand clinging to Togger who somehow provided an anchorage in a place of whirling strengths rising to battle one another.

He leaned over the rail of the ramp, and then there came from his twisted mouth those ugly obscenities which had studded the language of the Limits. Farree cursed the crown of light, those night candles about it, and fear fought anger in that cursing.

As if his words, expanding outward, possessed some visible power in themselves, the flames flickered. But that which he had hailed as Staver's Bane swelled larger and larger, embracing more and more of the hillock on which it was the crest, the silvery radiance of it slipping farther and farther down the rounded sides of the rise. No longer did it resemble a crown—rather it was a wheel which began to spin, so that the lights of its spear points became circles undistinguishable one from the other.

Farree, hoarse from shouting, caught at the rail of the ramp. He had only to— No! another part of him shouted in his brain, drowning out the first—it was truly a bane to him who would lay hand upon it. For this was no crown of the blue moon, it was rather a trick, a trap, bait to catch the foolish! Of that much he was sure.

The circle now had reached the ground level, forming a wall about the mound. There was a haze arising from it—

Farree shuddered. With one hand still upon Togger to anchor him safely to the here and now, he fumbled with the other in the air, jerking fingers back and forth as if he were able to so erase what he saw.

High above the wall of the cup from where night had gathered with racing speed, there came a shaft of light like the force of a laser beam. It sped across the still gleaming candles and struck, full upon those who stood at the top of the ramp. Zoror cried out and slumped down. A rainbow of sparks shot from Maelen's fingers. Vorlund caught her as she stumbled back, and held her against his own body. In that moment the spacer appeared the strongest of them all. But Farree was held motionless, as if pinned within the space he occupied by that needle of light.

It came from the north, and, though he looked into the full glare of it, unable to turn either head or eyes away, he saw not the blasting of the light but behind and beyond. There was a balcony, set into a wall and on that stood others—he could see no faces, no bodies clearly, yet he knew them for what they were—these were the masters of this world and to them, all who came in ships were dreaded enemies.

9.

A moan sounded. Farree rubbed smarting eyes and turned his head. Vorlund leaned against the wall of the door port to Farree's left, Maelen was limp and motionless in the spacer's arms. Her eyes were closed and yet she moaned again feebly and tried to raise one hand.

Zoror had reached that point of what might be temporary safety before them. He was sitting up, his head clasped between his two hands, his fanged mouth open as he panted, drawing in breaths as if he had been on the point of being strangled. Still, as Farree glanced outward once again, the light was there, yet stopped at the port through which they had come as if some tangible force had cut it off. Zoror pulled himself up on his knees. He was still breathing heavily, yet it would appear that his condition did not keep him from the quest for knowledge which was the ever-present employment laid on his species.

From his belt he drew the talon knife which was both an

honor badge of his people and, most times, his only weapon. He caught the tip between the two fingers and tossed it out to clatter down the ramp towards the ground.

What followed was like being caught near the tail of a ship taking off. There was an explosion of searing light which again left Farree blinded. Then— Something which he had sensed—a compulsion, a stern will—vanished. He pawed at his eyes with one hand—they were still watering. However, that spear of light from the north was gone. The weapon of fire might have failed; he was sure it had not willingly been withdrawn. There remained—like a whisper in his head— unease—counter-fear—astonishment—all. Then that, too, vanished and there was nothing but dark and silence.

Those candles on the mounds had snapped out of existence as quickly as had the weapon of light. There was only thick dark outside now, dark and a rising wind which beat with an icy lash against Farree as he staggered a step or two forward to look out into the valley. At first he had a fraction of terror, the belief that he had been blinded by that last shattering of flame. Then, as he turned his head frantically from side to side, he saw that each of the mounds was still sending into the cold of the night thin trails of faint luminescence—it might be the breath of unseen monsters turned visible by the icy air.

There was no crown, no candle flame. Farree leaned against the side of the door opening and he looked beyond— toward the north from whence that spear had come. His teeth caught hard upon his lower lip—there—and there—and there—!

Not as bright as the mound candles, in fact tenuous enough to be only ghosts of those flames, there were pale lights. As his eyes adjusted he could count them—nine— They were too faint in color to be camp fires, and from each streamed a thread of grey unnatural mist. Outward to the south they were reaching over the valley, waving as might banners. The first of these now dipped down, as if to lap them out of their refuge, but it came no farther than the foot of the ramp. There it wavered and clung, sweeping back and forth, joined and fed by those other traces of vapor, which made it more visible.

It was trying hard to get to them but it was walled away. Farree heard an exclamation from behind him. A stunner clicked, aimed at that wavering tongue of mist. It did not vanish, no, instead it appeared to draw energy from the power sent against it, so that the tongue of mist spread wider, its movements becoming more energetic and threatening, though it still did not reach beyond the foot of the ramp.

"No—!" He heard Zoror's voice. "Cold iron—your boot knife—let that feel iron!"

His cry might have been for Vorlund but it was Farree who heeded the order first. He grabbed at his own boot top, caught the hilt of the weapon which Vorlund had taught him to use, though he had never done so except in practice. The hilt was warm in his hand, the warmth growing into real heat as he raised it. Then, as the Zacanthan had done before him, Farree threw, aiming at the tongue of mist. He saw the black spot that was the speeding knife, and then the whip back of the mist. It broke into tatters which waved wildly in the air. A moment later he was aware that Vorlund had joined him loosing the infighting weapon of the spacers.

That mist fluttered, a thing now of ragged, dissolving wisps. It drew back to the mound which had been crowned, but no farther than that, changing the direction of its advance, pointing rather to the ground than to the ship beyond. Once more it was rebuilding in shape and strength.

"Cold iron! That is truth then!" Zoror's hand fell upon Farree's right shoulder. The Zacanthan may have yielded to the strike of the original beam but now his voice was full and deep again. He was, to all appearances, his old self as he leaned past Farree to blink out into the night.

"Cold iron?" Vorlund demanded. "What do you mean?"

"Mean?" Zoror's voice carried all the force of one who has

chanced upon a long-hunted treasure. "That once more there is a kernel of truth lying snug within legend, brother. It was said many times of the Little People that the one weapon they could not circumvent nor withstand was iron itself—iron which made man the master of the worlds where, one after another, they disputed his lordship."

There was a moan which was closer to a sigh. Farree swung around. Vorlund was down on his knees now, supporting Maelen. By the ship's lights her face was pale and drawn. She might have lain for long in the hold of some illness. Then her eyes opened and she looked up at the Zacanthan.

"They have power—such as even a Singer cannot summon—"

Zoror nodded. "It was always said of them that they were not to be easily overcome. There is something here, though, which we do not know—why should they attack without warning when we mean no harm?"

"Because of me!" Farree said bitterly. "And I do not have the knowledge to be able to discover the why of that either." Once more that ache in his head strengthened. There was something—something to be done—and the need for doing it gnawed within him; only he knew not what it was or why he must do that unknown act.

"We are safe within here," Zoror glanced around at them, his gaze lingering a moment on each as if he measured their strength and abilities. "Let us rest the night in iron-governed safety and see what the morning will bring."

Farree, half blind again from the pain in his head, lurched obediently into the corridor beyond the port. Somehow he got down to the level of his own cabin and there collapsed into his hammock, aware of nothing more than that his body rested and perhaps his head might follow. One hand moved restlessly. His palm felt sticky and not knowing nor caring what he was doing he brought up his hand and licked at it, so gathering into his mouth what was left of the bruised leaves and berries of ill-bane. He chewed and swallowed that harvest. The pain which had been a tight band about his head eased. He slid, as he might have on the ramp had he lost his footing, down into darkness.

There was a great hall, and panels in its walls were a-glitter with light, cold light, in spite of the fact that some of the colors were the red and yellow of flames. The pavement underfoot was silver, perhaps even true blocks of that metal. He did not tread there so much as waft above it, yet he did not feel any expansion of his wings.

Between the glittering panels were others of the same silver as was underfoot. Those were wrought with patterns in high relief. Some depicted strange creatures such as the fire-breathing snake which had hunted him back to the valley. Others were humanoid in form, yet differed one from the other. There were bodies like his own, winged and plainly traveling aloft. But there were also other things, grotesque, some monstrously so, and more merely strange, exuding no menace, as did a few.

There were no torches or lamps within the room—the radiance seemed to flow from the flooring beneath. Then he became aware of swirls of a milky mist which was coiling and recoiling, reaching every time farther out into the middle of the chamber. From somewhere there sounded a single trilling note. Two of the pictured wall blocks vanished sidewise into the flanking wall and there entered two whose wings were furled about them like colorful capes, even as he himself went where he trod the earth.

One was slightly taller than the other; since the wings sprang from the shoulders, they concealed most of the body, and were of a deep crimson shading into a silver as glinting as the pavement. His head (for the features on that calm and nearly expressionless face were ruggedly masculine, with a seam of scar across one cheek) was held high and there seemed to be flickers of fire in his large eyes.

His companion was just as plainly female. Her enclosing wings were the delicate ivory of the ill-bane flower, but they were also touched with silver which glinted gem-bright as she moved. Her long hair was braided about her head and woven in among the pale yellow of those coils were gem-set threads. Once in the room she loosed the tight covering of her wings to show that she wore a short, form-clinging robe of pure silver, girded by a wide belt of gold and brown gems. To the first glance she might look like a girl only on the verge of womanhood, but when one saw more closely, especially her eyes, there were signs of years of knowledge.

The man moved on into the center of that hall, his wings, too, now rising. While his body, even to arms and legs, was hidden in a glossy red mesh, he wore about his narrow waist a wide belt of silver scales which supported a weapon; Farree recognized it from pictures in Zoror's collection: it was known as a sword. The man's hands played with the buckle of the belt and he was frowning, his eyebrows near drawn together by a scowl. Now he stood staring down at the pavement as if he might find on the surface some answer to a problem which troubled him.

His companion did not come so far into the room. She held up her head as might one who was searching the sky and it was plain that her attention was caught by something which she sought aloft. Before either of them moved farther or spoke, if they did speak aloud, there sounded another note of summons, this time a double one which might come from within the earth. Two more of the panels opened, but those who entered thus were very different from the first comers.

They were small and they were wingless. Their shoulders were hunched a little forward, almost as if they were used to walking ways where the roofs pressed closer to the footing.

Both arms and legs to the knees were bare, showing rough brown skin, wrinkled and pocked with small dark splotches. Their bodies were covered with clothing almost the same shade as their flesh. And, far from being beardless, the faces of both were covered from the cheek bones down with mats of crinkled yellow-white hair, thatches of the same apparently covering their heads, as tufts appeared under the edges of dingy, rust-red caps. Their features—large hooked noses and deep-set eyes—were nearly masked, and as they drew nearer together and came forward a few steps, there was the air of suspicion about them, as if they were far from easy in this place or with such company.

The winged man looked about and jerked his head in a nod which both the gnarled creatures echoed. However, the woman continued to look aloft, now turning her head as if so to view the whole of the large chamber. She took no note of the newcomers.

A third sound followed speedily on those which had brought the bearded ones. A last panel opened and there came through a masked figure who, because of its muffling, could not be clearly named man or woman. The mask has been made to cover the whole head, fastened at the shoulders on either side of the throat with dull brown brooches. It had been fashioned to resemble the head of a beast, even to a covering of bristles, like needle spikes, planted along the large pointed ears and across the back, as well as along the drooping jowls, which helped to form the face (if one might term it that). There was no true nose, only a snout above a half open mouth. Small eyes were dark pits on either side of that snout, and there had been set in place within the jaw a full showing of greenish-yellow teeth with a rounded fore-fang sprouting out both to the right and the left.

The robe about the body of the newcomer was masklike also, falling in many folds. In color it was red, and over its surface were black lines which appeared to move with each step the creature took, sometimes forming patterns, only to dissolve at the next forward movement.

As the masked one advanced, ponderously, as if the robe covered a large bulk, the two capped men drew back hurriedly and shifted to one side so that the winged man was between them and Beast Head. Again the woman paid no attention to latest addition to their company, her head remaining up, her eyes searching.

It was Beast Mask who broke the silence. He spoke
gutturally, almost as if he found speech difficult for his tongue
and lips to shape. The words he spoke were slurred into a
monotone.

"Why the summons?"

It was the man who answered him, though somehow
Farree was surprised that he did so in audible speech:

"They have come in greater force. Also they have more
bait—one who has been turned to their service—"

"Where?" the Beast wanted to know.

"They have landed their hunting cage in the Valley of
Vore," the woman replied, never looking away from whatever
she must be seeking.

One of the small men laughed and the sound was like a
rusty bolt grating in a long disused lock. "Ah, and them what
sleep—they have stirred!"

There was a moment of silence. Farree believed that
perhaps of them all he could read the greatest surprise in the
attitude of Beast Mask.

"There cannot be an answer." That voice came even more
harshly. "The dead have long since returned their substance to
the earth. That which was the real part of them fled upon the
coming of the strokes which separated them from life—"

"Ho." Again the dwarf laughed. "Good teaching that. So
we can lie snug and not think of old ill acts and the payment
thereof. The earth hides much—but its doors lie open to us!"
He held his head back and as far above his bowed shoulders as
he might. "Bind the dead down with wand—even with
iron"—Farree noted the small start of the winged man at that
word—"and there comes a day when ties will break, for even
iron is eaten by rust. Do not think that you are rid of the
Hunters and the Shield men because they were planted with
the best of your spelling. Time may also wear that thin—"

He was interrupted by the woman. Her head had moved
down and now it seemed to Farree that she was looking
directly at him: her eyes widened with surprise and she held

out one hand towards him, her fingers crooked in what he guessed was a warning sign.

"There is one here!" Her words came as sharp as a knife thrust.

All the others stared in his direction now. The man had drawn the sword, the blade of which looked like a flame stiffened into a slightly curving length. Had Farree been able he would have fled. However, that which had brought him here did not release its hold on him.

"Who?" the man demanded of the woman. Beast Mask had moved up beside her, snout seeming to expand, as if its wearer could indeed pick up an alien scent.

"Atra—" The gross voice within the mask pronounced that word as if it were a loathsome oath.

The woman answered with a decided shake of her head. "Not her, no. They may have made her their tool, but she would carry then the stench of them with her. This one comes not in body—"

Beast Mask brought out of body wrappings a hand which was long and thin in contrast to the rest. This was turned palm upward. Farree caught a suggestion of glitter from a round disk which appeared fixed to the hollow frame of flesh and bone.

A finger of color, or colors, for it was rainbow hued, corkscrewed about, aiming in Farree's direction. The woman uttered a single word and that hand shook, while Beast Mask gave a short cry as from pain. The man was beside the woman with one stride, his wings fanning out so the tip of one came near to buffeting Beast Mask.

"Fool!"

"Fool, thrice fool yourself!" spat back the masked one. "How do we know what weapons the Hunters have made for themselves through the centuries of time? Can it not be that they have projected a defense to cover the incoming of a spy? What have we done? Gone behind our cloud walls, sealed ourselves in as a way of escape. I tell you that this will never rid us of these vermin who have trailed us on through space for more than five lifetimes of the Star!"

The upward gesture of that muffled head drew Farree's sight even though he felt as if he must be fastened there, easy food for the killing. The ceiling of this great hall was again silver—but it was a setting for something else. There depended a huge crystal on a single chain, as Farree had seen in miniature made into amulets favored by those who believed in the power of luck. This one was divided into three points—the two on the sides jutting out from the middle one as branches might grow from the trunk of a great tree.

Rainbows of light not unlike those imprisoned in Maelen's fingers played along its surface, and there were flashes from the pointed tips of the three branches. Inside Farree there was a sudden mighty surge of feeling. What had filled him on the hillocks of the valley—that sensation that he was a part of something he did not understand, that ignorantly he might lose that which none could control, was back a hundredfold.

"Atra!" He had certainly never spoken that. It was only a reaching thought which made him try to raise hands pleadingly to that triune of crystal.

"Here!" The woman's voice arose in what was close to a shout. "One of the blood here!" She ran forward before Farree could attempt to move and swung her hand as if she would seize him. He saw the flash of fingers close to his eyes but he felt nothing. So real had this all seemed that he could not believe for a moment that he was *NOT* there.

"Not Atra—" The man joined her again. He had reversed the sword which he held and was now prodding with the hilt, passing through the very space Farree seemed to occupy.

"No." The woman's hand had fallen by her side. "If it is not Atra—then who would be so spying? None else has been captured alive by the death dwellers.

"And none of those has the inner power to enable them to come here!" the woman added. "Who else or"—now her expression changed from one of astonishment and wonder to a smooth mask in which only her eyes seemed alive. Yellow those were like the ones which Farree faced when confronting a mirror—"has there perhaps been some greater folly—some attempt to bring forth Atra? Someone of the Icarkin may have gone against the oath. A second capture—"

"So oaths do not hold you flutterers—" one of the small men growled. "Are you then foresworn?"

"Aye," his mate echoed. "Is not Atra of the High Blood? Mighty close do you stick together, you flitterers! Did they not set the trap with her as bait as speedily as she fell into their hands? These 'men' are not fools and they are all sick with greed. If they have caught another such as Atra and set him or her to watching— Did not Sorwin here say that they may have new weapons to bring against us? You!" He swung his head toward Farree or towards where Farree would be if he *had* invaded this centermost defense in person. "By rock and rap, by thunderclap, by sword and stone, and voice alone—"

"By heart and eye," intoned his fellow, "earth and sky."

"Show you must!" Beast Mask's voice, more than half snarl, ended the chant.

It was as if he were one of the candles' flames on the crests of the hummocks back in the valley; Farree felt a pull from one side to another. He might be clasped in giant hands and so shaken back and forth—

Shaken back and forth. There was no more hall of silver and crystal—no more winged ones, no dwarfish workers of spells, no beast-headed monstrosity. Instead it was as dark as if a cloak had been flung over him. Then Farree opened his eyes.

He lay on his hammock in the ship and he was blinking into the eyes of Maelen, who was regarding him with concern. Behind her stood Vorlund, and the taller Zacanthan was in the doorway of the cabin. Under one of Farree's hands there was movement and he felt the well-known contour of Togger's spiky body. Dreaming—he must have been dreaming! Only the memory of all he had seen and heard remained as clear as the ceiling crystals of his vision.

"You have been—elsewhere." It was Maelen who spoke, and she did not ask a question, she stated a fact.

Farree licked dry lips. Part of him was still Farree the outcast of the Limits who had been given new life and hope, but another part was stirring into wakefulness, an awareness which was born in the familiar pain within his skull.

"Under the crystal—" That part of the memory suddenly seemed the most important. "They—they have fear—of us— No," he corrected himself, "of men." For the first time another thought came into his mind and with it a spurt of excitement. "Great One," he spoke directly to the Zacanthan, "are we—men?"

Zoror blinked. "Each of us has a name for our own kind, a measurement against which we rank others. 'Men— women'—to a fellow of my blood I am 'man.' To other Thassa"—now he nodded to Maelen—"she is 'woman.' To Thassa and perhaps Terran also, because he held once Terran identity to come by chance and fate within a Thassa body, Krip here is 'man' to those two species. Yes, to ourselves, our kind are 'man—woman.' What we may be to others—" He stroked his jaw with a taloned finger. "To those others we may be different. Extees is one word that is used. We have intelligence in common, and perhaps some extra natural gifts of mind or body—but we are not 'man—woman' in one meaning of the word with each other and his or her kin."

He was right, Farree knew. Here was a Zacanthan, two of the Thassa, and he who really did not know what he was. They were working for a common purpose but they were not a common species—'men—women' by some measurements— that used by those who pioneered in space.

"They fear, I think," he said slowly, "some like those of the Limits. But perhaps we can find an understanding—"

"With whom?" asked Maelen. "Little brother, where have you traveled this night?"

10.

Trying hard to make with words a picture of what he had seen, Farree outlined all which had happened in that dream that was not a dream; but he knew not what else to call it.

"Ah." Zoror was the first to break silence when he had finished. "Here then also are several different races. There are the winged ones, the small ones without those pinions, and this one who wears a beast head. Tell me again, little brother, the manner of the mask that one wore."

Once more Farree repeated his description of that figure. Maelen and Vorlund were looking at him intently as if they hoped in some way to enter his memory and view that scene for themselves. But Zoror was nodding as if some bit of unexpected knowledge had suddenly fallen into his hands.

"Swine—" He said when Farree was finished. "Another of the legends come into life for us. You speak of an animal which was known to the People we seek—one the keeping of such they reckoned part of material wealth. Perhaps this masked one was a—" Then he frowned. "But Zargo said in his twin worlds research that this was a matter of women's religion and that a priestess would play herder—though his authorities were few and very obscure."

Farree thought again of the masked figure. A woman—or anyway female? That one's voice had sounded harsh and low pitched. However, it was also certain that the masked one was not of the same blood as those whom he might call kin—it, or he or she, was wingless.

"We can take it," Vorlund said sharply when Zoror's words trailed into silence, "that there is another ship downed here somewhere. And that the crew or owner has captured one of the winged people and is using her as bait."

"Also," Farree broke in, "her people are not trying to rescue her— Ah—" Now it was his turn to lapse into silence. Then he added in a rush of words— "She—it must have been she who called!" Even as he said that he experienced some of the force of the compulsion which had carried him from their landing place off across the mountains until he was stopped by the haze.

The haze! Was that a barrier which the winged ones were using to cut off any of their people who would try to answer the captive's call? To him that instantly seemed possible.

Maelen read his thought. She reached for the far end of his hammock where his head had rested such a short time before. It was faintly alight with green and she clasped it tightly, her eyes once more on Farree's as if she willed him into some action. However, it was Vorlund who asked a question.

"You remember nothing else—nothing of these winged ones? Of how you went from here into the Limits?"

"If he came from here—" Zoror corrected. "There may be more than one world where such dwell. If it is true that they must have a world like to that which those of the old Terran blood required for settlement— Well, are there not numerous planets with such attributes, and not all of them settled, or, if so, only thinly. Our records report that these People have shared many different abiding places with those whom we well know. But there always came a time when the People of the Hills were forced to withdraw, to take flight again for the search for a place of their own, for they never lived in peace long with the human kind. Another planet may be such a home also—"

Farree rubbed one palm across his forehead. The ache was beginning again, becoming a dull torment behind his eyes.

"Guesses." Vorlund shrugged. "That Farree has found those like him may be the only answer. If we could only get behind that mind block which weighs upon you so, little brother!"

Maelen had leaned forward a little and now her fingertips touched Farree's forehead directly between his large eyes. That contact was almost as if he had taken a drink of water when he had been long parched with thirst. He saw that her eyes were closed and now her thought came into him.

"Loose—loose your thoughts, little brother. Do not try to raise any barrier—"

He struggled to do as she asked; the need of his own to find answers made him eager.

Farree whirled around and stumbled back until he half fell over the hammock he had just climbed out of. About him streamed colors and those colors were pain which he could not subdue. He clung to the hammock, feeling as if that flood of color strove to carry him away. Then it winked out and he was once more in the dark, shivering and weak.

"It is a lock which I do not understand." He heard Maelen's voice but it sounded very far off.

"My lady, it is a death lock!" That was surely Zoror. "You must not try that again. Such a lock is unknown to us—even to our records—"

"But perhaps not unknown to the Guild," Vorlund cut in

crisply. "Is it not well understood that they have secrets in advance of much of ours? Perhaps they held and lost him, and then only found him again when we battled on Yiktor and he came into his power of flight?"

"Possibly—" Zoror was saying, but Farree had his eyes open though there were tears wet on his cheeks. The ache behind his eyes seemed likely to blind him.

"Little brother—" Maelen touched his cheek, then smoothed his tumbled, sweat-slick hair. "There will be no more, this I promise you."

He was still shaky and weak when he joined the others on the bridge of the ship from which by the landing screens they could view the world about them as they ate ship's rations and watched the sweep of the outer mirrors. The ship itself was locked against any invasion and as an added precaution Maelen had alerted Bojor and Yazz, saying that their minds, being different from those who were seeking knowledge, might stand sentry into the bargain.

Those candles of light had disappeared from the mounds attendant on the large one, but every time the mirrors' report flashed on the last they could all see that there was still a pulsing circlet about it—no longer in the form of that wondrous crown, yet visible as a pale ring.

The ramp had been run out again for a short time, long enough for Bojor to shamble down, his thick-furred pelt, having been grown for the season of chill on Yiktor, making him look twice the size that he really was. But the bartles were never to go unmarked by anyone invading their native mountains. Although Bojor had been captured as a yearling, he still retained inherent in him the strength and cunning of a nasty fighter were he to be aroused. As all those Maelen called her "little ones" (which was a misnomer in the case of Bojor, for his breed was notorious for their handling of any would-be trapper and also stood taller than Vorlund when he rose to his full fighting stance on his sturdy hind legs), the mighty beast was able to thought meld with the Moonsinger to an astonishing degree, and had welcomed the chance to be a part of the active forces from the ship.

He melted into the dark as they tried to follow him with the ship's sighting equipment. However, he had been given directions to stay away from the hillocks and to head directly for the cliffs, prowling along the foot of those. Suddenly, as they sought to watch him, there appeared to burst from the ground itself a number of light dots. As if those, too, were under orders, they clustered, outlining the body of Bojor. He squatted back on his haunches, one of his huge paws, meant to deliver crushing blows, waving through the air. Yet he was unable to beat them off. They flashed so quickly that it was apparent he could make no contact with them. As length he went again to four feet and moved on, still revealed by the light dots so that now he could be easily watched by those within the ship as well as by anyone who might have summoned that form of illumination to keep spy sight on the ship and those within it.

Twice Maelen communicated with Bojor, only to report that the bartle had not been attacked, that the sparks of strange fire only hung about him. Yazz, who had come up into the cabin to watch the mission of her furred companion, whined deep in her throat, her attention all for the screen. She raised a forepaw suddenly as if she could scrape the surface of the view plate and so release Bojor from his strange escort. Even Farree, who had only limited rapport with her compared to Maelen's ability, felt her uneasiness, a kind of foreboding. Though the bevy of lights had made no really hostile move, it was plain that Yazz did not trust them.

The bartle's speed was deceptive. Though he appeared to amble along at hardly more than a strolling pace, he had almost finished a quarter of the wall's length. He had passed well beyond the carpet growth of ill-bane and was into the withered land overlaid with the pattern of the hagger web.

Yazz once more whined. Farree dropped a piece of leather-tough dried fruit on which he had been chewing.

"Back!" he cried out. The advancing lights gave only a partial sight of Bojor, not clear to ground level. Farree had felt through his body, as clearly as if he stood out there beside the bartle, that beginning of a stir; not what had moved earlier beneath the hillock but something of the here and now. It was like an evil stench projected to his mind instead of assaulting his nostrils.

Yazz threw back her head and gave voice to a growling which was her own battle cry. She turned swiftly and pawed at the door of the control cabin, at the same time looking over her shoulder to Maelen, her whole attitude expressing her need to be loosed to join Bojor. In the days they had spent together these two, so different in species and early training, had thought themselves into a team, a team which had drawn Farree, too, into its being.

Farree had pushed past Vorlund and was busy with the door latch, Yazz crowding in beside him, ready to leap when that portal opened.

It must have been their united fear which reached Bojor. For the bartle had halted and was standing now, back to the cliffs, facing outward to where that webbing lay across bare earth. Maelen accepted the warning of them both. With no questions asked she pointed directly to the screen where Bojor was to be seen.

The light sparks shifted as the bartle settled back, again on his haunches, a favorite stance to await attack. His paws hung down before his barrel of body and, though Farree could not see them clearly in the minute flashes of light, he knew that the bartle was extending to their fullest length those broad punishing claws which could tear apart any attacker who got too close.

"What—" Vorlund moved, planting one booted foot over the fastening of the trap door in a stride so swift that Farree had only an instant to get his fingers out of the way. "What are you doing?"

"The hagger— Underground!" Farree returned impatiently. "They can attack, never coming into sight, from below! Lady, call him back!"

Maelen's fingers blazed, building up, as Farree knew, power for her mind sending. But if she reached Bojor, the bartle gave no sign of having received any such orders. His mouth was a little open and they could see his head more clearly, for the sparks were now clustering tighter there about. Though those within the ship could not pick up the sound, Farree knew that the bartle was roaring a challenge. He grasped a fleeting mind picture of a dark tunnel in the earth and things moving along it. Had he or had he not also glimpsed for just a second just such a figure as those small men he had seen in his "dream"?

He thrust his shoulder against Vorlund's leg, the suddenness of his move pushing the spacer off the door even as he struck a fast blow with the side of his hand against the latch. With his other hand he jerked up the plate which formed that barrier and Yazz, snuffling and whimpering beside him, leaped down, not touching the steps of the ladder.

Farree swung, folding his wings as tightly as he could. But it was always difficult to struggle through such passages with what he bore on his back.

Vorlund was following, but he could move no faster than Farree lest he push before him, perhaps disastrously, the smaller, hunched body. He asked no more questions and Farree would have had few answers for him if he had. There was only one thing true—that Bojor was about to face such an attack as none of his kind had ever known and against which all his strength and native knowledge would provide no defense.

They were in the lower corridor now and Yazz was on her hind feet against the wall, pawing at the controls of the ramp.

Farree reached up also and snatched from the rack mounted there a stunner kept for just such emergencies when trouble awaited outside.

He brought the butt of that against the ramp controls just as Vorlund caught him by folded wing edge. Farree glared at the spacer.

"Out!" he said between gritted teeth. "Bojor will be taken else."

The ramp had answered; the hum of its expansion vibrated through the ship and the scent of ill-bane was wafted in to them by a brisk breeze. Yazz had already taken the lead and was riding the ramp out and down, her formidable rows of teeth locked around one of the railings to steady her as she was swung by the motion of her footing.

Vorlund loosed his hold on Farree. "What and from where?" he snapped.

"Hagger and from underground! Their webs already lie out there. But those are old. Now they are being led!"

Farree leaped ahead, free of the ship port. His wings expanded and he was airborne in the night, wheeling about to face that part of the cliff where Bojor waited at bay.

The spots of light were larger and brighter here, making a beacon easy to see. Farree shook his head a fraction; having left the interior of the ship, he could feel better and stronger that warning of the coming of the attackers. Beating his wings against a strong flow of air he headed toward the splotch of light. A moment later and he himself gathered up attendants. For the same sparks of fire which had hailed Bojor sprang to life around about him, outlining his body, gathering in a tight cluster over his head.

At the same time his wings faltered in their beat. He was nearly sent earthward as their power failed for the pace of a heartbeat of two, while in his mind the old ache steadied into an ever-growing pain. He forced himself on but it was as if he were trying to beat his way through some viscous invisible flood in which his wings were being tangled and slowed until he was brought down so low he was skimming across the ground, the toes of his space boots caught now and again by some higher tangle of growth.

Yet he refused to answer a compulsion and go a-foot, for there grew in him the strong feeling that as long as he continued to fight so he was free of another entanglement, this one ready to grip his mind. He was able to pick up Bojor's rage now. Not since the bartle had helped to retake their ship, captured by the Guild fighters on Yiktor, rescuing Maelen and Vorlund from imprisonment, had Farree known such anger to fill the brain of the huge furred one. However, threaded through that anger was puzzlement, for Bojor as yet faced no visible foe, only sensed, as did Farree himself, the threat growing ever stronger.

Those sparks of light which clustered over his head and followed the likeness of his suddenly too-heavy wings were glowing brighter. Pressing against him was the power which attempted to bring him to earth, perhaps to render him useless in any confrontation to come.

As Farree fought on, throwing all his strength into the struggle with the pressure, he was suddenly shocked by such a spear of thought as he had not felt even from Maelen, the acknowledged leader in their own communication.

"Come—die! Traitor, losstreek, demni—"

Loud and firm as that rang in his mind, he could not pick up, save as a wavering and faceless shadow, who thought that. But that opponent had erred for, by the very storm he so loosed, he gave Farree himself a goal for a counterattack.

At the very edge of that part of the valley floor which was crisscrossed by the web lines, Farree settled, though he kept his wings spread, and kept so little of his weight on the ground that he hardly crushed the last straggle of ill-bane.

Instead of concentrating on keeping aloft, he now bent all of his strength on a mind thrust—dragging out of the depths of himself anger engrossed by fear—a fear he projected on that other. Because he had no other clue and very much needed a target, he pictured his opponent firmly—one such small man as he had seen in the hall of the crystal—giving that vision all the details he could summon.

Above and around him the points of light blazed—no longer white, but green as if the ill-bane itself had become a fire and he had wound the flames about him as he might a cloak. The green motes swirled now, all gathering above his head and moving so fast that they appeared to form a ring. But Farree was more aware that his mind touch had vanquished a shield. It was not a shield like any he had met before—either the science-produced ones the Guildsmen had worn on Yiktor, or those he had encountered with Maelen, Vorlund and the Zacanthan when they had tested him in hope of finding some answer to the barrier which he found so crippling.

Having damaged it, Farree now threw strength against it. At his second raging attempt the barrier went completely down. He was caught up in a chaos of thoughts but the greatest and clearest was intelligible enough. The one who broadcast was afraid, yes, but under the spur of that fear was determination to act. It was true that the broadcast came from underground and the general direction showed that he who was coming into attack was heading toward Bojor. Only the mind Farree was now reading in part did not see the attacker to be physically engaged in any battle.

There ran before this other mind and under his control, others, perhaps for their size the most dangerous entities Farree had ever known—and since he only had a half knowledge of them sifted through another mind it could well be that they were even more dangerous than he believed. Hagger!

The picture was clear in his mind, sharply clear so that he saw in only an instant or two of holding it a horror which made him shiver. Oddly enough in shape it was not unlike Togger, save the pulpy, fattish body was covered with mud-streaked hair. Like the smux, the foremost pair of feet were equipped with great claws, the inner side of which were saw-toothed, a visible threat to any likely to be caught by those. The heads were round, bearing to the fore flexible antennae on the tips of which were balls which he knew, from the thoughts of the enemy who had herded them ahead, served as eyes and had an astounding range of sight in the dark of the tunnel through which they traveled at a speed which was seemingly foreign to the fact that they crawled on three pair of legs, the armed ones held aloft as if ready for battle at any moment.

Farree quested ahead, seeing in a strange way through the eyes of the herder. The underground traveler was aware of him now, but unable to push him out and away, though his increasingly frantic attempts made him strive to read Farree as Farree had already reached him.

Farree struck. The command which he thrust deep into that other mind was already aimed at the grotesque army scuttling under the surface of the ground. But with the necessity of keeping hold on the herder, and, through him, trying to reach the other creatures, Farree had to sacrifice sight of the burrowers. Whether his push reached them, or whether they surrendered to his unvoiced command he could not tell. Something hit the ground before him with a thud. For an instant that broke his concentration. Togger had lurched out of Farree's jerkin to leap to the ground between two of the crossing web lines. The smux flung himself, with a powerful thrust of his strong hind feet, at the nearest of those lines. His foreclaws whipped out, cutting into the earth, and when he brought them together with an audible click there was a crinkling in the dry soil as if, freed from a very taut hold, the web lines had snapped away from that break, carrying part of the earth with them.

"Bad—" Farree caught that but he did not catch the smux whom he tried to snatch up again. Togger was running over the webbed earth in the general direction of that glow which marked Bojor's choice of battleground. Time and again the smux stopped for only an instant or two to snap the lines just under the surface of the soil, though for what purpose Farree could not understand.

However, that thickening of the air, or what had seemed that, which had kept him from speedy flight, was gone. He soared up and out across the web Togger was so effectively destroying, heading toward Bojor at the foot of the cliff.

Over his head the circle of lights had broken apart and now fell behind him like a headscarf blown by the wind. Twice he bent all the strength he could muster into trying once again to take command of the underground party, only now he encountered the blankness of a new shield, one strong enough to stand firm against his probing. Thus he concentrated on reaching the cliff, the ship stunner in his hand.

"Bad—come—" Not Togger this time. He had already flown past the smux, could no longer see him. That was Bojor. And if the bartle had assessed the enemy enough to add come, then indeed the attack would be a formidable one.

Farree reached the edge of the webbed country. Bojor squatted almost directly before him, the crest of longer and stiffer hair between his ears standing up. The light which had marked Bojor when they had watched him from the ship was now plastered against the cliff side some distance away from the stout body. Bojor's eyes were red and opened to their farthest extent. He looked up to Farree but did not hold that glance very long; his attention dropped quickly to the ground immediately before him. Farree winged a fraction closer and lit, not folding his wings, but feeling the security of the ground beneath his feet. He had the stunner in a tight grip and now dared once more to mind search.

Almost he leaped into the air as he met a surge of what was not thought as he knew such, but rather a great hunger, a need which came from many minds. He tried to separate one of those threads from another, to trace it back to the mind which gave it birth, but they were so entangled there was no hope of that; and they were very close.

"Togger—come—now—" There was that sending and he saw in the dim light sent off by the motes a blotch of shadow which sped in closer to one of the bartle's legs. Once there, crowded in against the bartle, the smux turned around, claws up and ready in something of the same stance that Bojor had taken in defense. Outdistancing the smux was Yazz; she was not running, but weaving a pattern with short jumps from one clear patch of ground to another. It was manifest Yazz sensed some danger which was inherent there.

11.

T heir only source of light were the motes hovering in the air, a patch over the head of each. When Farree, in one wing-aided bound, joined the other three by the wall of the cliff, only to whirl around and stand ready, waiting for the charge he was sure was coming, his attention was all for the ground. There was a swirl of light which whipped about him as the lash of a whip might have cut at his body. He gasped and choked. The lights were lower, circling about him at throat level, drawing in closer.

He flung up an arm to beat them off and small pains stung his skin as if they were in truth sparks from a fire. Nor could he so win free of them. The circle was at chest level now. Unconsciously he had furled his wings as the fire sparks flicked along their surfaces.

His left arm was pinned to his body by the sparks, but the right one still held the stunner. There was no way he could spray those strange attackers. Nor had he any belief that they were even insects ready to sting him into submission, for his mind did not pick up the slightest hint of life as he knew it in those minute flashes.

Farree tried to expand his wings again, to perhaps rise above the attackers. At that moment, as his struggles grew stronger, the ground itself burst outward, spraying earth and stones into the air as there boiled out of a crumbling hole the first of those things he had mind seen in the tunnel. He had already set the stunner to full strength and part of its beam, though his arm was unable to hold steady as he was being jerked back and forth, chopped across the first two of the ground runners. Yazz showed her teeth and made a rush at the third to climb out of the runway below.

Above her head the sparks which had accompanied her formed a ball aimed at her. However, like all of her species, her movements in attack were delivered so swiftly that her body became slightly blurred to the sight. Though the ball swooped, Yazz was gone, only her hind legs and thrashing tail visible, the whole forepart of her body now within the hole.

Farree kicked and twisted his body. At last there was an instant when he could bring the stunner to bear on part of the star ring about him. There was a winking and he felt a relaxation of the pressure which had been squeezing him. Bojor roared, that vast surge of sound echoed from the cliffs about. Farree stumbled back, one of his furled wings striking against the bartle's bulk. A vast paw fell heavy on his shoulder drawing him farther on toward the cliff. The lights, which had surrounded the bartle and brought him to bay here, divided into two clusters, one of which struck at each paw.

Yazz drew back from the entrance to the burrow. Her jaws were fast set upon a thick round body, just behind the head of the creature. It was beating its forefeet against the ground in a vain effort to win free.

Its efforts merely broke loose clods which the claws showered through the hole from which it had been so unceremoniously ripped. Yazz gave a quick snap and threw her captive to the other side of the hole. It landed on its back, kicked feebly, then was still, while its killer was already heading back into the hole after more prey.

As Farree was swept against the cliff, those sparks of light which had snared him before formed a new ball, drawing back several paces. He gasped air into lungs which had been compressed, took aim at that ball.

He never fired. Instead he gave a cry as the balled lights sped at his head. A solid mass, it struck an instant later with a force which snapped his head back. The sparks wheeled endlessly before his eyes. Then, on the tail of that strike there followed pain so intense he could neither hear, nor see, nor understand anything, save that the world was a place of torture. The brilliant, eye-searing white which had followed on the stroke of the sparks darkened and then even the pain, at last, also was gone.

As he had been in his dream he was somewhere else, not in his body, though he searched frantically for awareness of flesh and bone and could not find it. Yet he was able to sense that he was not alone. Bojor—Yazz—he tried to hail them—

Nothing of the warm sense of friendship, which should follow on his thinking those names, came to him. He tried to advance the mind search. As it had been when he met the haze he could not pierce the unseen envelope which appeared to hold him.

No, he could not reach out—but he could be aware— aware that he was not alone in this nothingness. Farree drew back into himself with a rush. For a moment he wanted to cower in hiding as he had in the Limits when some drunken and sadistic inhabitant of that hell was seeking him to afford amusement, for that which was without him projected a feeling of strength and ruthless purpose. Only he was no longer Dung, the outcast of the Limits; he was Farree, winged and—free? No, not free; he was caught in a trap, held to await the pleasure of those who had set it.

"—Langrone? But none of the guards survived!"

Thoughts, not voices. Only he could not send any reply. He was mind-dumb but not deaf.

"They were found—" Farree was granted an instant or two of a picture of a green hillside and on it lay forms sprawled. The nearest lay face down and dribbling down a bare back, from twin pools of raw flesh, was blood. Wing! The wings had been cut from the dead!

"—dead—" He had been so intent upon that picture which one mind broadcast that he had missed part of the sentence.

"Langrone," repeated the first mind voice emphatically. "Doubtless poisoned like Atra—bait!" There was contempt in that. Through the darkness there came a thrust of pain but it seemed far away—accompanying the body which he could no longer feel for himself.

"Blind!" The mind voice was very sharp, cutting into him as a knife could have cut his flesh—it was undoubtedly an order delivered to him. "Prisoner with no hope!" a second contemptuously delivered.

If he had for some reason accepted the fate the first comment had laid upon him there was still resistance in him against the second. Prisoner he might be—somehow dead-alive—but that core of him which had awakened with his wings, had been nurtured by Maelen and Vorlund, remained strong enough to refuse to surrender.

"—Selrena." Again he had missed part of the thought speech.

"We cannot carry— Ha—what is that thing?"

"What? Where?"

"It moved over there!"

There came a time of quiet and then the first of his captors spoke again: "It is one with the beasts that these death givers have brought to serve them. A rock finished it off. Now—we cannot carry him. Let Selrena lift him if she wishes. Or let him lie; he will be true dead soon enough. The winged people do not take well to the dark ways. If he is Langrone he is really of no matter to us."

"Say you that to Vaspret's face?"

"Langrone!" The other repeated the word as if he were spitting it out in a gob. "Air Dancers! What does it matter that they are being hunted?"

"Remember that which the death dealer from the other ship found? Do you think that they will let go of any of this world now that they have laid hands on that? Roxcit's lying place they are going to search for. With what they have in their ways of strange knowledge they are going to find the second cache soon. That they hunt the winged people—yes, there is no real harm for us in that. But that they break the guard we are set to—"

"Well enough, well enough! Remember, if this Langrone is one with Atra he has been blinded by those others. He will be able to draw them—"

"Not so. For them perhaps he shall be bait now." There was satisfaction in that.

The darkness in which Farree was closed drew tighter about him as if to force the air from his lungs, even as the lights had earlier done. He was aware of that frightening increase of pressure even if he was no longer aware of his body. Then—there was nothing.

Farree opened his eyes. There were no longer folds of black choking him—rather what he saw was grey—like the light of very early morning or the haze which had turned him back from his first scouting on this world. He rested on his side but a small attempt at movement told him that he was still the prisoner the mind voice had claimed him to be.

However, the haze of grey seemed to sway sluggishly in an odd way which made him feel ill. He was entirely aware of his body again but the ills of that were of less importance than what the swaying of haze revealed or obscured.

There was a chair which towered above him as he lay not too far away from it on a floor covered with a pavement of alternate green and brown blocks of stone, the brown blocks veined with threads of green. The chair was white and the legs, arms, and the frame of the back were heavily and intricately carved, the arms ending in balls as clear as if they had been solidified from fresh stream water. The chair had a padded back and seat of heavily patterned stuff, green leaves, flowers of every shade and here and there a band of what appeared to be such runes as Zoror had once shown him, saying that it was believed that the People he sought once preserved knowledge by such markings.

Before the chair was a footstool and on this sat a small creature which he could not immediately determine as a sentient being or a lower animal.

The small body was covered with spotted scales, golden in shade, but its contours were humanoid. A head which was round in the back and narrowed to a point in front crowned a long and sinuous neck. It had four limbs, stick thin, the upper pair of which ended in webbed six-fingered paws; the back ones ended in broad pads. Between the forepaws it rolled back and forth a tube of white which was patterned by a series of holes. Putting one end of that to the sharp snout mouth and fingering along the length, it now produced a series of notes which sounded like trickling water. The eyes were very large and were glowing like green flames, if such could exist.

Those eyes were regarding Farree and he knew that the creature was perfectly aware of him. Cautiously he tried mind touch—but was astounded to find that he had apparently been deprived of that sense—it was like the haze he had faced before. He met a wall.

The tinkling notes of the pipe grew louder and the room haze was thinning, disappearing. He could see more of the room now—the sturdy legs and lower surface of a long table, the color of walls where ran the runic patterns of the chair cushions; but these were clear, unhidden by any other designs.

Farree licked dry lips, preparing to use his voice as he was unable to mind touch. But he never got a chance to see if the creature with the flute would be able to understand vocal communication. There was movement beyond the table and he then saw fully the figure who came around the end of it.

To his first glance the newcomer looked like many of the spacers he had seen—tall, humanoid—perhaps taller even than Zoror. He wore tight covering on his legs and feet as if foot gear and clothing were one—above that a laced jerkin clasped in to a narrow waist with a broad belt which glimmered and flashed with a silvery radiance. His head was covered with hair which was mingled red and gold. The skin of his face and his uncovered hands was pale—there was no space tan to darken it.

There was something set and remote in his expression. Heavy-lidded eyes were half shut in a face which was as perfect as if it had been carefully carven out of a substance as white as the chair he now sought and settled in. Remote that expression might be, but he was regarding Farree closely, and there was that about him which suggested that he was in complete command here.

"So—" Though Farree had not been able to pierce the interference resisting his own thought, the barrier did not exist for this stranger. "Who may you be?" The feeling that question suggested was a cold curiosity. Again Farree strove to answer but for him the barrier held.

On the footstool the flute player leaned forward. It no longer played that instrument, but flopped down to its pad feet and advanced a step or so. As if it controlled Farree's body it leaned forward and tapped the captive's lips with the tip of its flute, clearly an invitation or perhaps an order to use vocal speech. Having done so it padded back to the footstool and once more resumed its seat.

The man in the chair had watched that action and now he nodded. "So—" He once more turned his gaze on Farree. "Who?" He made of that single word a sharp order.

"Farree—" To his own ears that hoarse sound was extremely loud as if he might be shouting—there was even a murmur of echo to follow.

"There is no mistake that you are that." The questioner's speech sped smoothly into his mind. "What name have you or *had* you in Langrone ranks? Or have they taken that away from you, cripple, along with all the rest?"

"I am called Farree." He did not understand what the other meant.

There was a faint frown on the man's face. Then Farree shook as a spear of mind send invaded him. He was no longer aware of the room, the man, the flutist—only of the same torture which engulfed him when Maelen and the rest had attempted to break the barrier which existed between him and much of his own past. He could not defend himself against the power this other projected, but neither could that one penetrate the shield which someone or something had used upon his captive. The pain became darkness and he was only aware of weak relief that the force was gone.

Breathing fast as might one who had nearly gone beyond the ability to breathe at all, Farree was again aware of the room and those two watching him. That frown had grown the darker on the face of his interrogator and the creature on the footstool had drawn arms and legs back against its body, shivering, as if it also had been the target of sudden assault.

"How did you escape?" The send did not ravage him now, rather it was softer. In the great chair the man was leaning forward, his hands on his knees, his eyes no longer lazy.

"They freed me—" Farree tried to summon up pictures

of Maelen and Vorlund as he had seen them first, when they had rescued Togger, and incidentally himself, from the filth of the Limits.

"No—" The man straightened in his chair to eye Farree with open surprise. He pointed a finger at Farree as if flesh and bone were a weapon. "No, you cannot be made to hold a lie such as that! Then there are two parties here!" He was out of the chair in one movement, walking at a swift pace away from Farree, out of the captive's range of sight.

Farree began to test whatever it was which held him so tightly prisoner. He looked along his own body and could see no sign of any bonds. The light particles which had entrapped him were gone, but still he could not move.

Move, repeated his aching mind, still weak from the force which had been used to try to pluck his past from him. What had Zoror said about glamorie—that it was a weapon, or a trick, which could be used to entice or deceive those who did not understand it? It was true that he could not transmit to another, but did that barrier also keep him from working on himself? There was certainly no reason not to try.

The flutist on the footstool was playing again. Farree moved his head slowly, trying to shut that music out by concentration, for it seemed to him that the tune filled that very part of his mind that he must use, lulling what was left of its power into uselessness.

His hands—in his mind he pictured his two hands as he had seen them last—not stiff and straight against his body but free to move in any direction he willed for them. Fingers—curving so! Yes, he could picture that in spite of the drone of the flute.

Move slow— He had a sudden small rise of triumph. One finger had indeed arched away from tight contact with the rest. Farree fought the euphoria of that triumph and held tightly to his mental picture. He felt the trickle of moisture, summoned by his effort, across his skin. Two fingers now—a hand! He shifted his hand and felt it move against his side.

Two hands— A snatch of thought—had the flutist noted this? Was he a guard sent to do sentry duty and summon help if it was needed?

While patches of sweat plastered his clothes to him Farree fought on. The flutist had made no move. But that did not mean that he would allow Farree to win this battle. Feet— Farree rolled over on his stomach and used his hands to lever himself up. He looked over his shoulder as he managed to rise to his knees.

The sentry no longer played, merely slipped the flute back and forth through its webbed hands, its head cocked a little to one side as it watched Farree's floundering fight to get to his feet. He expected any moment to see the man rushing in to put him once more under restraint—still that had not occurred.

He was up at last, though his wings were still folded into the narrowest possible bulk. The flutist continued to watch. Farree moved quickly, putting the table between him and the other. From the size of the table as well as that of the now empty chair Farree believed that the room was intended for the use of the large man's own race or species, since all was clearly too big to be easily accepted by one of his own stature.

The top of the table was crowded with a variety of objects, including a mirror. He hooked his fingers over its edge to study himself in the surface. Near him there were flasks, some of them transparent, so that one could see either liquid or powders inside. These were as rainbow-hued as the flashes from crystals, which were present also. Two had been carven into balls and were positioned on stands—one of them white and carven intricately, the other dark and plain; the ball resting on the latter was also murky in shade. Other crystals remained in their natural forms, holding jagged surfaces aloft. There was also a roll of greyish leather (which resembled those records Zoror consulted from time to time). This had been flattened out and was kept so by smaller chunks of crystal of a greenish shade. A little farther away was a second sheet of the stuff, and a pot of dark color with a pen made of a stiff feather lying beside it.

A brazier occupied the middle of the board. From its pierced lid there curled a faint coil of smoke, bearing with it the scent of spice. Plainly this was a work place for someone whose interests lay along the same path as those of the Zacanthan. Thinking of Zoror now brought Farree back to the matter at hand.

He tried to expand his wings, centering in his mind his vivid memories of free flight. However, though he might have freed his body, he was not successful with his wings. They remained cramped, as tightly furled as bones and flesh would allow.

Still holding onto the table Farree surveyed the room carefully. The haze which he remembered had now vanished, although all the corners of the chamber were dark and shadowy. Walls were cloaked with stiff panels which bore both dim pictures and lines of runes. There was another chair and a smaller table by the far wall, and, beyond the large table, a piece of furniture which he also had seen in Zoror's rooms: This was a tall standing rack, each shelf divided into a number of small cubbies, many holding rolls which matched that one outspread upon the table. Zoror had very ancient rolls fashioned from the skins of beasts (from many worlds and scores of years) which he stored so. Farree had seen some of them—those the Zacanthan had consulted in his search for the People.

To his left there was one wall bare of any drapery and broken by a large window, now curtained, though that curtain stirred as if wind plucked at it. Here was a bench fitted into place. Farree drew away from the table, testing his ability to walk alone. He staggered, grasped again at the table, and then, taking steps with care, he made for that promise of an opening beyond. If there was a door to the room it was hidden somewhere behind those lengths of stiff folds.

He reached the bench, ever listening for any cry of alarm from the flutist. However, when he edged partly around to see, the creature had not stirred, though it was watching him. The sill of the window was high, again not suited to one of Farree's small stature. He pulled himself up on the bench and then got to his feet, one hand to the wall to steady himself while with the other he tugged at the curtain, dragging it a little aside.

There was darkness beyond, the gloom of night, perhaps even a storm-summoning one. In spite of the fact he could not see much or clearly, Farree believed that this room was well above the ground and that there was no way out. For upon the moving of the curtains he sighted a barrier which was a web of silvery metal patterned in the form of entwined vines, the leaves of which glimmered as if drawing some light from beyond.

He shook the web, or tried to, but none of the metal shifted, being too well rooted in the stone about it. Then he flinched back, nearly falling from his perch. For driving straight at the window was one of the flying lizards such as had escorted him back to the valley where his ship had finned in. It uttered a grating cry and swerved just as it appeared that it was going to hurl itself against the bars of the vine. At its full-lunged screech Farree hurriedly loosed his hold on the curtain and dropped back to the bench.

The fluttering notes of the flute sounded. But the creature had left its perch upon the footstool and was moving in a queer way which was not a walk but a skittering kind of dance.

It was not coming towards him but rather was headed toward the wall behind the chair. And before it quite reached that goal it shimmered, its outlines becoming unclear. Then it was gone. Farree rubbed his hand across his eyes and drew a deep breath.

Of course this might all be a dream, as his other venture among these people had been. Perhaps they had indeed taken over his mind and he saw only what they desired to show him. Had he fought that battle which had freed him from what he believed was a trance—or had they only allowed him to do so in order to test him in some way? Was he waking or asleep?

He hunkered down on the bench, leaning well forward to accommodate his furled wings. Could one dream such reality? He clipped a good pinch of skin on one wrist between his fingers and applied full pressure. Pain—

Still Farree huddled where he was and fear such as he had never known, even in the worst days in the Limits, stirred within him. Who was he? Was he here at all or had some other mind taken over, putting all this into his mind? Perhaps he was even back at the ship bodily—and here in another form, no matter how real this seemed!

Sliding down from the bench he once more approached that crowded table. Deliberately he leaned forward and cupped his hands about the clouded globe, which was nearest. He had to draw closer to the edge in order to hold it.

There was an answer to his touch. Within the globe there burst a fiery circle. Then the flames died. He was looking straight at Zoror, but companied with the Zacanthan was the Lady Maelen. Her eyes widened and Zoror blinked. Farree was sure that even as he viewed them they could also see him. Then the Zacanthan edged aside, and only Maelen stood there. She raised a hand and from each fingertip there flashed a light which darted straight toward Farree. The globe trembled in his hold and such a heat seared him that he had to jerk back. But the flames continued to coil about in the crystal globe, slipping along the inner surface as if that fire fought for a way to reach him.

12.

There was a burst of the flame within the globe, and all sight of Maelen was seared away. From somewhere sounded a piercing note, sharp and jarring, bearing no resemblance to the tinkling music of the flute; this was an alarm. The globe moved in Farree's hold, seeming almost to twist itself into freedom. It forced itself between his fingers and fell, not to the top of the table but to the floor beneath.

A thunderous sound followed. The ball had splintered at impact, shards flying. The light it had held vanished and the pieces on the floor turned a dull black as if a real fire had burned within it. Only for a moment or two they lay so, then crumbled, becoming a pile of dust. There puffed from those last remains a strong odor of burnt meat. Then that, too, was gone. Farree stood, his smarting hands to his mouth as he blew upon them, trying to abate the pain, though there was no sign of any burns on his flesh.

Suddenly there was more light, this time snapping into

life in the clear crystal which had accompanied the murky one. This pulsed irregularly as once more sounded that piercing note. Farree dared not try to take the other one into his hands, but he leaned forward, staring into its flutter of light, striving with all his might somehow to summon again Maelen or the Zacanthan—to no avail.

However, the light began to take on form. He was again looking into eyes, but, though they were in a woman's face, they were not Maelen's. There was no age to her; she might have been young or old, for her skin was as fair as it was unmarked. What he could see of her hair was part of a dull brown braid which formed a crown above her wide brow. Her eyes were dark, so dark Farree could not have named their true color, while her lips were a brown-red, thin and tight at the corners. There was no brightness of welcome in her, only something of a faint expression which spoke of cold curiosity. Inwardly, Farree shivered. Even if he could not read her thoughts, there was a strangeness there. She was so alien he could not even think of a meeting mind to mind.

Still that was what followed, shaking him as if each word was a blow aimed at rocking him. Once more he saw only through a haze which clouded sight, and even cloaked his mind.

"You are not Langrone—" It was not a question but a statement. "Throstle?" That was a question but he had no time to answer it if indeed he could. Instead he felt as if he had been gathered up bodily and hurled through time and space in an instant.

Again he crouched in all his filth and rags against the wall in an alley of the Limits, suffering the hurt of Togger as the smux was disciplined by the master of that unsavory show of pitiful wild things beaten into submission. Once more Maelen and Vorlund came to him. Memory spun on—he was reliving in a series of flashes his life with those to whom compassion of the heart was abiding. He was in Yiktor seeking out some needful thing. There was Maelen about to fall from the mountain trail. His hand went forth once more, just as it had on that real moment in the past. He felt the split of that thick growth on his shoulders which had pressed him forward through all the time he could remember as one who went hump backed. He had a flashing moment of wonder once again, as that tightened, itching skin broke, releasing the wings he had never known he carried.

Once more he crouched in the stinking alley and now he was shot backwards from his meeting with the space people into the days before. He endured blows, starvation, all the evils one who was small and handicapped might know in the Limits. Now he arrived with a rush at the earliest memory of all—of looking out from his hiding place in Lanti's tent to watch the renegade spacer killed, which freed him from the first of his bonds.

Perhaps he screamed then—if so he did not hear his own cries. It was as if a great force was pushing him back against a wall which would not give, that he was about to be crushed, flattened against that hard surface. The force which inexorably thrust him so hard was crushing— He screamed again as pain burst in his head. Then, mercifully, he was in the dark—he was nothing within nothing and there was nothing—

"—Throstle?" Far away that sounded. "Selrena—"

"Tricks again. Do you doubt he should be dragon meat? Where is the globe of storms?"

Memory stirred, willing him back once again. There was an urgency to the attack upon him.

"He is empty—gone. It is of these others we must think now. In him there is no thought of harm—"

"You grow simple, Vestrum. Thoughts can be erased; they might also be inspired to confuse. We have learned much; through the same generations they have also. He is of the blood, yes. That could not be faked. But of what clan— Langrone? We can account for all of that kin."

"Atra has been brought to serve them. Why could this one not be shaped anew as she was?"

"His memories say that is not so. But you are right. Many things have been learned by those, our ancient enemies. We cannot count this one as any but a danger.

"He can be taken by the Hoads—"

There came a sense of outrage or strong denial.

"We do not waste the blood. What has come to you, Vestrum, that you would suggest that? Is it that the old blood *has* run so thin that we can think even as those do—to slay for safety? Do we not know of old that that would be a deed to break us forever apart?

"Are we then so great again that we can move mountains and roll up seas to confuse our enemies? If they have learned through the centuries, have we been in exchange dull of mind? Should he be their proposed key to our gate, then since he is in our hands let us study how they would use him. But he is not part of those in Dakar's Valley."

"True. So what do you make of this other ship?"

"Have you not read the answer to that, wrung out of this one?"

"They trouble the inner sight. There is among them such power as we have not found in the enemy for ages. They seek him now, their thoughts running here and there until they are a torment to all Listeners. It is true that they are not openly akin to the dark ones, and so far they remain a puzzle. It may be they who placed this one among us—"

"And he broke the Globe of Ummar."

There was a pause. In vain Farree tried to trace the thought pattern back to the last speaker, only to face a wall once more. There was a coldness in these words which shifted through to him—mind words. If they realized he could hear them, they did not care.

"You think then that that is what he was ordered to do?"

The asking came to him again, growing easier and easier to understand with every mind touch.

"There is no shadow of the Restless One on him. It might have been chance only—"

"If there is only a small doubt that it was not— Yes, you are right. Let him be prisoned—near the Hoad Ways. If he receives enough of their probing he will be weakened, the better for our purpose. Let it be done!"

That last was a sharp command. Farree expected some action on it, only he was aware of nothing at all. The darkness held him as tightly as if he were the meat within an uncracked nut shell. He was, however, gaining some strength of mind and that he hoarded. He could not understand the nature of the bonds which they had laid upon him. Yet it was plain he was again a helpless captive.

He was once more able to see by physical means, but dark first met his eyes. About him was a sourish smell, combined with that of fresh turned earth. For one moment of heart-thumping fear he thought he had been buried. Then, putting his body to the test, he strove to sit up and was able to do so. His upper wing curves scraped painfully along a rough surface and soil shifted down on his face from the hands he had put out to judge the size of his cell—if cell this was.

When the fingers of his left hand rubbed an uneven surface, he used that point as an anchorage, drawing near to it. It marked a wall right enough. Sweeps along that surface told him it was of stone, but sometimes he felt the ridges of what could be bunches of roots depending from above. The smell became foul once as his nails scraped across something slimy. From that spread a faint glimmer of light, enough for him to see a tuber clinging with hairlike roots to the stone—now oozing viscid stuff from a hole his fingertip had punched in it. He wriggled the tuber back and forth until the hair-thick supports were torn free, so he could carry it with him as he went on—though the light was very dim, showing him no more than the patch of wall immediately around his improvised candle.

It was twenty strides from the place where he had awakened to a corner where wall met wall. Halfway up the new barrier was a dark hole and from that trickled some liquid, which coursed down the stones to collect in a runnel at the wall's foot.

Seeing this suddenly awoke in him a raging thirst. How long it had been since he had eaten or drunk he had no way of knowing. Did he dare to touch this oily-appearing streamlet? He was not sure. Debating the safety of that he turned and edged along the side of the stream, using that now for a better guide.

In the end that disappeared in a round hole in the floor. His torch was failing him and he tried to find another such. Only here the growth from above looked more like ends of stout vines. There came a sudden sound. The stream had flowed silently, and the silence itself had pressed in upon him. He had not realized the full depth of that quiet until it was broken.

There was a kind of flutter, as if the roots from above swayed. He looked up. Overhead was nothing but the thick dark. Cautiously Farree tried to open his wings. Once more the edges scraped over his head. The passage was low of roof. He pulled his wings into as tight folds as he could manage.

The thirst which he had tried to put out of his mind was joined now by hunger. He longed for the pack of emergency supplies still back in the ship.

The ship! The Lady Maelen—what had happened to her when the murky globe had broken in his hands? What had those who had put him here done? Had they in some manner moved into that bowl valley and tried to fetter those on board as they had him? He had great respect and awe for Maelen's powers—even more for those of the Zacanthan. Through unreckoned time Zoror's people had collected knowledge, had developed latent talents. Not all of them had followed the same paths—he knew that Zoror had experimented with mind speech and mind control. But Farree did not know the scope of the historian's talent. He paused for a moment to put his own mind send to the test once more—only to strike that barrier.

Well, they might have bound his mind, but they had not fettered his body this time. During his brief halt those roots above seemed longer. For some reason that awoke a dread in him. Being under the earth was difficult enough; he had to fight an ever-present fear of being shut in—encased in this evil-smelling pocket of soil. The light from the tuber continued to ebb. Farree faced around to look back, although all there was blind dark.

Not quite. He sighted a small spark of light—fiery orange-red, like a minute, awakening flame. Two—close together—another pair slightly behind the first. At the same time an effluvium, a stench strong enough to churn his empty stomach, puffed in his face. He gagged and fought to control the nausea that awoke in him.

At the same moment his mind was touched. He was in contact with one of the things which had run the dark ways underground back in the valley. What he could read was ravening hunger, and a picture of this foul thing hurrying to seize upon his flesh.

The odor grew stronger, and the lights which marked their eyes brighter and larger. Hunger drove them and he was the food.

Moving backward, Farree edged as close as his folded wings would allow him to the wall at his right. His hand groped for the knife and then he remembered his sheath was empty. He had no defense except his two hands. Still he backed and the creatures followed. Now and again he gave a hurried glance over his shoulder to make sure that there were no other eye lights showing ahead, that he was not being driven into a trap.

He expected them to charge, but it seemed that something kept them from making that last run which would bear him down. They were coming up on him to be sure, but not as swiftly as he expected. The tuber in his hand lost its light. But he could still see the eyes.

As Farree went he was careful to test each step with his heel, making sure that he was not about to lose his balance. Then he kicked something and there was the sound of metal striking stone. He dared to stoop and seek to feel what he had stumbled upon. His hand closed about a chain.

Part of it was loose and yielded easily to his jerk but the other end appeared to be fixed. He pulled again and was answered by a glow of light. Again where his fingers pulled he saw a glimmer. The hunters had paused— Raw hatred and purpose still filled them but there was now caution, he believed, in their halt, as if he had chanced upon something in which they foresaw trouble. At the same time the links gathered into his hand began to warm, to burn as had the globe; but he refused to drop his find. The fact that the very picking up of the thing had slowed the others' advance made him cling to it the tighter.

Light sped from the links in his hand out along the rest of its length. This was a far better light than the tuber had given. He gathered the metal linkage up in both hands now to give a strong pull.

There was no give. Only more of the chain was alight, so that his eyes, already accustomed to the dark, could follow it to a wall. There it had been fastened to a loop apparently deep set in one of the stone blocks. Farree followed it up to that anchorage. He had to divide his attention between what he was doing and those menacing eyes. But the latter had stopped their advance.

Farree's fingers found a loop set in the stone. From his

touch there came a stab of agony as great as if he had put his hand into real flames. He drew back but he did not drop hold of the chain. Unlike the links he held the loop did not shine. Pull having achieved nothing, he tried twist, winding the chain as swiftly as he could to the left, its links clinging together and its length becoming less as he wound it into two strands together. Once more he jerked.

There was a clang and the link locking the chain to the loop gave way so quickly he stumbled back, his wings brushing painfully against the other wall. Now he held several arm's lengths of glowing chain free from its anchorage. Though it remained fully in his hand it did not sear his flesh as had the single stone-set loop. Winding a fair portion about his right hand he swung the rest back and forth as one would swing a lash. With a clank of metal against rock it met the pavement behind him. Only then did its light reveal something else—a skull, teeth a-grin, as it rested in the midst of a pile of bones. What manner of creature had been left to die here Farree could not tell, but to his eyes the skull looked as if it were humanoid in shape.

He took a stride across that mass of bones, striking the skull without intention with the toe of his boot. It rolled back along his trail, toward the waiting eyes. Farree shivered and began once more to edge along the right hand wall of this place, which changed quickly into a narrowed passage. The glow from the chain remained constant and he swung it back and forth now—not only as a warning to those who followed him, but as a method of seeing a little ahead on his own path.

The dim light picked up a heap of something and for the second time he viewed a pile of bones. But the method of securing this unfortunate prisoner to the wall had been different. The upward swing of the chain showed a small cage of metal secured to the stone about as high as a man such as Vorlund would stand. In that cage a second skull rested, with the bones piled below. Farree hurried on.

He passed two more chains looped to the wall but neither of these contained a prisoner held to his or her death. Then he came to the end of the way he followed to be faced by a flight of steps and a matching rise overhead to give that flight room.

It was at that moment that the hunters attacked. Farree must have been about to pass out of their territory and they would not allow that. He got up four of the worn steps and stood ready to face them, the chain dangling ready. They came and he lashed out. He struck solidly the one in advance of the other, then hit at the second with less chance to aim. For the first time the things gave voice—a shrilling so high and piercing that it hurt his ears. Twice more one leaped at him only to be caught by the lash. The first one he had struck lay struggling where the first blow had thrown it. Now its fellow joined it. One pair of eyes lost their light, and Farree thought that perhaps the creature was dead. Now it seemed that if not at that last state yet the second was badly injured, for it did not attack again, only lay near its fellow eyeing Farree with a hate near great enough to cancel out pain.

He watched it narrowly before at last turning away and beginning to climb. Farree still glanced back every step or two to see if he were again being followed. The heightened color of the chain dimmed to a light glow. He wound it about his forearm and held it out before him to light as much of the way ahead as it could.

Once started on that climb the upward path seemed endless. Twice he made his way through an opening overhead to come out upon another dark passageway. He was not tempted to explore, keeping rather to the stairs still reaching upward.

Used to the subdued radiance of the chain he was not aware at first of a faint light up ahead. At length the shape of a grey square drew his attention and he found by means of this some remnants of his decreasing strength to hurry on to the head of the stairs. This left him in a room of some size. There was a furnace at one end, and hanging on the walls at intervals were objects he had no desire to examine closer, for in this place there was such a residue of pain and fear as to make him shudder. Farree opened and flexed his wings—there was room here. At the far end of this chamber was another stair, while far above the reach of any one standing here, there was a row of barred windows, square cut along one wall. From them the mist-light of the grim place came.

Underfoot was a layer of dust in which Farree's tracks were very plain. The bitter cold here was that of a place which had been deserted. Farree wove the chain end once more about his hand as he fanned the cramps out of his wings and stood looking about. Here the glow of the chain was subdued, but Farree thought it looked like well-burnished silver. Certainly it did not show any rust, as had the anchorage loop and the cage of the skull, both of which had red flakes falling from them. He wound the length more tightly about his arm and started up the second flight of stairs. As had the one in front of the earth ways, there was a second flight beyond a first landing. A corridor ran off to his right but to his left there was a window—narrow enough that he had again to fold down his wings, and high enough that he had to loosen the chain from around his skin to catch the bars with both hands and pull himself up to look out.

He was staring into open air as he had done in that chamber of his first waking. The bars prevented him from leaning far enough forward to see what lay to either side. In the center crossing of those bars there was a plate of metal which was a dull red in color. Rust from the bars sifted off on his hands and his fingers jerked in pattern with twinges of pain until he loosed his hold again. The center plate had a deeply incised pattern, and there was no mistaking the picture it bore. He had seen in it some of Zoror's prized records—the ancient hand weapon known as a sword—longer than a knife and more difficult, he thought, to handle. The point and half the blade of this had been driven, point down, through the representation of a humanoid skull a-grin with teeth as long as fangs. Just as the room below had brought him the ache of pain and ancient fear so did this tug at him—but in a different way—as if there was an important meaning in it which he could almost guess.

Hunger and thirst drove him on, up the next length of the stair, and he came out at the far end of a hall which stretched before him as had the hall of his dream except there was no crystal brightness here. The walls were hung with tatters of woven stuff which were now rags, and most of them had fallen to the floor, lying at the foot of the walls in mouldering lengths. Down the center of this huge chamber was a table. Dust had reduced its vivid colors, but here and there some chance had brushed away the fall of years to show that the board was of a deep red stone veined with black and glittering. There were benches on both sides of the board, their supports carved of shining black, the seat hidden by the dust. At intervals down the table were set large footed goblets and these had a shadow of sheen. Perhaps if they were burnished they would show the glow as that chain which was his weapon.

There was a backed chair at one end of the table, also of the black glittering stuff. The top of the back was a mask of a skull, bone white and thus vivid against its setting despite the dust, pierced by a black sword. Along the left wall as he started down the length of the chamber, rotten rags had fallen from covering large windows, each barred and centered with the sword and skull device. Through these came air which was so fresh and sweet after the burrows beneath that Farree made his way to the nearest.

These were quite large and he found them closer to the floor than any of the others—as if they had been fashioned to accommodate inhabitants of his own size. Also, when he leaned forward he was able for the first time to see something besides sky.

Judging by the sun it must be after middle day, a clear day. The frightening gloom of the building through which he wandered was forgotten when he looked down. Below there were indeed walls. It was what was still lingered within the wall which made him gasp. For this was like a sea of green, although after a first incredulous glimpse it sorted itself out into a tangled mass of shrub and tree, with an inner core of what could only be a pool. A bird of clearest yellow arose from one of the trees with a burst of song.

Farree could see a terrace farther on, a stairway leading down into that miniature wilderness. He stumbled in the general direction now, trying to find the door which would give upon this freedom. He shuffled through a large mound of rags which became dust at his touch, puffing up to set him coughing and blinking his eyes against the flying particles. Then he found his door—closed. He jerked down on a time-fretted latch and came out on the terrace.

He was staggering, and had to make his way down the stairs crab fashion, holding on with both hands to the banister, the chain now looped around his neck. The water drew him—to find that pool locked within the green and drink from it—that was the only thing important now.

13.

Yellow birds were screeching over his head, expressing their anger at his plundering fruit from a tree they must consider their own. There was no sign here that any but the birds and a small furred creature who had scrambled out of his way, its teeth firmly fixed in one of the same pale green balls as the one on which he feasted now, had been here for a long time. He had dared to drink from the pool and to cram the fruit into his mouth, taking the chance that neither carried any seeds of death for off-worlders.

Only—he was not an off-worlder, Farree thought, as he reached for another of the fruits. There were those like him here. Also there were those odd small flashes which managed to work past the memory block which cursed him, letting him know that his kind were not strangers here, though this castle might be utterly strange to the Farree within its walls now.

His hunger for the moment satisfied, he climbed back to the terrace where there were no trees or bushes to impede the full spread of his wings. From there he launched himself into the air, the better to see the nature of this lodging which chance had brought him to.

The walled garden became a single bright green square as he spiraled upward, while the dark mass of the building looked all the more sinister from this height. It was not the height of the walls and towers alone which rendered it so for him. The fact that it crowned what might be a high-set plateau, with lower heights crowding about it, made it all more impressive. There were three towers, one large one springing from the bulk of the building through which he had come into the garden, two smaller and of less bulk to one side. The building was unique in that the pile of masonry rose sheer from the very lip of the level on which it had been built—as if it had sprung directly from the native rock.

He wheeled down closer to those two towers and the small open stretch before them. It was now plain that they guarded a gateway—one where a massive portal was firmly closed upon the outer world. However, from an open space there led downward a way which had been cut into the rock—steep enough in places to turn into steps of stone.

That was also closed he saw as he swooped downward, for not too far down that stepped path was abruptly cut off. There was only the rock of the mount on which the castle stood, though some distance below there were signs that broken traces of it still lingered.

Below at ground level there was a trace which might once have been a road, and that pushed between ranks of oddly twisted trees bare of any leaf or sign of life. Farree swooped lower again until he was near skimming the top of a dead forest. Limbs of all these trees were twisted as if they had been deliberately wrung and left contorted. There were splotches here and there of a sickly yellow and a disturbing red-brown, masses which clung to the trunks or to the spindly branches. As he had felt in the unpleasant chamber within the castle, so did the same faint fear touch him here. There had been evil here, strong enough to utterly defeat all that was of life and hope.

The dead forest spread out and away from the foot of the plateau on which the castle was rooted. There was no sign of green no matter how high he flew. And at the end of that stretch of tormented woodland there were again mountains such as stood between the ship and that other mountain hold which went veiled in haze.

He circled back and flew along the wall of the two towers, seeking again the garden with the food he needed. Between the towers on that gate which was so firmly set there appeared in high relief that device he had seen elsewhere in the castle—though this time the skull was red and the black sword had lost its hilt.

Farree's flitting was joined suddenly, as he passed the second tower, by a flight of birds, not the yellow ones of the inner garden but larger and more aggressive looking. If they were birds—Farree wondered as they circled in a wheel formation around him, taking turns to fly closer until he feared one of those curved beaks would strike at one wing or the other.

In color they were almost the same yellow as the growths on the dead trees, and, although their bodies were feathered, their wings appeared with patches of what looked like dirty grey skin exposed. Their eyes were always turned toward him—they might well have been examining a suspected enemy before they ventured an attack.

So wary did the sight of them make Farree that he almost sheered away from the castle, to wing out across the dead forest. Only the need for food and water kept him on his way toward the overgrown garden. He was above the bulk of the castle, the tallest of the towers to his left when the birds, which had flown in silence, suddenly voiced a series of harsh screams. The encircling flight broke apart.

Out of the uppermost slit window of the tower there shot a beam of light. It had not been aimed at him, but rather at one of the birds. That one screamed again and veered, flapping its ragged wings with frenzied haste, yet losing altitude.

The others were already on their way back toward the gate tower from which they must have first come, while that one which had fallen afoul of the light shaft landed on the roof below where it lurched along, one wing dragging, as if it could no longer be folded against its body.

Farree kept out of what he believed to be the line of fire. Who still defended a place which had seemed deserted for generations by all the signs he had so far seen?

The slit window through which that light had come was deep as well as narrow and he caught no sight of anything—or anyone—within, although he now discovered the sensation of peace within the garden disturbed. Certainly he had no wish to go exploring in the dark pile again. However, he selected a place where he could fit himself under the cover of a tree if he remembered to keep his wings well folded. There Farree busied himself with some tall grass he had wrenched out of a bed at the foot of the terrace. He began to knot the lengths together into a kind of net, with a care which seemed to draw into his fingers skills he did not know he had.

Sunset was already just ahead as he tied the last knot. He allowed himself a long drink at the pool and established a rude nest of leaves he had scooped up from under the largest tree. To sleep here was perhaps rank folly, but his flight outside had showed him no place better and he was very wary of ever entering the castle again. Having nearly gorged himself he settled down, not to sleep as yet, though the sun was lost behind the heights, but rather to test once more his ability to search by mind sense.

Surely it reached farther now! He fastened upon the far end of the tangled garden as his goal and went slowly, ready at any moment to snap back into hiding within himself if any danger arose. There were flutters of life, birds, and perhaps the small creatures that had raided the fallen fruit. Neither of those showed any trace of another purpose. He thought of trying to reach the tower and then decided quickly that there would be little profit in perhaps drawing upon himself once more the notice of the various owners of those voices he had not been able to answer.

Once he started up as a cry of one of the ragged birds sounded near, was even echoed back by the walls. His body was tired and longed for rest but his mind was like another creature, alert, prying a little here and a fraction there. He found another life form, ground dwelling, which was a night hunter and fastened a thread of search upon that.

As the thread spun out, he grew excited. The barrier about him must be either gone at last or worn thin. This creature he so accompanied scuttled along what could only be one of the inside hallways of the dark deserted bulk behind him. If only Togger were here! It was hard to keep in touch with a small mind which seemed to wander in and out at the lowest range he himself knew.

It was in the castle—and it was hunting, though what other life form could be discovered there he had no idea. The stone-set walls were too bare—there would be none of the possibly edible refuse which might be available if the castle were inhabited. Up—the creature was going up and the runway was a tight one. It managed to squeeze through places where it must flatten its body to half size in order to pass.

There was nothing in its mind but hunger and the anticipation of finding food. Also it was very sure that there was that food only waiting to become prey. As a fisherman might play some sea life larger than himself, allowing it to run fruitlessly, keeping only the thinness of a line upon it, so Farree followed where that night hunter went. There was excitement in the creature now; it was nearing its favored place for finding what it sought. He did not have Maelen's power or Vorlund's; he could not see through the hunter's eyes or even gain a picture of what it pursued.

It was slowing, showing more caution, advancing by short spurts which carried it apparently from one spot of cover to the next. Then—

Farree loosed his touch, whipped it back, hoping that he had not been detected. There had been another mind—not that of any of the creature's kind—powerful, overwhelmingly so, though Farree had only brushed lightly against it. Someone was on watch. He pulled himself to his feet, his wings compressed as tightly as he could hold them, and strove to look inward to the east—toward the tower which was only the faintest of shadows in the swiftly fallen darkness. Were there any windows on this side? He could not remember. His mouth was dry, and he felt his hands sticky on the heavy branches he had pulled into place before him. This was fear again, perhaps the stronger because the object from which it spread was unknown. He forced the barrier of mind nothingness on himself and waited—for what he could not tell.

Time passed. The throb he had fully expected to feel did not come. Still he dared not try such a search again. Togger— he longed fiercely for the smux. They had played games before, those which took the two of them for the playing. Still he waited for an assault, although there had been no light in the tower, no sign that anything but the creature was there.

At last Farree settled down once again in his leaf nest. His only defense could be to keep strictly away from any more such experiments. Scent from newly opened night flowers was heavy and there were insects in plenty which gathered around each of the large blooms now giving off a pale glow.

Glamorie—that strange word which Zoror had used. Farree thought he detected a new softness in the night air, a kind of defense against the harshness of the stone which walled in this place. Slowly he studied what lay around him, half expecting to see some change strike this spot.

His initial wariness was fading and with a start he recognized what danger might lie in that. He might be under the edge of some control which had not alerted him as it came. He loosed the mind send because he had to know—

He could sense the small lives of the garden, and there was no fear, no uneasiness in those. If something was striving to move him now, it was narrow-beamed to touch him alone. He looked up once more, sweeping aside a flower-studded branch to try and see again the tallest tower, for he was sure that all he sensed as intelligence must be located there.

Then he saw a round coin of blue, the same blue as had marked that beam which had swept the bird from the sky. This was not fixed, for, even as he watched, it swung a little to the right. Not an eye in reality, of course, it was too large. But that it performed for someone that function, yes, of that he was sure.

Now it had circled so far to the right that he could sight only the edge of it. Again it must have moved on for there was nothing suddenly. Could he, during the time it might be turned away, wing to the west and away? It might be possible but to him at that moment the chance was too thin. Instead he watched as now the eye appeared to his left and moved on until once more he could see the disc in its entirety. Then it did not shift any longer but remained fixed in the blackness of the night sky.

That it could look down to where he hid well below its level was another thing he could only guess at. Any moment he expected to be caught in some unknown trap. His presence here could have been sensed from the first moment that he had climbed out of the depths of the earth into that foul lower chamber. Surely he *had* been at least noted when he had taken wing out over the dead forest—

He had—What he had expected so long came—not with the force of a blow—but rather of a greeting. There was no danger—

Farree slipped out of his nest and reached the terrace before he took to wing—then as he arose above the scent of the night flowers a picture came full envisioned in his mind as to where he had been summoned. It was there—that landing place firm and square on a roof at the tall tower's base.

Furling wings again he went to a door which was a little ajar as if to greet him. He was only aware that there was need that he do this and as time passed that need grew more demanding. Once more he mounted stairs that wound around within the tower, the treads just wide enough to give him foot room, his furled wings brushing against each wall.

He hurried faster, a kind of breathlessness plaguing him. The need—he was needed! Time was so short—

Time for what? queried a deep-buried part of his mind. He was unconscious of the desire for any answer.

Light spilled down the last part of the stair—not the red-yellow of flame nor the glow from ship's walls, nor any other he could call to mind. Blue—as the watching eye. He stepped out into the room which must form the whole of the tower at top level.

She sat there in a chair of brilliant crystal which caught and reflected the light until it seemed that her resting place was formed of gems. Her full sleeves had fallen back from hands which were together so that her forefingers touched her lips, the arms braced with elbows on the arms of the chair.

Farree's wings trembled, half spread. He stared and met her stare eye to eye. She was certainly as tall as Maelen, and she wore no wings. Hair, which in this light was palely blue, must be really silver, fine spun. It lay loose on her shoulders, rippling down until it formed a shoulder cape above her robe.

Jewels as brilliant as the flashing throne on which she sat glittered here and there among the strands as if they had been threaded on her hair itself. And there was a device on the breast of her robe—wide wings of glitter outspread.

Farree stared. One hand went uncertainly to his head

where the pain once more built up swiftly. His sight clouded and his other hand went out in protest.

"So—the wheel has indeed turned." The words dripped through the pain into him. "What went down to defeat in darkness struggles to arise again. But not wholly, is that not so, small one? Fragon's seal is not easily broken. Tell me now—who am I?"

Farree's mouth felt as dry as if it had been scrubbed with desert sand. He whispered:

"Selrena—"

She moved her hands so that those forefingers no longer stayed at lip level but pointed straight at him as if to impale his body on their pointed nails.

"So—" She nodded and the jewels spun into her hair danced to dazzle him. But the pain was lessening, and he could see her clearly once more. "And what am I, little one?"

For that he had no answer. The wall within his head was as intact as ever.

"I—I do not know."

She did not frown but he sensed a momentary impatience in her.

"Fragon!" She spat that word and then appeared to school herself into patience. "At least you are Langrone. Look!"

So impetuous was that command, the pointing of her finger, that he immediately stared floorward to see that between them was a circle of the blue shining surface. The eye—but—?

She appeared to catch his thought. "Eye? Yes, it is something of an eye. However, we must make sure—"

He was invaded. There shot before and about him fleeting pictures. Once more he relived what he knew of his life. Then, feeling as if he had been caught up and sucked so that most of the strength in him was stolen, he stood again, swaying, at the edge of the blue disc.

Selrena had not moved out of her chair but she had placed her hands on its arms and for the first time there was real expression in her calm face.

"From off-world"—it was as if she mused to herself— "and those with you—What is planned can be changed when there are new strands for the weaving. Now—" There was the same force in her voice as had been in the command which had been given for that brief return to the past. "Look—reach—"

He went down on his knees, mainly because he could no longer stand erect, and he leaned over to stare down into the disc even as he had stared at her upon their meeting.

There was nothing to herald the scene which flashed instantly into sight. He was almost as much a part of what he saw as if he did stand in the control cabin of the ship. Zoror sat in the pilot's place, but Maelen and Vorlund were on their feet and now both their heads swung around and they looked in his direction, but their expressions were puzzled. There was another will uncoiling inside of him. Even as he had used the creature from the garden for a chance to seek out what might be of danger, so now he was being used in the same way.

Vorlund continued to look puzzled, but Maelen held up her hand and the fingers moved. Farree was shaken by a sense of surprise—that which was using him did not expect such a response. Beneath the surprise was now a thread of uncertainty.

Farree's mind sense was commandeered, thrust at Maelen, and flattened so against a wall. Then he was hurled against Vorlund and found entrance, but only momentarily. There came a wry twisting and he was once more outside. The Zacanthan then—

Again the defense was too much for him to hold.

"Farree!" Maelen had returned the sense. "Farree— where—" She did not complete that question.

Between his eyes and the disc a white hand passed, fingertips brushing the surface. The scene which had been so sharply clear was erased. Slowly he lifted his head to look again to Selrena. She was one of the Darda and they were always set to keep their own council. To them the winged ones were as children: this was another weight of knowledge from the past.

She was standing now, towering above him, no longer looking down but at a narrow opening in the wall to the west. Her lower lip was sucked in between her teeth, and a lesser person might have been thought to be in a state of indecision.

He felt as tired as if he had gone for days without any rest, and he had to fight to keep his eyes open.

"New one—with power!" Selrena said slowly. "And not come against us but—for you!" She swept her robe about her and went to a small table which stood a short distance away. Picking up a bowl which she cupped in the palm of one hand she shook into that the contents of two small boxes and added liquid from a tall bottle. In her two hands she tilted the bowl slowly from side to side and then brought it to Farree, stepping around the side of the disc.

"Drink!" she ordered sharply.

He found that he could do nothing else then but obey. The contents were thick but fluid, and the taste was tart, nearly fiery, so that he swallowed hurriedly to get it out of his mouth. Heat sped down his throat and suddenly he realized that the grim walls about had forced a chill not only on the room but into him so that he had been tense against it, whereas now he relaxed.

Selrena had reseated herself in the crystal chair and sat watching him with the expression of one striving to solve some problem. As he put aside the bowl she gestured again to the disc on the floor. He leaned forward a little, wondering if he were again to face his companions. The fatigue which had ridden him ever since he had come upward from the ways beneath had somehow vanished; neither did he feel as if he were under any compulsion. Perhaps this was more of Zoror's glamorie, but he had no desire to fight it.

"Who are these friends of yours?" She was direct and to the point.

Though she must have learned from her mind hold the major parts of his story Farree retold it again, partly by mind picture, partly in speech. Though he used the universal trade talk of the star lanes it would seem that she had no difficulty in understanding him any more than he found her words untranslatable.

When he talked of their adventures on Yiktor she stopped him several times, mainly to ask that he repeat something he had said concerning Maelen or those of the Thassa whom he had encountered.

"From whence did they come?" she again asked abruptly, "these who share thoughts not only with each other but also with the animals and other life of their present world?"

Farree shook his head. "I do not know—only that they are an old, old people who once lived in cities but who now travel over their world, having no true homes."

"Yet they have power." The hand resting on her knee clasped itself into a fist. "Now"—she switched to another subject—"tell me more of this Zacanthan—from whence did he come and why does he comb old legends? Does he hunt treasure as seems to be the goal of many races and species?"

"The Zacanthans hunt knowledge. In their own world they store all that they can learn—"

"For what reason?" she pushed him.

"I do not know, except that they find knowledge itself treasure. Sometimes they go off-world as Zoror has done—either to stay, as he does, on another world where many ships planet and where he can gather the news from many far places—or sometimes they explore ancient ruins to hunt there some clues as to who built them and when and why—"

"And it was this Zoror who told you of the People—who came with you seeking them—merely for the knowledge he could add to his gleanings? Or had he some other reason—perhaps to hunt for the Doomland? Only death comes to those seeking there for any treasure. There are many stories of what can be discovered, but those are rightly distrusted. Death guards its own.

"However, that the People are still remembered and that someone seeks them"—again she was looking over Farree's head toward the wall of the round chamber—"that is something to think on."

"He does not hunt treasure—" Farree began and she laughed, though there was nothing but chill in that sound.

"No, he comes to return you to your kin. Is that his boast then?"

"He does not boast. Yes, he wished to follow the need which brought me here. And the Lady Maelen and her lord—they were of a like mind."

"A pretty tale." She laughed again. "So here you now sit in the hold which was once Fragon's and give me puzzles to be solved. I am always one needing answers, wingling. However, there is"—she tilted her head a fraction and eyed him intently—"this is just— Yes!" She brought her hands together with a clap of sound. "How better can you all play our purposes, wingling? Since you are here, be sure I shall make good use of you. Come—" She had arisen from her chair and beckoned. He got to his feet.

She waited for him to draw level with her and then laid one hand firmly on his shoulder, compelling him to walk with her. They were facing the wall when she halted to set her other hand to the stone. What she did there he could not tell, but a large portion of the wall fell outwards, providing a ledge open on three sides to the night.

Swiftly Selrena lifted the hand on his shoulder to touch his forehead between his eyes.

Farree lunged outward onto the platform. There had come a question—one only he could answer and that he must—now! His wings expanded and he leaped out and up into the night.

14.

This was the same call which had drawn him earlier from the ship, and he could not do anything else but answer it. Under him the earth was dark; an evil greenish glimmer from the dead forest provided all the light except the very distant stars. No birds arose to fly with him or harass him during his flight. Farree tried to reach ahead, to pinpoint the source of the call but he could only learn that it lay to the west. While to the east—He thought fleetingly of the ship and those waiting for him there, but there was no way he could escape the urge which kept him flying directly away from what might be safety and help.

The fatigue which had enfolded him in the castle was gone. Perhaps, he thought fleetingly, banished by the drink Selrena had pushed upon him. He was flying with some speed. Now the dead forest was overpassed and he was above another line of cliffs which towered to match the heights on which the

castle was perched. There came an end to the glimmer of the
fungi-like growths, and once more he was over bare stone.

Farree was well out across this, discovering that he had
more night sight than he had ever been aware of before, when
ahead he caught a beam of a far stronger light than the forest
had produced. At the same time the cry which drew him
swelled up into what was like a mighty moan before dying
away completely.

After that was silence, and some of the urgency which
drove him on was gone. He slackened speed, once more
somewhat in control of his own movements. The beam of light
head became just that, a column pointing skyward. Ship's
light! That must be it!

A ship in this direction could not be the one he longed to
home in upon. With the cry no longer ringing in his head,
deafening and deadening his other senses, he could think
clearly again. To rush straight for that beacon was to be a fool.
He tried to break from the compulsion, to head east once
more. But he had not been released to the point that he could
do that.

The heights over which he had been flying curled away to
the north and he discovered that he could vary his advance
enough to follow their broken line.

"Limit! Limit!"

That might have been shouted in his ear. He swerved a
little under the shock of that mind send, the strongest and
most punishing he had yet felt. He headed left and there were
four strong and frantic beats of wings before he could escape
the punishment of that ringing in his head.

Torment or no he was not allowed to go free. He flew in
and out, heading always northward against his will, striving
again and again to cross some invisible barrier which set off,
each time he tried, that burst of ringing in his head, even
affecting his sight so that he could not see as clearly as before.
He veered once more to the left and gave a leap in the air.

"Limit!"

Dazed by the pain in his head accompanied by a feeling of all beneath him whirling madly around, Farree winged on. He must have broken through, but he was only half conscious that he was still aloft, flying again towards the pillar of light in the distance. Slowly Farree recovered from the latest sharp encounter. He was again in the open, leaving the cliffs once more behind, as he headed, whether he willed it or not, towards that distant finger of brilliance.

There was no more of the crying which had pulled him here, yet he was sure that it was associated with the light. Shortly he was circling what was manifestly an off-world camp.

The ship which had finned down in the open was somewhat larger than that which had brought him here. Its ramp was out and there was a cluster of planet shelters set up about its foot, which suggested that this planeting had been established for some time. The beacon which had attracted him was aimed from the nose of the ship, straight up into the night sky. Perhaps it was more of a guide for those traveling on the planet—a warning or a summons.

There were lesser lights at ground level. Farree coasted down, slapped wings hastily together and trod earth again. Was his arrival still unknown as far as those in ship and camp were concerned? He had seen too many ship devices to believe that there were no guards set against strange arrivals.

The principal light at ground level shined at a place where a flitter—the light exploring craft—rested. Farree could see the forms of those working about that ship; repairs, he guessed. There were five of the planet shelters. Four of the smallest size, hardly large enough to shelter two men at the most, clustered about a single one three times their bulk.

His eyes had adjusted quickly to the glare given off by the beacon and the working lights at its foot. Now he could see who labored there—or stood looking on. From this distance they all looked humanoid. However, there were no recognizable uniforms among them, certainly nothing that marked them as perhaps a Patrol scout that had come to some grief and had only the chance of making a landing and setting a beacon to call for help. Certainly the ship was no broad-bellied freighter, even a one of limited tonnage such as a Free Trader crew would bring in.

He counted seven men—three hard at work on the inner parts of the flitter, two watching, and two more stationed by the entrance of one of the small shelters, their attitudes suggesting they were guards—which should mean a prisoner. His memory fed him a quick flash—could this be where that unfortunate Atra he had heard spoken of was kept?

As if the thought form of the name released a tight grip, mind send reached him.

"Help, oh, wing-kin, help!"

The plea did not strike hard nor very deep: rather it was a whisper which he had to strain to hear. He snapped up mind shield instantly and pushed himself further into a nearby mass of brush for hiding.

"Wing-kin—" The cry was piteous, the reaching out of someone deep in the grip of some peril who called against all hope for succor. It did not have the compulsion which had brought him here; the last of that had been burned away in his battle with that which had cried "Limit" to him. Still it held him uneasily, making him uncertain as to what he did here and why.

A man came at a run down the ramp of the ship, pounding towards the shelter which was under guard. The faint echo of a shout reached Farree. The guards whirled, one facing the door, weapon in hand, the other hastily circling about the bubblelike structure to view its far side.

The runner pushed past the guard and jerked up the tent flap. While both of the guards now prowled about the circumference of the shelter, their heads turned outward, weapons at ready.

Farree longed for Togger. If he could have sent the smux in, seen through his eyes as he had before—! Only there was no Togger within the front of his jerkin, and no one or nothing to depend upon save himself.

"Wing-kin—Farree—come—come—!"

The wail in his head was strong enough nearly to drag him out of hiding, lead him down to the camp. Bait! That was bait set to entrap. However, in this second call for help there was a difference—something which overrode any anger or fear he felt.

"No! Noooo—!"

His hands twisted in the branches about him. Pain, real pain, hot and sharp. Farree felt as if a lash had been laid across his back as had often happened in the old days. The one who summoned was forced to it!

Farree strove to build a barrier against the send. It was meant, he knew, to set him running or flying in to its source, unmindful of anything save the need to help. Perhaps that would have worked well had he been indeed wing-kin, raised here among those who certainly appeared to be of his own kind. Only he possessed no real ties with any he had seen or heard. The Darda, Selrena? To the Darda winglings were of no value—the Darda lived by different rules. And that animal-masked one who had been in the palace of crystal? He had picked up no suggestion that he, she, or it would be moved by any desire to go to the rescue. The one who cried, that must be the Atra they had spoken of—

"Come—" The mind voice was a frail shadow of itself. He could feel the waver in it, believe that the one who called was failing with the plea.

There came a silence which made Farree shiver in spite of his fight for control. Such a silence could perhaps fall when death came. Was the prisoner dead? His hands curled about branches in a grip which broke twigs, sent their sharp ends digging into his flesh.

The guards who had been on duty below separated and two of those by the flitter joined them. They fanned out—two going west, weapons at hand, and the next two coming toward his hiding place on the east.

That mass of brush behind which he had taken refuge was separated from any other chance at cover. And he was without any concrete form of defense. To take to the air should make him fully visible, and Farree was well aware that the off-worlders might well have very sophisticated tracking devices. He could already be within a trap, but he had not fallen into their hands as yet.

One thing to do was to blank out all mind send. Once before he had come up against enemies who were well protected by artificial thought dampeners which protected them, yet also left them well aware that there was someone near at hand to be reckoned with.

Farree began a slow crawl to the right. The hunters were coming at a very deliberate pace. Now and then both men halted for a moment or two near some thick growth of vegetation. Then both would bring left wrists in at waist level to stare down at something they wore. He wondered if perhaps they were even seeking underground for the source of the alarm. Underground—were those who had seized him also busy hereabouts, either building traps or spying?

He was at the inner edge of the bushes now, crawling on a parallel path which he hoped would eventually slope upward so he might reach the foot of the cliffs. The high stand of the vegetation would, he hoped, provide him with a screen.

He was trying, so far vainly, to plan what must be his next move after he did gain the bare earth beneath the cliff. Then, without warning, darkness snapped about him. That beacon of sky-pointing light was abruptly cut. There was a long moment or two and Farree desperately took advantage of that.

He leaped into the air with a wild beat of wings, climbing up and up. Not a moment too soon, for a smaller shaft of light now shot from the nose of the downed ship, not vertically this time but rather horizontally, flicking through a rapid circling of the camp site.

He rose above it until the camp below was small enough to be covered with the palm of one hand. This was his chance—to get back to the cliffs, out of a trap which apparently had its limits after all. Yet even as he turned west, there came the knowledge that the force which had brought him here might have relaxed, but it was not totally gone. Below him the light was now not only making a circle but reached skyward in fast jumps. He was barely able to avoid one. It was plain that even as the guards had appeared to fear something under the earth's surface, they also watched for what might come from above, out of the air.

Farree threw himself toward the cliff crest, but it was as if he tried to fly with wings beating through a viscous flood; it was difficult to keep airborne at all. He fought both for altitude and then more speed. So far he had been very lucky that he had not been caught by the wandering beam, though it seemed to be focused lower than he sought to fly. Farree was nearly to the cliff edge when there were other movements in the air. Birds—? The dragonlike creature which had once herded him back to the ship?

The light stopped suddenly, then flashed, and caught in its glare the edge of what could only be a wing as large as those he wore—only it was black, and it was gone in an instant.

Farree tried to soar higher, sure that the light would be back. Yes, the sweep was already returning! Now it was one of his own wings that was revealed, and by more than just its tip. As he climbed out of that edge of beam, the light flashed up to transfix him.

A downward drag seized him, which he could not break. He was coming down too fast, having no control any longer.

Farree could only hope that he would not smash against the wall of rock which the cliff offered. A last beat of wings, a mighty effort on his part, and he reached the cliff, managing to make a forceful landing on a spur of the rock, scraping his body painfully against that ungiving substance as he struck. But he had a hold, in spite of the pain in his hands, and he scrambled up a little, coming onto a fraction of ledge where he just managed to turn, pushing his wings back and apart to give him the most room possible.

He had freedom only until those men he could hear now shouting one to another, reached him. The light was centered on him, to keep him where he was, while the brilliance of it made him blind.

There was a sudden flicker of the light: something had swung between him and its source. Wings again—dark wings—invisible in the night—then something else flew through the air. At first he thought something had been cast at him, but it was jammed into a crack beyond his reach. He saw a rod which quivered from the force of its strike.

Farree crept along the ledge. The beacon no longer pinned him so tightly, for it was swinging back and forth again, striving, he was sure, to pick up that other winged one. As far as those below could see it might be that they thought him safely at their mercy, and they were now endeavoring to bring down a second captive.

Farree reached out, swinging his arm and hand as far as he dared extend his body. Those groping fingers closed to meet around the rod, which still moved a little. Exerting what strength he could, Farree deliberately added to that quiver, fighting to pull the shaft free from the crevice. At first he thought he had no chance, then it yielded so suddenly that he was nearly tumbled off his perch.

What he held was a hollow rod almost the length of his body. For all its size it was light of weight. The beacon had not caught his move to free it—instead it had risen yet higher, sweeping along the edge of the cliff, once more catching part of a wing which was as quickly gone.

Farree ran the rod through his hands. It was smooth for most of its length, but at one end there were protrusions like buttons—four of them. He had a strong guess that this might be a weapon of sorts but it was totally strange to him. Huddling as far back on his foothold as he could, Farree shifted the rod from one hand to another. There was no cutting blade which he could discover, nor was it either a stunner or a tangler. A simple staff of defense, he believed, one which would be less than nothing when used against such weapons as those the hunters below carried.

The light was swinging back and forth at a high rate of speed. Then a flash of brilliant red cut the air. Though he had not seen any trace of wings again, some one of the men must have fired a laser. However, that single burst of lethal flame, for Farree was sure by the depth of color it had been on kill strength, was not followed by another.

All at once he uttered a small yelp. The light had not turned but, out of nowhere, there had sprung a force which beat upon him, shoving him hard against the rock, making him entirely unable to move. That held for only a few breaths—breaths which his lungs labored to draw in and exhale. Then it was gone. Farree guessed that whatever it might have been must be being used methodically against the cliff, striving to catch and hold the unseen flyer.

He fought to see. There were small lights below now. These spread out along the cliff side. Like the beacon they swept back and forth, also up and down. Twice they flicked over him but did not linger. He was judged, he thought, a core of anger starting to glow within him, to be safely pinned—they were intent now on locating possible other quarry.

With those beams, the great and the small, playing back and forth so close, he dared not try to climb. If he took again to wings he could well be burnt down by the lasers. In his hold the rod moved, turned of itself. He gripped it the tighter, not letting surprise rob him of what he had thought was a weapon if a very weak one. His finger caught upon one of the buttons, and his tightened grip pressed a second one.

From the opposite end of the rod sped a small projectile, or so he believed because he saw a chip appear on the wall. From where it had struck a small bead of glitter grew rapidly into a tiny hollow of fire. Farree loosed his touch on both buttons hurriedly. Whatever chance or the concern of that other winged one had brought him was far more potent than he had expected.

For the first time his anger grew to equal his sense of caution. Let them try plucking him down and he would now have some kind of an answer for them.

"Come—come—"

Out of the silence that had fallen the plea came again.

"Come—" The mind touch trailed away. Then it was back, sharp, urgent— "Go, no, go! They come with nets—"

For the second time that communication was silenced as if the one who sent it had been out down. He dared not try to search for it.

Suddenly into the very center of the great beam there winged a flyer and another behind, two, three— Behind them shot something even stranger—charging ahead, unheeding of either light or those below. It appeared to be flat platform unfitted with wings, far different in shape than any air sled. On it stood a single figure.

Searchlights caught and awoke glitter from the tight clothing the rider wore—she might have been encased in metal. Farree did not mistake the face of the one who dared test the strength of the enemy with such a disregard of their power to attack. This was Selrena.

The speed of the platform on which she rode brushed back the long streamers of her silver hair until it seemed to be a cloak stretched behind her. She held close in both hands what looked to be a twin of the strange weapon Farree grasped.

Her attendant winged ones were of his kind, save that their pinions were black and their hair was the color of a starless night sky. Each of them grasped a silvery chain such as that which Farree had taken from the dead in the underground ways. These chains stretched downward, but hung very stiff and straight, as if their other ends might be anchored. And there was something there—a mass which piled up against each chain in near invisible folds, but able to be glimpsed against the gleam of the silver.

As they came, so did the beacon swing around to keep centered on the airborne party. Laser beams cut high—but the ends of those beams veered outward, as if the firing had been aimed against the surface of a wall. Yet no wall or any construction of which Farree had ever heard could have held off a laser attack of that intensity.

It was certain, however, that the newcomers had the full attention of the attackers. Farree teetered on the edge of his ledge. If he could even reach the top of the cliff he would be better able to take care of himself. He leaped from the ledge.

For a moment he thought his wings were not going to support him. The heaviness which had weighed him down before was again a burden. He could not make it to the cliff top. Nor had he any intention of following behind that strange entourage which had already passed his ledge, skimming serenely along, as if they had nothing to fear from laser flashes which cut below, above, before and behind them, but never touched them.

There was one way he might go while those others took the attention from him—and that was out over the camp, heading still farther west. He began to believe that such a maneuver might well be a good choice. To go west and then circle north and east—

Thus he chose a path which carried him over the heads of

the ship men, fighting for altitude. Their full attention was still centered on the group in the light.

Selrena broke her calm, tempest-riding stance to point to the ground with the rod she held. Farree had just time to see that her escorts were aiming their weapons downward in obedience when a strong blast against him brought him to the ground. He was angry at his own folly in trying such a reckless ploy. On wing he stood out to be picked off by any who sighted him.

He expected to be either burned or jumped when his feet touched earth. It was darker here. All the light was gathered near where the other air invaders were traveling.

Out of the dark span a loop snaked about his body at waist level and then set off tendrils to bind his arms tightly to his body. A tangler! He was indeed trapped, forced to yield to the will of the trapper as he was snapped back, losing his feet, and then dragged face down across the ground where the vegetation had been worn away. Those portions of his hands and knees which had been skinned by his cliff landing were rasped raw for the second time.

He blinked. That drag had brought him up beside one of the bubble shelters and the flap curtain closing that had been pulled aside. Out of the shadows came his captor. He was a tall man, matching one of the Darda in size, but there was nothing about him which suggested those cool and distant ones. He wore the clothing of a spacer and that was stained, grimy. From him as he moved there came an animallike smell which was like that of one of the drifters in the Limits. His skin was nearly black from space tan and he had a wide mouth which now gaped as he grinned, showing spaces of missing teeth.

Now he reached down and caught Farree by his hair and dragged him up and into the shelter with one strong pull.

"How'ya, lady? Got you a friend for now."

Farree, helpless in that hold, looked to one who was not only more helpless than he but who had suffered from her fate.

She huddled on the ground, her thin body seemingly drained of substance, curiously flat, showing bones beneath the skin, for her clothing consisted only of a few rags, and those left enough openings to display old lash marks and new. Her hair was a matted tangle and her small hands and feet nearer to claws than normal appendages. She did not lift her head nor look at the man and Farree.

The spacer took from one of the loops of his belt a thin tube. Crowding past Farree he held that over her head. She stirred and lifted a face so twisted in torment that Farree struggled vainly in sympathy and fear.

"Come on, you. Give us an invite now," her captor ordered.

She stared past Farree as if she did not sight him or understand his presence, if she did. If his mind broke full voice, filled with pain, the cry he had heard before.

"Come—come!" Around him he sensed a strange eddy, as if there were more than words in the mind plea. She moaned a little, her hands going to her head. The tall man laughed.

"You got your wish, lady. Here's a friend come to you. Not that it's going to do either of you any good."

15.

The jailer stood aside from the girl, but she did not show any more awareness of him nor of Farree then she had before. Her wings were fastened together and over them was a near transparent film packaging them so. They were the same color as those Farree wore—shades of green—but the sheen of the furlike covering was masked by that which imprisoned them. The guard stepped closer to Farree now and tapped one finger against the wings tangled in the cord which kept him prisoner.

"Prime!" The man licked his lips. "Prime stock. Vass will like this. You've brought him luck, flying boy. At auction these will fetch a good round of credits and Vass, he don't forget them as has done a good job. Yessss—a prime pair."

Now he ran his fingers along the edge of the near wing and Farree shivered. There was something in that touch which promised worse than he had expected. There came a clacking noise and the guard hurriedly unhooked a disc from his belt, listening to staccato speech Farree could not identify.

The off-worlder barked an assent into the disc and stowed it away again. For a moment he stood looking at the two of them, a leering grin on his face. Then he spoke to the girl.

"You, little lady, don't you think as how you can get out of here with him." He stabbed a thumb in Farree's direction. "You want th' silencer?"

Something in that question pierced through the daze which held her. She gave a little moan and shook her head. The guard laughed.

"No, I thought as how you wouldn't want that! As for you"—now he looked to Farree—"don't you go threshing about. Because there ain't anyway you can get yourself out of that tie up!" With that as a parting shot he left the shelter and dropped the outside curtain behind him.

Farree already knew that there was no way he was going to get out of a tangler. Only fire might shrivel those bonds away—unless the proper signal was thumbed on the stock which had spun it. He looked to the girl. She crouched as if she wanted to bury herself in the earth under their feet, her head bent and her attention all on her balled hands.

Then she spoke and there was a sharpness in the quality of her voice—as if she were thoroughly aware and unmarked by any ill handling, but knew exactly what she would do. Only the words she voiced in a thin croon, hardly above a whisper, meant nothing to Farree. It was not the universal trade tongue with which he was the most familiar—rather it sounded almost like a song.

"I do not understand." He curbed his own voice until it was hardly louder than hers. Perhaps there was no hope that she would understand him in return. He guessed that to use mind touch here might be the worst of all.

She did not raise her head but glanced up at him through the sweat-wet tangle of hair which fell across her forehead. The dazed stare was gone out of her eyes, replaced by inquiry which was as wary as if he were about to add to the wounds and scars which patterned her body.

Now her fingers stretched apart from the tight fists into which she had curled them. She pointed a forefinger at him and her lips shaped a word which again had no meaning for him, but he took a guess at the question.

"Farree," he answered with his name.

The girl looked impatient, started to shake her head, and then winced as if at the bite from one of her hurts. Again she pointed, stabbing the air as if to emphasize the seriousness of what that question was.

He could shake his head only a fraction in the bindings of the web which held him fast. If she did not want his name, but rather his reason for being there, he was unable to satisfy her.

She had settled back a little and was eyeing him intently. Then she held out both hands. Her fingers slowly moved as if they wrote on the air.

Farree sucked in his breath. Just so had he seen Maelen gesture once or twice in the past; yet the prisoner was plainly no Thassa. He could not lift his own arms, which were bound tightly by the tangler. If he could what might he do—only copy her own gesture?

Maelen! He built up a mind picture of her without thinking.

The girl threw herself forward, her one hand out to his head, one emphatic shake warning him.

But that came too late. Skittering in and out of his thought bands was the touch he knew well—Togger! In spite of the continued emphatic warning the girl pantomined, Farree deliberately pictured the smux, down to the last curve of the poison-feeding claws. Once done he held to that—not trying to reach any other of their company. It might be that his call for the smux was on so different a band of mind sense that it would not be detected by any of the sensors, mental or mechanical, which these killers used.

He put into his own call all the force of his frustration.

"Friend—friend!" Togger had made contact! Where was the smux—how far away? Farree forced all such speculation from his mind and continued to hold only on the picture of Togger, and to keep in touch with the smux. From the clearness of the touch, and the fact it grew continually sharper, he believed that by some freak of chance fortune was with him—Togger!

The girl was on her knees before him, staring straight into his eyes as if she could see through those into what stood in his mind—the squat body of his first and closest ally.

She brushed aside the locks of hair dangling about her face and then she held out both hands, touching his body between the loops of the cord which held him so motionless. Into him streamed a flow of strength. There was amazement in her expression, a recoil that almost caused an involuntary withdrawal from contact with him. Manifestly she had not expected what her touch was accomplishing.

"Togger—" He strained his mind touch as far out on the scale as he could. And touched now another—!

That these two had managed to reach him, and yet he had not felt any call from the Zacanthan, Maelen, or Vorlund, was surprising to him. Perhaps some device activated by his captors prevented this. But the party from his own ship must not be allowed to come within range of these who had established camp here. They in turn could be swept into captivity.

The near witless look that the girl had worn while the guard was with them was swept away by her continued attitude and expression of wariness. Her touch on Farree changed. Now she gripped each of his hands, even pinned as they were against his sides by the tangler, in one of hers and a stronger force flowed between them.

"Bad—bad in the air—" Togger broadcast. And repeated even more firmly, "In air, bad."

Still keeping touch with the smux Farree listened. There were more shouts and he could hear the crackle of lasers. Did that mean invaders were still trying to shoot down Selrena and her black-winged escort? Or were the three of his own comrades riding the flitter of their own ship and now taking a part in the battle?

His back was to the door of the shelter but he saw the girl's eyes widen, felt a small added pressure in her hands. Someone was there. Then Farree caught a whiff of the acrid odor given forth by Togger when he was aroused and his claws were ready to deliver poison to an enemy. There was another smell, too.

"Yazz!"

A furred body pressed against his back for an instant and then rounded into his sight. Mounted on the back of the slender hunter rode Togger, holding on to a strip which had been fastened around Yazz's body just behind her forelegs.

"Togger, Yazz!" Farree would have liked to have shouted aloud, but he remembered to keep his voice down. Yazz raised her slender nose, sniffed in direction of the girl, who stared wide-eyed at the pair of newcomers.

"Friends!" Farree, unable to even point because of his bound hands, nodded to the two newcomers.

She dropped her hold on his hands, edging back into the position in which he had first seen her. Still she looked from one to another of the three of them with wonder in her face. Yazz moved in closer and opened a mouth well equipped with teeth, ready to snap at Farree's bonds.

Hurriedly he sent a thrust of danger at Yazz. To touch those might well entangle her in turn. He must have his freedom—but how long they might have before the guard returned Farree had no way of telling. Fire—but there was no fire to shrivel the tangler cords into black strings as he had seen done before. Nor was the whip stock which controlled the spread of the sticky cords here. How then—?

It was Togger who answered that. The smux dropped from Yazz's back and scuttled forward, his large foreclaws slightly raised. There was the shine of poison showing on those, even one or two drops falling as he came to Farree.

Was that the answer? Could the caustic defense of the smux work to burn in another way? Farree clutched at that thought. Togger might not be able to nod in agreement as he squatted momentarily before his friend, but Farree was certain that that caustic burning was just what he proposed to try.

He clicked his claws and Yazz came to him. Using a dangling end of the strap by which he could ride on the larger animal's back Togger pulled himself up to that place he had occupied before. Yazz turned sidewise and with small, cautious movements she drew as near as she could to Farree without touching one of those white cords. Togger held on with his back legs and his small claws, and reached out to Farree, straining his whole body as far as he could to reach the prisoner.

Despite the growing stench of the poison and the threat of those claws should Togger aim badly, Farree stood as still as he could hold himself. Selecting a length of the bonds which was as far from any bare skin as he could find, Togger clasped it with a light grip.

There came an even stronger whiff of the poison. But the touch of the smux had not tied him into captivity, too. Instead there was a black ring where the claw had clutched as the smux loosed it. That blackness spread, in both ways, from the ring.

The cord loosed suddenly, fell down, while the black spread up the surface of each end of the cutting. Farree started once as part of the blackened stuff which touched his own skin gave him a sharp thrust of pain, as if he had held his arm in an open flame. His hands were free and the darkened portions were falling away. In moments he could shake himself and the last of the smoking tangler loops dropped from him.

He kicked those away and stood steady as Togger now leaped from his perch on Yazz to his favorite riding place in the front of Farree's jerkin. The girl's hand was at her mouth as if she were chewing on her knuckles.

Farree held out his hand to urge her to her feet. He might have very little hope of winning free from this camp but that was no reason not to try. Then she shook her head vehemently and pointed to what lay along the floor, which he had not noticed before. She was tethered to the large support in the middle of the shelter by a chain and a ring about one slender ankle; her ankle was much darkened by bruises, as if she had tried for freedom on her own.

The anklet was of the same silvery metal he had found in the deeps below Selrena's castle. But the chain itself was darker in hue and looked as if it might be steel. The end which was clasped around the support was even darker in color.

He reached for the nearest of the chain links to test the hold. She caught at his hand and shook her head sharply. He drew as gently as he could of her clutches and knelt, taking the chain up between his hands. The links were warm, even hot to the touch, but it seemed to him that when he jerked the loop around the support, it gave a little. Togger's acid poison had bitten through the tangler cord; could it also act on this?

Farree threaded the chain through his hands, until his fingers were near that other ring about her ankle. The longer he held onto the length of metal the hotter it became, until he had to push himself to touch it. But he straightened it out against the trodden earth and mind sent to the smux.

"Cut!"

Togger slid down from Yazz once more and scuttled in his half side-wise advance to study the chain. His eyes shot out on their stalks to the greatest length, nearly touching the chain, and for a long moment he did not move.

"Back—" The order reached Farree. Obediently he hunkered back on his knees. His smarting hands had gone to his belt pouch to bring out some wilted ill-bane, near crushed into a wet mess. Catching this up between his palms he turned it around and around. The first hurt of moving the reddened skin across his fingers was swallowed up with the healing coolness of the herb. Togger meanwhile squatted down and closed claw about the chain.

How much venom remained in the claw pockets? Could it corrode metal as easily as it had disposed of the tangler cords?

Togger closed both claws on the same link and held it tightly. The smart of his hands reduced, Farree leaned forward to set fingers to the chain on either side of the link the smux held. He pulled at that with all the strength that he had.

There was no change; the chain held. The effects of the ill-bane were wearing off, and Farree's hands felt the scorch of the strange heat rising again. Togger sat back, supported by his hind legs. It was plain that he, too, was bringing all his strength to bear.

The smux dropped the chain out of his claws.

"Hurt—" his complaint reached Farree. There were no more bubbles arising along the edges of the claws. It was plain that the venom pockets were empty. Perhaps half a day—or night—might lapse before they would be filled once again. Farree himself gave a last defiant jerk, in spite of the pain in his hands, to the chain.

The link snapped. Farree looked at the two ends for a moment and then he caught the girl by the shoulder and dragged her to the entrance of the shelter. Unfortunately, it was also apparent that she was in a very weakened condition, and had to hold to Farree or fall face downward. Yazz crowded in upon his right side, Togger once more in place on her back. The girl caught hold of a roll of the loose skin immediately around Yazz's neck and used that hold to balance herself, while Farree, making sure she could stand erect for a few moments, carefully pushed back the shelter curtain a slit to look out. They could hear the crackle of lasers and the night sky was lit by constant flashes—but the main part of the disturbance was some distance away. He wondered if Selrena or any of her winged crew had been caught in the vicious and deadly darting of the beams.

How had Togger and Yazz gotten there? Had they tracked him somehow clear across this country of which he himself was not sure? How had he gotten into the depths of Selrena's castle, by the way?

"Not here! Them Darda will claim anything, 'tis truth enough. But Fragon never built nothing for no one but his own self—"

The words in Farree's mind gave the impression of guttural sneering. Involuntarily his gaze fell from above to below. Beyond the next shelter bubble there was what seemed to be a well-like opening of dull black lying flat, only to be noted for a second or two when the firing above came near. A figure hunched on the lip of that and Farree was aware that the send came from there.

"Go!" Togger's urging was sharp enough nearly to touch another level of mind send.

Though he might be journeying from one trap into another Farree did not hesitate, but turned to pull the girl through the curtain. She was plucking at the transparent substance which covered her wings, without achieving any freedom. Grabbing her hand Farree propelled her toward that disc of darkness. The hunched figure arose to full height, proving as tall as Farree if one did not count the arch of wings overhead. From the glimpse Farree caught of him this was like the leader of that pack which had been traveling underground to attack Bojor. He longed for the strange rod he had lost when he had been captured, for any weapon to hand. From the shadow came a grate of what might be laughter but did not sound like honest mirth.

"Gonna get outta here, wingling? You gonna try up through that?" The underground dweller flung a hand high to indicate the sky, though the light was such that Farree could not tell how many of the flyers were still engaged. To rise into the midst of that Farree knew would be the same if not worse than going back into the shelter to wait spiritlessly whatever fate the enemy planned. He tried to see deeper into the hole, distrusting its size when he had to count on the folding of his wings.

Again that cackle of laughter while mind speech accompanied it. "Not winging will you be this time, wingling! Nor she neither. 'less she puts those flappers of hers down."

The girl was pulling once more at the edge of the transparent covering which held her wings pressed as tightly together as hands palm against palm.

There was little of the night left, Farree noted. Instead a distant greying of black sky suggested that dawn was close upon them. They must waste no time.

Though his hands were stiff and painful after his ordeal with the chain, Farree tried to help her tear off that covering. Then he caught up Togger. There might not be any more venom—nor could the smux have used it here—but his foreclaws still had their sawlike inner surfaces and these Farree put to use, holding Togger while the smux moved to open a hole in that tightly fastened length. Once that was breached it was easy enough to strip off the stuff in lengths, hurling it away from them.

"Make it quick, winglings!" The underground dweller had popped down into the hole but his mind speech still reached them. "We ain't gonna wait around for any of them Big Folk to come-a-lookin'. Get in here with you!"

Farree dropped Togger back with Yazz and steadied the girl beside him. He still dared not try mind send—with her; Yazz and Togger "talked" in another level of communication, at the very edge of what he could pick up. Maelen was better

at communication with all those she called "those little people
in fur," but his long connection with Togger made Farree able
to pick up the smux easily enough. The fact that somehow the
people of this ship were able to force the girl to talk to their
purposes kept him from attempting other channels—though
the send of the earth dwellers appeared much like Togger's on
a lower level.

He touched the girl's nearest wing even though the pain
in his now very stiff fingers made that a difficult gesture,
pushing gently at the edge to attempt the suggestion that she
fold them back. Perhaps she picked up the earth dweller's
order, she was flexing her wings, stiff from their long imprisonment, though she jerked and shook as if every move caused
her pain. But at length she got them as furled as Farree had
brought down his and, as she was ready to enter the hole, he
held her by the wrists to lower her. Yazz and Togger had
already gone in.

There was something of a drop; Farree had to lie belly
down until he felt her come to a stop and her fingers moved to
free themselves. Then he swung over hurriedly, having to let
himself fall until he plopped down on earth and smelled the
sour and musty odor which seemed to hang in these underground ways. There was a dull light some distance away
towards his left and Togger's send reached him again:

"Come—"

The passage was none too large and it must have been
recently dug, for his wings, as tightly folded as they were,
brushed clods of earth from both overhead and from the walls,
until he feared that the whole way might collapse on him. The
light was not stationary but ran ahead as he followed and he
guessed it to be some kind of a mobile torch in the hands of
one of their party.

Then he passed by a hollow in the side of the tunnel and
heard a whisper of stir there. He chilled. Though he was not
sure how he could be so sure of it, he was certain that in that

hollow, well within reach of him as he pushed hurriedly past, were the furred, leggy creatures who had opened the other way in order to attack Bojor in the valley of his ship.

There was a rustling behind and he called on his sense as strongly as he could. Yes, it was the burrow lurkers, but they were not trailing him as he had feared, rather scuttling back toward the hole which led to the camp. Surely they would be a surprise to any who would come after them, but also they might now be engaged in filling the entrance to this escape route.

Farree quickened his pace as best he could, his arm up and ahead of him to feel out anything which might catch on his wings. But he did not touch any of the tubers which had hung from the roof in that other way.

Twice the passage took an abrupt turn, and on the second one he caught up with the rest of the party, hardly more than shadows in the very weak light which came from a crooked stick carried by the one who had overseen all this rescue. His head, in that dim light, looked nearly too large for his body, and his forearms and legs, which were incompletely covered by dull grey-brown, skintight clothing, were nearer stick thin. The rest of his body was haired with coarse black and thick clumps of bristles. His nose was nearly a snout, for his mouth was very large and he had no visible chin. In some ways he looked rather like the animal-masked one Farree had seen in his dream. His ears were pointed and placed well up a naked skull, the ends of them curved over a little. Farree, who had seen many strange wayfarers during his days in the Limits and a-travel thereafter, thought that his ugliness well passed the common.

Having once made the escapees free of this secret way he paid no more attention to them, but stamped ahead flatfootedly, leaving them to follow or not as they would.

The girl was behind Yazz, and she kept hold on Yazz's waving tail as if she needed touch with some creature less disagreeable than their guide. There was no room here to push up closer, so Farree continued to bring up the rear. They passed walls now where the soil rained down and there were streaks of moisture showing. The earth dweller hastened by those spots and they had to hurry, Farree very uneasy at those signs of possible disintegration.

One more turn and their path was much brighter. Unconsciously they all speeded up once more toward that and so they came out into a place so different from the cramped ways down which they had come that Farree stopped short, once he was through a break in the wall, just to stare about him.

16.

The light was as brilliant as the full day's shine but not steady. As the lasers had flashed in the air earlier, here also shot shafts of rainbow glitter. He might have been back in that crystal castle of his first dreaming.

Only here the crystals were untamed. They had not been quarried or shaped by any will save their own. Great, sharp-pointed spikes stood taller than Farree, sprouting from the rock as if they had grown like trees. Some were as clear as mountain water save that they cut the light into rainbows. Others were footed in color—amethyst, clear yellow, smoke-silver. In the midst of this vast cave or hall there were many of grey but these were murky, not silver, resembling the ball, the Globe of Ummar, which had splintered.

These alone showed that they had been worked upon for a purpose. They were packed together, flat sides uppermost, a wall of high points at the back of a level stretch on which someone was seated.

The earth dweller who had led them here forged ahead, but those he had guided remained just within the entrance of this place of colored light, dazzled by its brilliance. Their guide shambled on, to stand at the foot of the piled crystals which had been fitted to serve as a seat—or a throne—

He bowed low and then looked up into a face—

Not a face, Farree thought, the chill once more upon him, but rather a countenance close to a skull, even if there was yellowish skin laid across the thrusting bone. The eye holes were not empty; there were tightly drawn lids across their sharp edges. And the skin on the two hands resting on flanking crystals was deeply wrinkled, showing long nails, curved beyond the ends of the fingers as might claws, all emblazoned by a bright scarlet which the play of the crystal light could not disguise.

The rest of the figure was muffled in a grey robe which did not look as if it were of material substance, but rather as if an armful of haze had been pulled about a skeleton body. Between the knees of the enthroned one was the massive hilt of a sword and at the hidden feet lay a skull, this one far larger than that of any man Farree had ever seen. Struck well into the dome of bone was the point of the sword—the device which had been so plainly displayed in the castle where Selrena had had her lurking place.

At the same time he noted that, Farree was aware of what might be the first stroke of a very strange battle—the throb of an invading mind send.

"Glasrant." That one word pierced his head as the sword pierced the skull before the seated one. There was a stirring, a pushing—such pain as he could not have imagined before strove to split his head open. Through the tears gathering in his eyes and running down his cheeks Farree saw that those tightly drawn eyelids were no longer flat and closed. Somehow they had vanished and, as he staggered forward to answer an unvoiced command his gaze was caught and tight held by what lay in the dark pits so uncovered: cores of flame, red, yellow, near white-hot— They reached into his head, hunted, sought, appraised, dropped aside as without value, summoned what the mist-robed one wanted and formed that into something which could think, and thinking, hear again.

"You were dead," observed the robed one.

"I was not dead." Farree felt as if some other had taken over his body, his mind. "Your earth grubbers were not thorough, Fragon. Then there was Malor—you were not well served, Fragon."

He kept his feet by sheer will; there was a burning hell of released thought and memory, which strove to carve more room that it might fill its proper place again.

"Ah, yes, Malor. One must often be reduced to using tools which are flawed." Now the skeleton's red-nailed hands met and bore down on the sword hilt. If that gesture measured some emotion it was not echoed on the skin-and-bone face in which only the fire of the eyes was alive.

"So Malor did not gain by his treachery?" There was a face in Farree's mind—sculptured to resemble his own, so much so he might have been the other's son—or brother?

"For a season he profited," Fragon said indifferently. "As a quas fruit he had that much. Then there was a naming and challenge; he thought himself invincible. The learning otherwise took but a short space. Quaffer had the better of a yield flight."

"And what then happened to Quaffer?" Farree asked as in his mind a second face formed, one for which he held no liking.

"Quaffer was a fool!" That answer had not come from the dead-alive Darda on his smoky crystal throne, but from one Farree had forgotten, the girl.

She must have followed him, for now she drew level with him, her eyes also on the Dark Darda.

"Quaffer was a fool." Agreement rang in Farree's mind.

"Fools and knaves, they rise like scum on a meat pot when it is set boiling. Quaffer made a pact with those of the Cursed Ones who had discovered this world. It was he who bought their aid with an offering—you, Glasrant. They sought you the world around. After that star ship rose from the earth, Quaffer swore you dead of the Cursed Ones' malice when the Bright Lady and the Sword Lord threatened him with a coat of iron.

"Yes, youngling, there was a blooding of many shields and a tramping of feet after that. For that the Cursed Ones would return, as was their fashion, all knew; and this time it had been sworn by Light and Dark, Night and Day, Sun and Moon, that we of the Folk, Darda, Winglings, Hodlins, Wisser, Thorm, and Wend, would swear a pact to hold, though there be bad blood 'twixt clan and clan, folk and folk. Still that would be forgot until our time of the last trial would come. Thus we have wrought what we could since the Cursed Ones did come again. Now you appear, Glasrant, and from a star ship with Cursed Ones—" There was a pause.

Farree found himself thinking of Maelen and Vorlund, of Zoror, and of what they had meant to him since his escape from the Limits. His other memories, those that almost vicious unlocking had doomed him to, he pushed away.

Fragon leaned forward a little, his hands on the sword hilt supporting him.

"They know—" He shaped those two words as if he chewed upon something which he found as bitter as the poison of Togger's claws. "These know!"

It was the girl who swung half around to stare at Farree. Her fine greenish skin did not disguise a flush, even as her anger burned him along the send between them.

"You—" she began when Fragon's heavier and clearer send cut over to drown hers out.

"No, Atra, Glasrant has not played your role. You who have been the Cursed Ones' bait can lay no such guilt on him."

Her flush grew deeper and then faded, leaving her cheeks

so pallid that Farree guessed she was deep stricken. Then her head drooped and all touch with her was gone.

However, Fragon was not yet done with her. "So, sky dancer, you wish to deal a blow with what you believe to be truth but cannot face such yourself? It seems that Glasrant has found something anew—that there are those of the Cursed Kind which court our trust. The one who is scaled, even as the wisser, the two might be Darda, they have brought you here. But the treasure they have come seeking is not to be ripped from our earth, strained from our rivers, lakes, and seas; instead it is found within skulls!" The hilt of the sword moved in his hands and appeared to dig even farther into the skull.

"There is a very old saying which has come out of the far mists of even our time, which is very long as the Cursed Ones reckon it. And that is—we who share an enemy may stand together without hindrance, even though not all of us are of one race, one species. These who have come with you, Glasrant, perhaps are part of some such a pact."

The girl's head rose again. "Those from the stars all carry the curse."

"Say you so? Now let us see." On the rack of bones which under the mist robe marked his shoulders Fragon's head swung a fraction; he was looking beyond her to the opposite side of the carven hall.

Selrena strode between the up-pointing crystals. There was a reddened line along her arm, and on the tight silvery garment, which covered near all her body except for her arms, were blotches of dull black. Behind her came two others, a little taller than she, one the man Vestrum, who had faced Farree in the room of the crystals, and the other that cloaked one who wore a bristle-rooted mask—the face hiding the one of Farree's dream.

Behind these three there was a gathering of others, each keeping with those of a like kind. Here was a winged lord who had wings of red, and those whose pinions were as dusky as twilight on a starless night. Behind the masked one shambled creatures such as the earth dweller who had brought them here, and others varying in size; four at least were tall enough that they had continually to duck to escape from striking down-pointing crystals. Vestrum had two of the small flutists capering behind him, piping as if to set all dancing, and three ladies, tall as Selrena, their flowing hair red-gold, and their robes girdled and looped with wreaths of flowers no wider than ribbons.

"You called." It was the Beast Mask's harsh voice which rang out, as he was the first by a few steps to find a place before the crystal throne. And he made no obeisance to Fragon, though those of his hideous and motley following all bowed to the Dark One.

"And you have chosen to come." Fragon did not speak—he thought that. However, it would seem that Beast Mask did not choose to follow that form of communication, for he spoke again. Farree did not feel it queer that he could understand. He was assured by Fragon's very presence, by his own, that here he had once a place, and tatters of memory which might never reweave gave him power he had not yet tried to understand.

"You are free—" Selrena spoke, not to Farree but directly to the girl. "There is"—she held the fingers on her right hand wide and came up to Atra, setting her hand so on the crown of the winged girl's head—"is, however, something of *Them* about you." Her fingers burrowed into the girl's matted hair and Atra gave a small cry of pain, wavering where she stood. Farree turned, caught and held her. Out of her hair Selrena had drawn what looked like a very loosely woven cap of thin wire. It was held tight knotted and she had to tear it free, each tug of her fingers bringing a gasp from Atra. Selrena threw it from her with the gesture of one who had held foulness.

It struck the pavement and Fragon studied it for a long moment. He nodded to the earth dweller who had been their guide. The creature aimed a kick with one of his outsize feet, setting the circlet spinning until it brought up against one of the smoky crystals which helped to support Fragon's throne. There was a flash of light bright enough to be seen even in this place of many lights. Nothing was left of the cap but a wad of smoking metal.

"Ahhhhh—" Atra's hands threaded through her hair back and forth. She might have been seeking some other bond which held her. Her wings expanded, brushing Farree back and away. They swelled and small silvery designs were visible along them as they moved. Head held high she looked to Selrena.

"Thanks to you, Lady. What debt does Langrone now owe you—or is there still any Langrone kin to offer such? I saw many fall to the mutilating knife and their blood guilt rests on me—for some I called to their torment, being captive to *Them!*"

"True enough." Beast Mask faced her, and there was nothing but coldness in his or her harsh voice. "There is more than one debt, Daughter of Langrone, since it was Noper here who had you go forth—"

The creature who had led them showed a row of yellow fangs in what might be a smile.

"Not so!" That was the lord of the red wings. "Come the inner ways perhaps she did, but it was this one of her own kind who had her go forth." He nodded to Farree who noted that the winged people were edging away from any contact with the strange beings who followed Beast Mask.

"Have done!" It was not a roar of a voice but one which cut through the mind like a blow, and Farree was sure he was not the only one to receive the force of that order. "This is no time to remember old troubles between our people. Glasrant brought her forth from the first bondage. Sharp Nose sent to him those who served him well. It was a thing done together. It is of more importance that Glasrant tell us what may come from this other ship which brought him— Who are these slave dealers, Son of Langrone? And what new injuries do they think to deliver here?"

Farree shook his head violently. "No injuries—they brought me—"

"For bait!" hissed someone among Beast Mask's company.

"No." It was Farree's turn to sweep his hands across his aching head. That wall within his mind may have been shaken, shattered in places, but still all he could remember came in faded bits and patches as if he looked upon some chronicle in Zoror's collection which had been half destroyed by damp and the nibbling of insects. He knew that it was true he was of the winged people who stood in companies here, and that he had been handed over to smugglers by one of his own people who wished the power Farree, once an adult, might claim. He had an instinctive dislike for Fragon, as if he sniffed now and then some foul odor which puffed from the mist robe. Also he was wary of Selrena and the black-winged ones which made up her escort. But even now he could remember so little—

Selrena must have been following his thoughts. "What you remember—do!"

That was an order Farree discovered he must obey. He began with the misty half life he had led in the Limits, coming into clarity only with the death of the spacer who had kept him in bondage and his own escape. The dangerous days which followed were so much alike in the constant peril which they offered that they were a single blur of misery, in which only his tie with Togger made one small patch of light. Then there was the coming of Maelen and Vorlund and the seeming miracle that they cared enough to lift him out of the foul mud of the Limits and admit him into the tight circle of their friendship.

There came the voyage to Yiktor and the meeting with the Thassa after the Guild had made its move to take them over. When he thought of the Thassa and of Maelen's people there was, for the first time, a stir among those who listened, who read from the pictures in his memory. It was Vestrum who broke through what was nearly a trance in which Farree spilled out the past.

"These Thassa—of what world are they? From whence do they come? And what powers have they?"

"Why not ask that of they themselves?" Selrena countered. Those who followed her broke apart to form a pathway and down that came Maelen, the flickering lights of the crystals seeming to center about her slender body in the sober-colored space covering, making it resemble the robe of one who was equal to Selrena or perhaps more than the Darda. At her shoulder walked Vorlund and he, too, appeared kin to the Darda, as powerful in his way as Vestrum. While behind the two was Zoror looking eagerly from right to left as if to crowd into memory every small detail of the scene.

Maelen and the two with her made a small gesture to Fragon, no more than they would have used in greeting one of their own kind with whom they had little to share. But Maelen smiled at Selrena and raised her two hands before her, her fingers moving in intricate patterns as if she wrote some message on the air.

For the first time Farree saw an odd expression on the Darda's face—a trace of confusion. Vestrum stepped to her side and his eyes were intent on the off-worlder. One of his small flute-playing creatures made a sudden quick movement, squatting down before his feet between him and Maelen.

From its pipe there arose a thread, thin, sweet-noted air. Maelen listened for a breath or two. Then from her own lips there came a song without words, note matching the note of the player. Wonderment was on Vestrum's face. Selrena's hands moved of themselves, her fingers lifting and falling to the measure of that wordless song.

Among those who were winged there was a stirring, a

fanning of pinions as if they would take off to the spaces above Fragon's seat, though none of them did. In Farree there was also an answer—a lightness of heart such as he had not felt since they had started this venture. He found a hand slipping into his and he knew that Atra also was making her own answer to the weaving of this spell. Only Fragon, the beast-masked one, and his crooked company did not move. The faces of some of them were screwed up into masks as ugly as that their leader wore.

"You are—of the Blood!" Vestrum spoke first when the piper was finished and Maelen's own song died away. "Of the lost ones, the far travelers who are apart!"

"I am Thassa," she answered him. "My people are so old that we have forgotten our far past. Long ago we put aside what we had held to—settled homes, land, save for riding over it, possessions, all which had weighed down our spirits. We cut ties with the past—seeking only that which would give us life with the Little Ones—knowledge which brought good, not harm—"

"You are of the Blood!" Vestrum repeated. "And of the Lost Ones! We are few here. There only half a hundred of us left. And of those many have withdrawn into worlds they have created where they choose to be gods, or heroes, or"—he looked to Fragon and then away again—"devils. We age with weariness and the knowledge that wherever we go *They* will follow to bring their deaths and their ills, and, at last, all destruction of what we know. Do you now take to the stars and seek distant kin? If so, you have succeeded—I will say that you are of the Blood!"

"Of the Blood," Selrena echoed him, "but, I think of a different path. You have power but never have you used it to the full—" Her head was up and her dark eyes seemed to grow ever the larger. "You have chosen another way. And"—she hesitated—"perhaps your choice has brought greater content than we have known. What do you with *Them* when they come?"

"We live apart, and because we have no treasure and because we walk another road, we have lived without darkness for long and long. Now there are others who have set up laws that none may be troubled if they live in peace." Maelen looked to Fragon. "What is your peace, my lord? Rule by your order alone? And you"—she turned her head slowly that her gaze could go around the half circle—"until those from off-world came was there peace here?"

Farree remembered the skeletons of the dark ways and that room of shadowy horror through which he had gone.

"We have had our disputes." Fragon made answer first. "Of such ploys there always comes an end. One tires even of power. This I shall say first, I of whom much ill has been said and perhaps with truth. There comes a time when one has fulfilled every wish, answered every desire. Then"—his grasp of the skull-piercing sword must have shaken a fraction for there was a clatter from it—"one is as nothing." Now he deliberately rattled the skull by twisting the hilt of the sword back and forth. "*They* have found us and with us they have played games—setting one against another as they have done countless times before. There are old hatreds which they aroused on their coming. Why not"—it was plain that he spoke to the others behind Maelen—"give them what they want—we are done—"

"That is not the truth." Zoror's slightly lower mind band came alive. "Never yet has one door been closed that another does not wait the unlocking—"

"So?" Fragon asked. "You are not of them, nor of the Blood, or else our records are not complete. What part of this do your people play?"

"We gather knowledge, hunt for the beginnings—"

"On the belief that the ends may be better marked?" Vestrum locked eyes with the Zacanthan and stood still as if they were now bound together. Then he added: "What are you that you can see so far into others? You are—"

"A Zacanthan."

Farree knew that these were claiming him, and that perhaps those he had been comrades with were acknowledging that claim. However, at this moment, he felt no comradeship with those others with wings, though he had sought such ever since his own had broken out of their casing.

"We search for knowledge."

"Knowledge can cut two ways—" began Selrena when, for the first time, Fragon loosed hold on the sword hilt. His talon-fingered hand arose to make a small gesture which ended Selrena's speech almost in mid-word. "Knowledge is never to be neglected. Tell us, hunter of the lost, what do we face now? For out of past roots grow present troubles."

"What you and your kin have faced before." Zoror nodded. "You have said here that, though you have not been friends in the past, you have now drawn together—"

"Drawn together?" Atra said, her voice high, almost shrill, as she interrupted. "Ask those who winged out of Burdenholm at a sending for an ingathering how that drawing followed! Well did the Earlier Ones name you in-cursed, Fragon!"

"You see"—the ancient Darda did not reply to her challenge, rather he continued to speak to the Zacanthan—"there is little upon which we may build anything which approaches true comradeship. The Langrone are near wiped from our history as we make it now. It is true that there was treachery and ill dealing which began that. This one"—now that free hand pointed to Farree himself—"can be witness to that, even though the memory was near burned from his mind. He is in truth Glasrant and right lord to those same Langrone who are near gone. All happened to him because there was a settling of blood between two who held false honor above the good of all. And Atra who speaks so plainly now, she also has been used as a weapon against her own kind—but not by any will of ours, wingling, earthling, or Darda.

"These Cursed Sky-Riding Ones who have made near a quarter of our world a place of blood and killing—always have they followed after us from world to world. They turn against us the metal which burns and various powers of their own, born in turn of artifacts they make of that same iron. Our wits they can rift from us—Atra can witness that. They fight with fire and all we can do is to call on skills such as we have long known and make what defenses we can. At this hour we do stand together, power with power, that we may not be mown down apart and have no defense at all.

"Now you come also from the star ways and you are not as *They*, for you have that in you which is far nearer kin to us. You brought hither Glasrant and him we have read—to know that in you is found none of the poison that *They* use to besoil all they touch. There are three of you and you are of different races— You, Lady"—he spoke now to Maelen—"are of a people we can call kin after a fashion. And he"—now Vorlund was indicated—"is also of a mind with you, though he is not born of your blood, and within might be one of *Them*. And you, Zacanthan, have no malice in you toward us, only wonder and pleasure at finding our kind. So we are not enemies, though we may not be friends—"

Vestrum shifted a little. "Words upon words, Fragon! You summoned us hither for deeds. We had Selrena and her winglings go up against these enemies by mind will alone, impressing upon *These* who slay without mercy the phantoms which can be summoned by mind—"

"True," Selrena cut in. "Have we not spent too long a time on words? While Atra was with them we had no chance to attack, for she would have known and by their trickery must have given us away. So when that one"—she nodded at Farree—"was near within our hands we had no trouble closing fingers upon him, and using him as a key to open Atra's prison—as he did very well. Now what do we next? Once more summon up ghosts of ourselves to ride the sky? There is little ghosts can do and already we know that *They* have doubts about us. So, I say again, Fragon, Vestrum, and also"—she indicated the Beast Mask,"what do we do?"

Fragon spoke directly now to Maelen. "What do we do?" He repeated the question.

17.

"What do we do?" Fragon had asked of Maelen. Perhaps he had not expected her to produce an answer, but she did.

Farree—he could not yet think of himself under that other name they had called him, nor even wholly accept that he was a part of their race—lay belly down on a rock ledge. His outspread wings were the same color as the lichen which grew in patches among the stones here, and now served him as disguise. Togger squatted just under the edge of the right wing. The smux's sight could not reach as far as his own, but Farree was aware that Togger was using all his own senses to the highest alertness.

Behind the two were others of the winglings whose natural pinions were of a color to blend in with the rocks—there grey patched with silver, and the darker ones who had accompanied Selrena. What they spied upon was the off-world ship and the small temporary settlement by its fins.

It was well into afternoon and there had been a great deal

of activity down there to be observed. Three days ago several of the spacers had tried to take the path underground in search of their freed captives, only to discover that most of it had fallen in; after a few feet not even its course could be traced.

They had taken to the air also. The repairs on their flitter had been speeded up so that it could continue to carry laser-armed patrols out over the surrounding country in a gradually widening circle. Twice those Farree had met in the crystal cavern had summoned up the haze which was their most constant defense, only to have the flitter bore directly through it, seemingly unaware that there had been any blinding fog projected. They had not attempted another mass hallucination such as they had used to cover Atra's rescue.

It was plain from the probing Fragon and Maelen, two unlikely partners-in-arms, had used, that those in the camp were well guarded by devices which protected against either mind search or lasting illusions—the two ancient and tolerably efficient weapons of the People.

Nor could they compete physically. Swords and force-charged wands, the other arms which were theirs and had been for untold generations, could not stand against lasers, tanglers, even discordant sound. When the latter had blasted out of the camp earlier that day most of the winglings, the Darda, and several others of the old stock had been rendered helpless for awhile. Only those born of the earth who had immediately retreated underground kept their full senses. Then Zoror had loosed a small shape like a winged tube. That, arching up above the waiting ship and its camp, had blasted back, as a mirror might return a reflection, the same ear-piercing sound, drawing it up the scale as if each note were threaded on a cord and jerked out of reach.

In answer they had seen the men spill out into the opening, staggering here and there, hands pressed over their ears, some stumbling to their knees and then falling forward to roll across the ground, plainly in agony. At length some one of the enemy regained sense long enough to shut off their own broadcast and the ensuing silence was like that of death, so complete was it.

The spying party, in hiding along the upper reaches of the great valley in which the ship had set down, revived sooner than the opposition. While Farree and his companions stirred and came back to themselves, at least three limp bodies had been toted into the largest of the ground shelters and several others had made a difficult business of getting back to the ship itself.

It was not much later that the flitter had taken off and began to fly its spy circles around and around, each one farther than the one before. That the invader might be equipped with detectors was a point Farree considered when he had witnessed the first flight. They had had Atra long enough to run a sensor on her, set her pattern as part of the "memory" of such a machine. Thus any of her own species could be instantly detected when caught on the flitter screen. That the enemy did not coast down the wind and spray them all with laser fire as they lay in hiding was something which Farree himself could not understand. He cringed flatter to the ground—his fingers digging deep into the soil as if he were an earthling used to disappearing quickly from sight into that sanctuary.

Atra herself was up in the heights with Maelen and Fragon, submitting to their examination of her mind sense as they sought any traces of future attack which might have been placed within her, as a buried and unpleasant form of weapon, providing she did execute an impossible escape. Farree did not envy her that; he had too many times in the past undergone such delving into what was a sealed portion of his own mind.

If the invaders had taken a reading of Atra, it must have been too closely turned to her own personality to serve now to locate any of her own species. The flitter was already on a much farther circling out and had not slackened flight speed when it had crossed the place of concealment where his own party lay in wait.

Those three giants who had come into the crystal cave in the company of Beast Mask had left hours ago to tramp back with Vorlund to his ship, their supply of strength meant to transport certain equipment which both Krip and Zoror had selected for this voyage. Nothing had been chosen which would not be permitted for use on a primitive world—if this, which the first comers had named Elothian, might be termed primitive. The People had long ago set up their own defenses, recalled lessons from their history, to make as secure as possible this new world. Their inability to handle heavy metals, especially iron (Farree need only look at the bandages on his own hands covering burns the chain of Atra's captivity had left to understand what damage even that could cause) had handicapped them always when facing off-worlders.

The crystals of the caverns they had uncovered here had provided an array of weapons as deadly as lasers. Only lasers could kill at a distance far beyond that which any of the people could send elfshot, small needle-shaped and sharp fragments of the dusky spikes, which buried themselves within flesh, eventually causing clouded and diseased minds. There were other weapons, mostly mind linked. Those again required a careful assessing of the mental strength of the enemy; but Atra had been under such control while in the off-worlders' hands that now she brought her people a clear picture of their powers.

Zoror was prowling the upper heights—a good distance away. Equipped with a beamer suited to a Zacanthan's greater strength, he was busy sealing up any way through which the People's own holdings could be invaded, except from the air.

The Zacanthan might be so engaged physically but Farree was sure that mentally Zoror was busy in a different direction, that of searching his vast memory for anything of the past which could be turned into good use in this present. As for Farree himself—

He stared at the scene below, now so familiar with it from hours of observation that he was sure he would never forget so much as the curve of each and every one of the shelters. There had been lookouts before him and what they had learned from this intent study of the territory was little enough.

That the beacon which had lighted the scene at his first coming was a recent addition to the scene he understood quickly. This ship was, in the opinion of Vorlund and Zoror, but a scout for a larger force. The nose beam from the ship was set each night as a guide to lead that force in.

To have the invaders thus reinforced would be the end of any successful defense—that was already understood. Thus— the beacon would have to be taken care of, and that was Farree's part. His answer to that pillar of light in the night rested now just under the curve of his wing—a flat box slightly larger than one of his bandaged hands.

Vorlund had spent nearly the whole of a day fashioning what was inside, helped by a pair of misshapen earth dwellers who worked metal in fire with the ease of those who were master smiths. They had looked at the pictures the spacer had drawn, listened intently to a jabber of firm instruction from Beast Mask, leader of those dark dwellers—who were of a devious and often treacherous turn of mind. Metal had gone into it, but that was silver poured from clay ladles, and thin streams of gold fed into narrow tubes of clay, to be later hammered and twisted into wire near as thin and supple as thread.

Months ago, the winged race among the People had discovered, at a bitter price, that to approach the camp by air was folly. There were various disturbances invisibly cutting the air about the ship able to paralyze wings, dashing the flyers to their deaths; or else, if those wings were to be harvested, bringing them immobile and helpless to the ground where another form of death waited. However, all such flights— and there had been very few of them after their end was witnessed—had occurred only when the winglings had reck-lessly soared out over the shelters or that part of the ship which was open at a high altitude.

Farree's body now was fitted with two wide belts. On each were seamed pockets into which Vorlund had fitted more small devices he had urged the smiths to make in haste. In the seven days since their meeting in the hall of crystals, they had all been driven by that need for haste. For how long would it be before that beacon would lead in larger forces?

Their one bid for victory depended on so many ifs—*if* Farree could indeed penetrate the air above the enemy encampment successfully undiscovered, *if* he could affix the device he carried to the proper place on the ship, *if* it would really work. All was founded on hope and the best that memory could supply from the observations and lore of the People, the encyclopedic recall of Zoror, the ship knowledge of Vorlund, born to be a star rover, and of Maelen and the Dardas, who had drawn together as they never had in the history of their colony on Elothian. So many *ifs*, Farree thought, but perhaps their only chance now. He watched the slow coming of sunset and his body ached with the strain of waiting.

The flitter swung back at the coming of the dark, landed in the twilight not far from the ramp of the ship. Those who manned the smaller ship, four of them, clambered out—three heading for the shelters and a single one trotting up the ramp into the ship. Farree rose to his knees and Togger gave a short leap, to burrow in beneath his jerkin. Farree sensed the tension of those who remained in hiding about him. There had been neither the time nor the proper material to equip the rest of them with the hereto untried method of defense he wore. However, they had their own duties and were already taking wing, to establish the trap which would be the next defense.

Between two of the night-winged leaders hung a netted bag and what weighed it down was bait. Piled in it were vessels and ornaments of gold and silver wrought by smiths who delighted in setting crystals where they made the bravest show. They had already learned from Atra, as well as from reports of some of the groundlings who had gone spying on their own, that the invaders equated the People not only as raw material for their trade (when they could rip free the wings of the dying) but also with a strong tradition that all the People were guardians of treasure. To this Zoror gave credence, saying that such stories were an integral part of many tales he had ferreted out.

There was a place where a bank overcurbed a stream, the flood waters of which had cut away a large bite of soil. There the "treasure" was to be half hidden, a piece or two dropped into the shallows of the water itself, waiting for the invaders to spot. Selrena had overseen this part of their preparations and would be moving now into place at the foot of the rise where Farree was poised for take off. She had reports from the groundlings as to the invaders who slept outside the ship. Two such she had selected her own prey. They would have dreams this night, for she had been testing her ability to sow hallucinations by subtle mental touch. As she had led the supposed entry of the airborne attack wholly by projected images, so she could reach any of these below by a dream. The "reality" of the dream would enforce itself most strongly on certain temperaments, and both Vorlund and Maelen believed that such temperaments were to be found here. Two down there would dream vividly tonight, so vividly that they would be swept into action with the coming of the morning. Also, they might strive to conceal that action, being who and what they were.

Farree was airborne now, the device he was to plant on the ship clasped tightly against his breast with both hands (Togger crept up to cling just beneath Farree's chin) as he climbed steadily into the cold of the upper night air and moved out towards that beam of light which had already burst from the nose of the ship, spear-straight up through gathering clouds. He winged forward in desperation, not knowing if he would be beaten from the air by some silent defense. Even though that attack did not come in the first few moments when he was out in the open over the edge of the camp, still he could not be sure that his flight was not being recorded by some intricate device below.

He must come up against the outer shell of the ship well below where that beacon sprang. Now he held firm in mind the information Vorlund had drilled into him. The spacer who had voyaged in star ships almost since birth knew well the danger spots and where a ship could best be assaulted.

Farree's fingers caught in the rim of a small port used for the workmen during an overhaul. There was no hope of his gaining entrance here. All such places must be under spy screen since the night of the escape. But this was the guide for him and he had reached it with no sign that he had been sighted by any of the sentries the invaders must have on duty here. If he could have dared mind send he would have been better content—touching any foreign thought patterns would have been warning. Only he must go blind.

He pulled himself up with one hand and now his toes found a small resting place on the nearly invisible seam which marked the door. One of those discs on his belt gave a sudden jerk forward and planted itself tightly to the surface of the closed port.

There were small surges of heat about his bare feet. The fabric of the ship was indeed not cold iron, that deadly metal, but there was enough of it in the alloy forming the surface to make itself felt. He forced the pain to the back of his mind and brought out the case he carried, slipping the cord about its top between his teeth so he could use both hands.

At the same instant the warning came that he was indeed being picked up by some alarm. A trickle of jumbled thought whipped across his mind. Farree clung to the almost invisible seam of the hatch and frantically edged upward as that questing picked and prodded the natural thought defense he had developed.

He slapped the narrow box against the surface of the ship, perhaps the length of his body below its nose. It instantly became so closely a part of the surface that nothing could free it—or not without a lengthy period of careful work with tools, which time those here did not have. Even as the box welded itself to the wall, a touch of Farree's forefinger activated what lay within. Farree pushed back and away, his wings beating almost frantically as he tried to put distance between him and that which he had brought.

He was away from the ship, even past the circle of shelters, when the device Vorlund had labored on blew. Flame torched through the sky, rising to join with the beam of the beacon. That went out abruptly, and Farree heard a roar. There followed a second outburst which might have singed one wing had he not, in his dread, flipped sidewise, no longer in a direct pattern of flight outward from the camp.

Below there arose a clamor. Two laser spears cut the air, which made his body quiver so he near lost the firm beat of the wings which bore him. However, the lasers lanced the air far enough off that Farree believed that he had not been detected, that they had been unaimed, fired only as the result of fear.

He was away, flying with desperate wing beats in the direction of the place where he had hidden during the day. He passed over that, to flash on into a place of broken rock pillars which guarded one cave entrance to the lower ways in which there lay the hall of crystal, their agreed-upon meeting place when this piece of action lay behind. Farree alighted at the mouth of that cave and smelt the mouldy stench which told him at least one of the underground people was present. He did not go forward, but wheeled about to look out toward the ship.

The beacon might be gone but there was still light about

the nose, hazy as if there were clouds of fire roiling about. Still he could catch now and then clear sight of a splotch of true incandescence which must be cutting itself into the ship's skin immediately below the level of the control cabin.

Such vagabond and wandering spacers as this company carried with them means for some repairs, but Farree believed that the hurt this ship had taken could not be mended by any improvised work as the crew was trained to do. Vorlund himself had learned by default—helping to keep other lone ships flightworthy—just what would do the most harm, which also could be delivered by the materials as were at his disposal.

There was a far-off sound which could have been caused by the hungry flame, or perhaps by the voices of a number of men raised in wild shouts. As if in answer, the dark clouds overhead, which bore a reflection of the fire, massed the tighter and then released such a pelting of rain and earth-tearing force of wind that Farree pushed back into the cave, knowing that with wings wet through he could not hope to fly, however much he wanted to join with those winglings who had gone to set the trap, or else beat an air path to where Maelen and the ancient Darda had gone, to an almost forgotten lookout within the body of a mountain.

There came a snarl out of the dark behind him and the stench grew stronger.

"Wingling"—the word was spat like a curse—"get you out of the path—we are not afraid of wind and wet even though you may be."

Farree folded his wings as tightly as he could and edged against the wall to his left. His eyes, still somewhat dazzled, took time to adjust and twice he was prodded by a sharp elbow as a groundling crowded by. He did not count them but he was sure that there were quite a number, and he wondered what was taking them out into the storm. That some of the Darda were supposed to be weatherworkers, that much he did know. But there was purpose in this gathering he did not understand—not that more than the bare skeleton of what was to be done this night *had* been told him. What had been important for him to know was his own part and that seemed now to be over.

In the dark there was no sighting where the groudlings went, nor did he, he decided, have any particular desire to learn. He hated invading their odorous hole any further but he was bound for the appointed place of assembly so he went slowly along a way which sloped inward. Here and there one of the tubers gave light which revealed hardly more than the area immediately around it. As long as he could see those pallid spots ahead he was more willing to walk a way his whole nature detested.

Togger's head wriggled from the front of his jerkin and the stalked eyes of the smux were advanced to their greatest length, revolving slowly as if to make very sure of their surroundings.

Farree rubbed his hands together. The pain of the iron burns lingered on though ill-bane salve had been lavishly applied under the adhesive leaf bandages Selrena used. He thought of the Darda—three only of that race had he seen, unless whoever hid behind the beast mask was also of that company. Fragon had commented that they were very few.

How many of his own kind—winglings—still existed? Those who were of his clan, or the clan claimed for him, had apparently been near wiped out by the invaders. The other clans had not been so devastated, for the fate of the Langrones had come upon them soon after the enemy had finned down. Since the winged race were widespread over territories they claimed, most of their co-species had managed to escape, save for a few surprised when they returned to their territories by crossing the ravaged land of their sometime kin.

It had been easy enough to understand that the People had been divided among themselves when the off-world danger had struck. He himself had been of some importance, not for himself but because of the state of kinship he could claim. However, he had, at the same time, been practically defenseless, condemned to the ground until his wings were fully grown. While he was so helpless, Farree gathered from the scraps Fragon, Selrena, and Atra gave him, he had been a victim of jealousy among his own people. His father, who had led the Langrone, had been brought down during the clan-species dispute which had flared between his people and the groundlings (due to some incitement on Fragon's part for what reason Farree could not guess). He, Farree, had then been taken into captivity by the Museyons, night dwellers and hunters of the dark, answerable—sometimes—to Beast Mask but mainly going their own crooked ways.

From them he had been freed temporarily by a traitor—brother kin to his father and sour-blooded because the rule had not passed to him. Naively the traitor had attempted to bind the star invaders to his cause and had delivered Farree in turn into their hands, hoping so to remove him in such fashion that his trail could not be traced.

Those of the ship Farree had just attacked had not been the first to fin in here—there had been earlier ships. The first one had had none of the defenses which had rendered this one and its crew so formidable. That earlier crew had been made free of some treasure; in fact a "safe-hole" of groundlings who were considered Langrone enemies had been betrayed. But that treasure had been hardly won. Star-based men had died, and, in turn, burrows of groundlings had been stormed, their owners trapped and slain. So that at last, having in turn suffered a loss of nearly half the crew, the ship rose again, with its hard-won cargo, determined to return better equipped for the tearing of the last scrap of precious metal or new-found gem from one-time owners.

How he, Farree, had come into the Limits with Lanti, reduced by drink and graz chewing to a sodden wreck unable to get another berth, was part of the memory which still eluded him. Not that any of that mattered. This was history as far removed from him as Yiktor from the earth into which he was advancing steadily downward. There had been another visit here of an off-world ship, and that had stayed for some time. Traps had been set—they had gathered captives—even one of the Darda. What they did with those they took none could discover, for their ship was blank to all mind probing. In fact the use of this talent could and had led to more captures— the invaders seemed able to home in on any trace of mind search.

Thus, unable to use what they had come to depend upon as one of their most important weapons—the power to contact mentally and even overcome the wills of others—they had realized that once more they had been overtaken by the old, old enemy and against off-worlders they no longer had much chance to win. They had been on Elothian for centuries, so free from the ancient menace that they had no longer had the knowledge nor the materials to prepare for another flitting. Here they must stay and face a losing fight. Furthermore they were not of one mind, for the groundlings considered that the invasion could not move against them—they had their ability to burrow and hide in places too remote for the invaders to follow, unless they were willing to creep or wriggle on their bellies through the dark, unable to stand against ambush. It was easier to battle winglings and the Darda castles. It had taken the fall of one of their cave cities, its inhabitants overcome by fumes from smoke released from balls of metal which had been brought back by some of the smiths, to bring the under-surface ones out against the enemy which thus became a common one.

That ship, too, had vanished in time. But the Darda had not released watch, nor had the winglings and the others. Their history was too plain—with the coming of such invaders their day of defeat was upon them, and there was nothing to do but wait for that to arrive.

Except this time there were other players. Farree thought of Maelen, of Vorlund, of the Zacanthan, who had the results of centuries of learning behind him. What of himself also? He was Langrone but more beside. Having survived the horrors of the Limits he had proven that there was a good measure of strength in him, while his journeying with Maelen and Vorlund had brought him knowledge his kind might never have gained before. Yes, he might not be Darda but neither was he pure wingling.

Before him burst the great light. He now moved more quickly into the chamber of crystals, eager to learn what he might of what the others had done.

18.

Fragon again occupied the throne of dusky crystal. He might not have moved since Farree had last seen him. There were others gathered about, some finding perches among the lighter crystal outgrowth. He saw Selrena seated so. Her head was upheld but her eyes were closed. On one side of her Maelen was also seated and she held one of the Darda's slim hands between the two of hers. Her eyes were open but there was a remoteness about her face which suggested that she had fastened thought elsewhere.

At their feet was Atra, so removed from the others of her race; they were clustered in a burst of color apart from the center of the cave chamber, their wings folded, their attention on the three they did not approach.

Well to the other side of Fragon's chosen seat stood the Beast Mask, but for the first time Farree saw that mask thrown back, to lie along the shoulders as a limp hood. The features so disclosed were not entirely unlike those of the

Darda, save that the skin was dark—greyish—like unto Fragon's, and this was no skull head. That dark skin was puffed and so distended on the cheeks that the eyes seemed very small and near hidden by the rolls of the unpleasant-looking flesh. There was no hair on the puffy ball of the head. Male or female? Farree could not be sure. He felt an instant disgust and beyond that—fear. This one was as powerful as Fragon in his or her own way.

The other Darda, Vestrum, and his flutist were missing. However, even as Farree stepped into the crystal lighting, so did Zoror enter from another angle. He laid down the power conductor which he had carried up the slopes and, doing so, noticed Farree first, beckoning to him. Of Vorlund there was no sign; perhaps his mission to their own ship was not yet finished.

Atra opened her eyes, meeting Farree's with a strong compelling stare as if she had been waiting for him. Farree paused. She edged away from Maelen and Selrena, to cross the cavern toward Farree and the Zacanthan. Her torn and filthy clothing had long since been changed for a short robe of creamy white, girdled with a mesh belt of silver into which had been set small gems of green-blue. A circlet of the same material held her hair in place at the nape of her slender neck.

Farree noted that in her coming to him she made a short detour which took her away from close contact with the other winglings, those whose wings pulsed, rose or blue or yellow. Nor did he escape picking up a flash of thought—just as he had found himself aloof from their company so, it would seem, she, too, had been placed in exile. That she had been released from any enemy mind bond, he was sure, or she would not have been here. However, the shadow of what had been done to her, and through her unto others, still wrapped her in.

There was a small flare of anger in Farree. He moved out from beside the Zacanthan and held out both his hands in a welcome he had not consciously meant until that moment. Her delicate hands, still dark with bruises and rent by seams of scratches, lay palm downward for a moment, resting on his, and into his mind sang words.

"Welcome. Greater that the Seven Deeds of Malfor has been yours! We thought that the days of the Thrice Named were gone." For the first time she glanced away, her eyes sweeping over those of the company which were the closest. "Tallen can we of the Langrone claim, and Asdir, Tullusa, and Rond. You have joined a high and fair company, kinsman!"

At those names, very faint and broken memories stirred in him. He shook his head.

"You do me too much honor, kinswoman. It was not my own powers that I used." His hands dropped from hers and went to his belt to indicate what the smiths and Vorlund had made for him. "The Langrone—" He hesitated. What would it be to her that that word did not mean kin to him—that it was but a name?

"A name, yes." The words were in his mind. "And perhaps only a name—for the clan is gone. See?" She nodded towards the winglings in their ranks. Then her hand went up and smoothed the edge of one of her own wings and he caught her meaning. That color was not to be seen among the others gathered here, save in his own pinions.

"Lanquar and Lis, Lystal and Loyn." When she beamed him those names he knew them even as he would have known something long set in his mind. "But Langrone have no more to answer, unless those by the Far Rim scattered in time. And of those how many were there?" She held up one hand between them and extended the very slender fingers, once and then again.

In his mind he saw what she had willed—a threatening mountain, rock bare and radiating from it a gloom which was a leaden weight upon the heart. If any of the kin had been driven or had fled despairingly there—

"They have not answered the call—"

Farree was startled by that other mind voice breaking in almost harshly upon his thoughts. It was a wingling who wore red-white wings, and he had left his own people to come to them. Farree could sense no congratulation, nothing but a forbidding chill in his words.

"If they come not at the Great Summons, then they are either dead or overshadowed by thought far and faint. You have no true kin, Glasrant."

"So do you wish it!" flashed Atra. "Who closed the upper flight to Amassa when she was heavy with child? Who sent forth the Doom Singers in that hour?"

"What had to be done, was done. Sometimes one dies for many—"

"That I have heard before." This roused Farree. "Was it not that very thought which this kin-sister"—his hand touched Atra's shoulder and almost he gasped, for that touch had united him with a source of warmth he had not known could exist: it had nothing of the burn of fire but was rather a caressing, a healing—"Was it not that same thought which held you all," he began again, "when this sister lay in the hands of *Them?*"

"As bait—" the other returned. "Better she had taken up the fire metal and wreathed around—"

Farree moved. He stood between Atra now and the chief of Lystal, another scrap of memory supplying him with a use for that name.

"Do you speak now, Qua, for all?" he asked, narrow-eyed. Though he still felt apart from these who appeared so like himself, he was also aroused that they seemed so uneager to welcome him either. That denial angered him even more. Granted that he was mind blind, so he could not remember when he had been gathered close into the circle of kinship, warmed and sustained by this whole world. Yet that was a loss which he pushed aside. Nor could he fit into any other clan!

But that was it, he knew suddenly. There were the Lanquar and Lis, Lystal and Lyon— He saw them standing there. However, save for Qua, none had approached, nor was there any welcome mind send from them. Only Atra—

His hand slid down her arm to the wrist and there his fingers closed as if it were a matter of utmost importance that he keep her here. As it had been on the ship when he had depended on Vorlund's device, here was it now—she only was his anchorage and that which he had sought could be found only with and by her.

"I speak—" Qua hesitated and there was a shadow of a frown on his handsome face; his folded wings stirred a fraction as if he would expand them and so employ all the stature he could command. "Yes, I speak for all. You have both been within the shadow, the very hold of *Them*. *They* have blinded and bound you—therefore shall we not always wonder whether there can be any trust placed with you henceforth?"

"You speak well, Qua." Atra smiled coldly. "Have you in truth matched words with Slitha of Lis, Usern of Lystal, and Cambar of the Loyn?"

All the gathering of winglings was watching them now. Farree knew that those others had been following all which was said by mind touch. There was a stir among them at Atra's naming of names. Again his remnants of memory gave him what he needed. He did not wait for Qua to answer that, but instead took the lead for himself.

"If you speak with one voice for all, Qua," he returned, "then put your fears to rest. This is not the first time Langrone has stood alone. Valfor bore green wings—and went to his brave ending because of that. However, we intend no ending. Langrone lives, under the ancient rule, as long as either of us flies—" He drew Atra a little closer. "If you covet our Two Plains and the river land, then take it, Qua. We shall not dispute you for them. But neither shall we be forgotten when the Great Summons goes forth at Year's Ending.

Remember that, Qua!" Farree now looked beyond the Lan-quar to the others who were waiting. "And you, Slitha,"—he looked toward a slender wingling with a queen's proud stance and wings of gold—"and Usern,"—blue wings quivered as his thought struck home—"and Cambar." The pinions of that leader were grey shading to white and he was much darker of countenance, thicker of body, than the others.

"Remember!" Atra's reinforcememt of his speech was more than a warning, it was an order.

Qua stared at the girl and then he smiled as coldly as she had done earlier. "There is now a common enemy; we fly no direction but that." He, too, might be only giving a reminder, but Farree was certain that there was also a warning to be read there.

"As Glasrant has already done!" she flashed. What more the spokesman for the winglings might have said was never uttered, for Maelen opened her eyes, and the skin tightly covering the eye caverns in Fragon's face quivered and also showed a slit break.

"It is done!" Both voice and thought came from Maelen. "*Their* beacon has been quenched, and even more, many of those traps and defenses set up by *Them* are gone. And the dream holds those two we need to make trouble for each other in thrall!"

Selrena spoke to the unmasked one.

"Loose your followers now, Sorwin!"

The robed one raised both hands to mouth and with them shaped a hollow like a horn. The puffed cheeks expanded even more and from that horn there pulsed a cry which echoed through Farree's head. It had savagery in it, a lust and a hunger which was like a call of doom. Groundlings growled and left with a rush and a slapping of huge bare feet, and after them came a following of things whose very bodies, swinging and swaying, seemed to alter as they went—and always the forms they wore, forms which slipped from one to another and then another, were those of the blackest terrors any night might know. Ironically it was true that those who were fashioned as entirely threatening to each other marched now against a single enemy.

They were gone, and it seemed to Farree that the whole of the crystal cavern was the lighter for their going. He wondered what harm they might wreak on the invaders, for many of those who had swept on seemed hardly more solid than a cloud of that haze which could spring into being at command of the Darda.

The Zacanthan moved for the first time, turning his sharp-jawed head to watch their going. Farree knew that Zoror was filing in his head all which chanced here. What names would he give to those who had just gone? How many more were there that had long ago been listed in the records he thought he knew so well?

However, if there was an exit of a force there was also an entrance. Farree heard the now-familiar tinkle of flute notes. So heralded came Vestrum. Gone was the clothing he had worn before. In its place he wore silver fashioned in small supple rings so that it moved even at his breathing. He carried a length of crystal rod which was headed by a hilt much like that of the sword which was never far from Fragon's hands. The flutist scampered back and forth as might an eager hound only waiting to be dispatched against some quarry, while the two women who walked a pace of so behind had laid aside their filmy robes and flower ribbons. They, too, wore chain mail and on the out-held right wrist of each there sat a flying lizard, smaller than that which had accompanied Farree on his first trip across this land, but manifestly of the same breed.

Neither was this all of the party, for Vorlund followed but a little behind the Darda and, with him, two of the giant folk, bending heads as they strode ponderously, striving to avoid and painful meeting with down-pointing crystals.

Vestrum spoke, but he did not seem to address any

particular one of them but rather the whole company, from Fragon to the smallest of the winglings.

"This one"—he indicated Vorlund, but as if there was nothing in truth between them but what might be a distant enmity—"has done as he swore that he would—he has launched forth his messenger."

"And you, Vestrum, how has it been with you?" Selrena was the first to break the silence on the tail of that message.

"I made sure that there was no treachery in what was wrought!" returned the Darda coldly. Now his eye caught on Farree for the first time, and with a lightning-swift gesture the hilted rod swung up, its end aimed for Farree's head. Along the length of that sped a dot of rainbow light. More memory moved in Farree. He took two steps forward and his bandaged hand swung up, his fingers caught and held the end of the rod. It was chill, seeming to generate a cold which bit into his flesh, but he did not loose it for ten long-drawn breaths. Then his hand dropped and he met the measuring stare of Vestrum with as level and probing a gaze.

Was there a faint trace of disappointment in the Darda's tight held eye to eye measurement? Farree could not be sure, he only held a suspicion.

"Well and now, Vestrum." This time it was Atra who broke thought silence just as the capering flutist settled down at the Darda's feet and made the instrument it carried give forth a trill of notes. "Do you believe? Or is it your claim next that Glasrant has power to hide the cast of all his thoughts from you?"

"Have done!" For the first time Farree saw Fragon rise to his feet. Standing, he was near as tall as he was spare, almost shoulder to shoulder with the giants who had come with Vorlund. "What may have been in these two—it is gone. This night Glasrant has done what Valfor in his day might have lifted hand to—save that, mighty as our Elders were in their own time, they had not the knowledge of *Them*. We have been given that which we have not held to us since the days of incoming upon this world. We have lived, we have built, we dwindle, we earth dwell or keep jealous council with one race, even one kin, only our kind. We have lost much and now we are too old and few even to defend ourselves against *Them*. How many more times must their star ships come—each adding death to death? *They* are as many as a hundred times the number of sand grains now under our feet. There will always be more to come and less of us at their going. *If* they go, for their signal was set to guide others this time. Look to your delving in the ancient knowledge, Vestrum. What discoveries have you made? Small things, things of half life— Can you bring forth that which is no larger than your hand but can rock a star ship?"

The trickle of notes from the flute ascended higher and higher—until they sounded almost like a cry for help. The Darda in his coat of mail stood frowning, his two hands sliding back and forth along his hilted rod.

"And you, Sorwin." Fragon thrust his head a bit forward, his now widely open eyes seeking out the unmasked one. "Well for you—yes, that has been your thought for a long time. Your groundlings and your wraiths—they have little to fear from *Them*. You and yours think to go into such hiding that no off-world mind or body can scoop you forth! We already know that is less true than you would like. And I say to you that *They* have always sought knowledge, more and more of it along paths which we do not or cannot follow. We can summon a storm, set against them the land itself. Only we cannot hold—there are too few of us and we are too wearied with time. What other secrets have *They* uncovered? Do not think you can lie safe hidden."

Sorwin did not reply but Fragon was plainly not through. He gestured with one hand while with the other he still kept his fingers in tight hold on the hilt of the skull-piercing sword. It was a summons and one they had no thought to disobey.

The Zacanthan came, and Maelen, and Vorlund, edged by his giant helpers, and Farree reluctantly dropped his hold on Atra's hand to stand with the other three. Fragon moved again, down from his dusky throne. He came to wait on a level for their coming to him.

They did not approach him too closely for he was now swinging the sword back and forth and the skull was smoothing out a patch of the sand. When that seemed leveled to his liking, the Dark Darda fumbled at the breast of his hazy robe and tossed out upon the patch of readied sand a ball of the same clouded crystal as Farree had taken up in Vestrum's chamber, though this did not break when it landed. Instead light spread from it. Then it was as if they were all a-wing, looking down upon a scene of constant, almost frenzied change. The star ship no longer stood tall but was canted, and its nose was oddly concave at one side. Hail and wind beat at both the ship and the ground about it. The wreck of the shelters flapped forward and back in the wind. Of any men there were no sign.

Then there appeared to burst out of the troubled air itself a flight of such winged snakes as those Farree had seen before. Only these were four, six times the size of those, and they whirled in a mad circle about the canted ship, one after another in turn darting down to skim the wreckage on the ground.

Then night and storm vanished, and with them the disabled ship and what was left of the shelters. What they were looking at now was a stream swollen with storm water, and it was day. A knot of men gathered on the bank of that stream. Several were on their knees digging into the soil with their bare hands. One jerked free from dark clay a swinging length of shining metal. The one nearest him snatched at it. Their mouths were open and they might have been shouting at one another. In moments a frenzy seemed to grip them all, and then there was the flash of a laser which itself banished the scene.

"These will not trouble us again—" Vestrum's thought came, and there was satisfaction in it and triumph.

"There will be others." Selrena broke that thread of satisfaction. "Always there will be others! It is as Fragon has said, they are as many as the grains of sand. Short-lived they are but they breed and breed and among us the young are very few. Long have we fled before them—now we stand with our backs to tall mountains and even the star roads are lost to us. We are already dead though still we struggle—"

"That is not quite the truth."

They all turned to look to Vorlund.

"You have wrought with your own strengths." He gestured to the ball now lying quietly on the sand, no longer beaming forth pictures. "We have wrought with ours. Not only as we have done these days and nights just passed, but for the future. You have been long apart—do not believe that now you are standing alone. You have your rites and customs, your laws and punishments for the breaking of them. There are also laws and punishments beyond this world. You believe that I have brought from our ship that which will serve you now. Yes, in truth that is so. Only we have more to offer—"

"Look you at us!" The command came with clear force from Maelen. She held out a hand and it was taken by the Zacanthan. In turn his other hand went to close upon one of Vorlund's while the spacer's second hand was with Farree in hold. "As you differ to the eye and yet decide on a single purpose, so it is with us among the stars. There are those darklings whom you know as enemies: not as many as your sand grains are they. And there are powers known to us which can destroy them, can bring you a defense that no ship of theirs can crack."

"That also is the truth." The Zacanthan's mind send was heavier but as clear. "There are other worlds where those who live upon their lands and within their seas can be easy prey to those of evil. Only there is no fear there—"

"Why?" Vestrum crowded a little closer to make his demand, his chin thrust forward, about him the sharpness of hostility.

"Because in the space about those worlds there are protectors. Not ones who live and breathe and are of our form of life. No, these are like small, very small, ships set to travel in patterns. If a star-roving ship comes near, these sweep swiftly to match its path and loose a warning. If that is not heeded then that ship will speedily become, while still aloft, like this invader that you have just seen. Only those who know and can think the proper words can pass unharmed. Once each four years one of these who know the signal will come here and land where you yourselves shall appoint and there you and the people of that ship may meet. So through the years to come you will learn of us and we of you and when the time comes we can share peace."

"Thinker and Rememberer," Fragon made answer. "We know that what you say is truth, as you see it. But truth wears many faces when it abides with different peoples. Truth also changes as lives change and what may be right at one time is wrong at another. However, we have little choice. If we are not to be meat for any strange ship which lands here we must accept what you promise. Still, how do you bring this forth? You have a ship and can run to other stars. We are earthbound, and, in the time we must wait for this you promise, we may attract more spoilers."

"Not so." Vorlund shook his head to emphasize his thought. "There has been set up among your mountains a defense—like that of the ship which was trying to beam in their fellow thieves, there goes forth now another beam. All may fear death, a death which cannot be withstood or treated with any ill-bane. There are certain worlds—your people were star travelers once, perhaps you can remember—where death awaits any who dare to land there. On such worlds the law keepers have set up that which will warn off any ship approaching a landing orbit. You need only tend well this warning and you shall be free of those who discover your world by chance. This will serve until we can come again with the more certain defense I have spoken of—"

It was Sorwin's harsh-pitched thought which interrupted him. "So we wait for the coming of those who will set up rule, a rule of those unlike us. They well hold us in a new bondage—"

"No." Zoror answered that. "I hope to come again, for there is much I would learn. Am I one to put the searing iron on you? There may be others like unto me—like these—" He nodded toward Maelen and Vorlund. "Ask of your own." Now he indicated Farree. "Can we be trusted, are we rulers with orders?"

"They are in their way kin," Farree answered. "Me they brought out of the Deep Dark and they call me friend. Even as I am friends with this one." He freed the smux from his jerkin. "It does not matter the form, only that which lies within it. Also "—he put his thoughts into order—"I swear this by my body after the Great Memory—I shall be with you here where you can do with me as you please if you believe I have twisted truth."

Vorlund laid hand on Farree's shoulder. "This one has been much to us, more and more each passing day. We shall give to him all the knowledge needed to keep you free. He is kin-friend and will always be."

Sorwin grunted but Fragon was nodding slowly. "There is no falseness in what you have said. You believe it. If we are minded to accept slowly it is because we have known it to be otherwise many times over. Glasrant has been beyond the stars as one of you. Indeed we can learn from him. Therefore we accept this much, that you will leave with him such knowledge as you are willing to trade. But to you we offer nothing now—save our thanks for what is already done. Let time prove whether you are right."

Farree stood where his wings had borne him at dawn. He was looking down into the cup valley. They were already aboard. All except two— He glanced down for a moment at what he held, felt the familiar pinch of the legs upon his arm and wrist.

"Cold—" That plaint was familiar too. Togger did not relish the kind of wind about them here in the heights.

"Lady Maelen?" A thought swift sent, an answer.

"Lord One Krip?" A second hail and farewell.

"Lord Zoror—?"

"Only until we come again." The Zacanthan's thought was swift to answer.

Farree watched the flame of the jets, the rise of the ship up and up, out of the cup which had held it, back to the stars.

"Do you truly wish yourself there?"

She had alighted on the grassy surface of the cliff top just too far away for him to be aware of her until the thought wove with his.

"I do not know— Here I am one."

"Here you are kin." Her send was clear and strangely soft. She had folded her wings and now she walked towards him. In her hands was a gathering of ill-bane flowers, and the scent of them was also hers.

"Kin, Kin," she chanted aloud now and each word was like the scented and healing breath of the plant.

Farree threw back his head to the dawn-colored sky. He could only see a very distant trail. Then it was gone.

"Kin!" Atra was beside him and the scent of the flowers brought with it a softening of all sadness.

He no longer searched the sky for the past but looked into the face of the future, and his smile was eager.